THE LAST

By

Anthony

March 2018

The ancient county of Durham was gripped by a dense fog that clung to everything in turn, nothing escaped. Dew laden grasses, bushes held by some haze and silver threads of gossamer left ethereal by the people of the night. The north west of the county is very rugged in its nature, high hills and wild moorland surround steep gorges and valleys. As a result of this harsh terrain the land was sparsely populated, a few sheep farms and the odd isolated hamlet here and there.

The morning was a one of dampness and misery as Peter and Kim Thorne rolled their car to a stop outside of the Three Counties Inn Elersly, aptly named as it is at the junction of Durham, Northumberland and Cumbria. "Do you think the car will be alright here?" Peter asked.

Kim looked at the notice on the inn door. "The inn doesn't open till one o`clock, we should have ample time to explore."

They locked the car and made their way the short distance into the village. The fog was no better here as it clung to the stone built cottages like a silver shroud, grey stones reflecting the sky and the universal atmosphere of melancholy. The whole place was silent and appeared to be abandoned as no sound or movement. They rounded a corner and there it was directly in front of them, Saint Andrew's church, they opened the heavy Iron Gate which squealed its displeasure and entered the church yard.

Through the iron gates they went and into the waiting arms of the dead, along the and rutted path, past the weathered headstones coated in shades of grey and green, unto the place of rest the earth wrapped ruins of the people of this parish. The graveyard was quiet, gripped firmly by the frosted hand of early spring. Apart from a bird scratching in the bushes, nothing moved; all was still. They began look at the grave stones, a lot of them by now weathered beyond recognition but some could be read.

"Elizabeth Jackson, beloved wife Robert, 1621- 1674."

"Martin Linn, 1640-1691."

"My God Peter these are very old!" Kim exclaimed rubbing away the moss from a stone.

Peter was just about to respond when they were interrupted by an old man seemingly in his seventies in a blue overall and a garden hoe in one hand. "The church is closed, Can I help you?"

Peter looked at the man a little surprised but apologetic, "oh sorry we did not realise."

"Are you looking for something in particular?"

Kim interrupted and spoke with some eagerness and authority. "Yes we seek the grave of Eliza Swann, could you help us?"

The old man grinned taking off his cap and rubbing his balding head. "I see it's a bit early for tourists, spring comes late in these parts. I'm Fred Spink I do odd jobs around the place, keeps me busy. Follow me I'll show you something you might be interested in."

They followed Fred around the other side of the church until he paused and pointed.

"See this stained glass window, it was paid for by the people of this parish in 1670, it is the eye of God. By installing it the people hoped it would keep away evil spirits and especially Eliza Swann, the last known witch in the county, is this what you are looking for?"

Peter looked at the window with its different coloured pieces of glass in the shape of an eye all held together by strips of lead. "There is no grave marker, why is that?"

Fred sighed and shook his head, "Because we do not know where she is buried somewhere on these grounds but the exact location was kept secret for fear of luring evil elements. You seem very interested, are you researching something?"

"Yes Fred we are researching my family tree and it has come as something of a shock." Kim replied.

"Oh, in what way?" Fred inquired, somewhat puzzled.

Kim glanced at him nervously and with some uneasiness answered. "I am a direct descendant of Eliza Swann, the last witch!"

CHAPTER 1

April 1599

The village of Elersly in the county of Durham was and always had been a small and uninteresting sort of place. The poor people of this parish did what they always did, the men worked the fields, the women kept house. They tended to children, washed their meagre coarse clothes and prepared meals for the men folk. The food on offer was as dreary as the village and the life of the poor peasant.

Poor people lived on a routine diet, in the morning they ate coarse bread of barley or rye, cheese and onions. They only had one cooked meal a day, they mixed grain with water and added whatever vegetables they had and now and then strips of meat.

Lowly people lived in lowly houses, simple huts with one or two rooms. The floors were of hard earth and the walls basic wattle and daub, furniture was very basic such as benches, stools, a table, and wooden chests. The poor slept on mattresses stuffed with straw or thistledown. The mattresses lay on ropes strung across a wooden frame.

Rich people's diet was more nutritious and of higher quality, bread was made from fine white flour and supplemented with meat such as goose, pork and venison. Sumptuary laws laid down what each class could and could not wear, which said that only people with a certain amount of wealth could wear certain expensive materials such as velvet and silk. These laws, of course, made no difference to poor people since they could not afford costly material anyway! However, the laws were supposed to keep the classes separate. You were supposed to be able to tell which class somebody belonged to by his or her clothes.

This day in this ramshackle hamlet was Sunday, a day of rest for the weary legs and twisted bones, no work would be done today and it was the Sabbath. The weather on this early April day cared not about the day or its importance as overnight the heavens descended upon the village and deposited their contents on the sodden, saturated, weary place. Moreover it had not yet ceased as heavy clouds of grey and black hung over the hills, it seemed that all of the rain in heaven had chosen to fall on this unfortunate locality.

Everything was soaked a sodden mass of mud and lying water which seemed to find its way into every crack and crevice. Roads and footways turned into muddied disarray and the land was littered with dirty brown puddles, an old dog shook the maelstrom from his hair sending a fine spray of coloured, dirt filled moisture in all directions.

Bad weather of whatever nature did not and would not discourage the good people of this place from their duty, it was Sunday and as proclaimed by the toll of the church bell as its muffled peel peculated through the gloom. A steady stream of villagers mad their way to Saint Andrews church, men, women, children, the old, the healthy and the crippled, beleaguered, dishevelled, but there all the same. The church was a simple affair with a basic wooden structure and thatched roof just like most of the dwellings but bigger. Inside was much the same although the floor was covered in wooden boards. The pews also made of rough-hewn timber and were modest in their nature and not of the best comfort. This was the Church of England; its parishioners were not here for comfort.

At the front on a raised platform a wooden table stood with a simple crucifix, beside it stood Reverend Adams resplendent in his vestments. The congregation filed in and took their pews grumbling about the weather and their drenched condition. Reverend Adams observed his flock, his sermons were typically robust in their message and the villagers expected nothing else.

"You may be seated." He spoke calmly.

"It is better in prayer to have a heart without words than words without heart." "Whether we realize it or not, prayer is the encounter of God's thirst with ours. God thirsts that we may thirst for him." "Prayer enlarges the heart until it is capable of Containing God's gift of himself."

Reverend Adams spread his arms wide. "Kneel now in the presence of the Lord, let us pray."

A young girl protested, "Mother the floor is wet!"

"Shush now lass! "Came a muffled reply.

"Lord, I didn't know what lay before me today, but I commit it all to you. Please give me strength and courage to get through the joys, challenges and happenings of the day. I thank you for my life and for all that I have; I commit this day to you. You may be seated."

Reverend Adams continued: "We are at any point subject to the word of the lord; he controls every aspect of our lives, good and bad. Yes we may fear him as well as praise him, for he and he alone will save us. Fear, what of fear we fear many things, poor harvest, pestilence but the real fear is evil. The presence of the devil is amongst us every day, we must keep him at bay always, be you peaceful but vigilant, let us now pray for salvation."

The congregation knelt down and prayed in solemn silence. It would be barely a minute later when this silence was broken as a horrific wail spread through the church, echoing around the walls as if it were trapped. Eyes opened from concentration, heads turned. In every direction as the people jumped to their feet some screaming, some running out.

Reverend Adams spread his arms wide in in a desperate attempt at peace. "Behold we have a sign that the Devil be among us even in this holy place, pray to the Lord Above!"

The night went long and slow for the people of Elersly, doors fast shut and bolted. God fearing folk cowered inside hoping for a quiet night, dreading what waited outside in the darkness. The wind battered and assaulted the humble wooden homes as if the lords of nature were angry. Children recoiled under coarse blankets that didn't feel so rough on this night shivering in trembled dread as the rain pounded the land like liquid bullets.

The morning came to the village of Elersly, even as the dark desperation of the night subsided into the light of another day as a sapphire sky marbled with red climbed over the rolling hills. Mercifully the rain of the night had abated and the morning sun lit the hamlet in a flushed radiance of new life in an old land, storm and bluster had diminished, all was calm. However the mood among the villagers could not be described as peaceful, there was unease and disquiet in the atmosphere. People regarded each other with a type of distrust and curiosity that was not typically apparent in this place. However, nervous people were still speaking but in discreet and muted tones.

Martin Howe walked into the centre of the village, bedraggled, dishevelled and sodden to the bone, tousled grey hair protruding from his bartered hat as if it didn't have the strength to come out or climb back in. Some of the men gathered observed him closely as he approached and where to a man surprised at his appearance, he was indeed an unfortunate spectacle.

Adam Smith looked him up and down, "where have you been Martin, you look ill?"

Martin held out his right arm, his hand gripping a large axe as if he did not care to part with it in case of unpredicted predicament, he waved it about a few times before he spoke.

"That noise last night, you all heard it, the howl of dread that stained this place. While others retired to their shelters, I went looking for the cause of the yowl; I believe it was that of a wolf and a gigantic one at that."

Adam shook his head, "pray tell me Martin, did you find such an animal?"

"No I did not but it is a creature of the night it could have relocated anywhere."

"Martin there have been no wolves in this area for many a year!"

Martin realising he had been on a pointless hunt for something that by all accounts did no longer exist in the area, even in the county, they were long gone. So, as the wind wrapped its chill fingers about him he trudged off through the muddied ground saddened and sodden in his misery. In the past local land owners employed men to aggressively hunt down and kill wolves as they had a tendency to kill and devour the sheep and cattle, bounty was paid for every wolf pelt handed in. There had been tales of wolves forty miles away over the Scottish border but in all probability just that, tales.

A man strode into the village with an assured presence about him, quite well dressed, well somewhat better than the local crofters. He took out a parchment from his coat and nailed it to the notice board before turning to walk away, a group of women were standing close by.

"Hey, what's all this about then, who are you"

"I am a member of the ealdorman's staff, I was ordered to display this notification."

"What does it say?" The woman continued.

"Well read it or do you expect me to do that also?"

"Yes!" Was the reply from more than one quarter, "We cannot read!"

"What none of you can read or write I presume? Very well I suppose I must," he began.

"Let it be known to all that Mary Swann of this parish gave birth to a daughter last night in the year of our Lord 1599 and both are well. Signed, Mathew Hudson, Ealdorman."

It was within seconds the gossip began and within minutes it had infected every corner of the village as the people spread the word to all who would know and those who did not care.

Ann Simms was somewhat uneasy, "Mary Swann has never been wed, she is a spinster, every person in this village knows that, there is something amiss here, mark my words!"

Ann parker looked somewhat fearful. "Maybe Reverend Adams was right, evil be among us, the devil hath taken her from our very midst, what shall be done?"

Janet intervened with a Deal of irritation. "Shush Ann, enough now I say, I will go and see Mary and the child, put a stop to this nonsense forthwith!"

t Janet urned away and made her way to the house of Mary Swann which was situated on the northern edge of the village. She knocked on the door and ranked it open with a scrape and rasp of discontent as if the place was not to be disturbed. The house was like most in the village, a simple wooden structure with a thatched roof. A simple opening in the wall was the nearest thing to a window, glass was very expensive and not for a lowly peasant.

Janet peered inside; a shaft of sun light sliced the gloom with a radiant beam of light. The room was meagrely scattered with furniture as it was costly. The floor was hard packed earth flattened over the years with the feet of common folk, these were simple peasants and carpets were for rich folk.

"Mary, are you in here lass?"

A voice came in reply from a dappled corner of the room. "Is that you Janet?"

"I have just heard the news, I thought I would come and see how you were keeping. I also heard that you have been blessed with a daughter, where is the child?"

Mary motioned with a finger to a simple wooden crib in the corner and there laid an infant girl wrapped in humble cloth on a bed of straw, she was asleep, sound and quiet.

Janet leaned over and stroked the child's hair and smiled. "She is a fine girl Mary, beautiful blond hair she will be bonny when grown I foretell that now!"

Mary sighed with a sense of emotion that spread through the room like a damp draft.

Janet approached the bed and gazed at Mary. "You seem sad, what troubles you?"

"I don't know Janet; this whole thing seems like a dream or a nightmare!"

"Whatever do you mean Mary, you have been born of a fine daughter, be proud."

"You don't understand, this is no simple tale of woman giving birth, yes I have a healthy girl but that is not the whole story there is more and it is terrible in its nature!"

"What are you on about Mary Swann have you been on the mead?"

"No listen Janet, I must tell all and I trust you not to inform the whole village."

"I promise that I will not divulge anything I know what they are like for chatter, they wait for news outside as we speak and I will need to tell them something, who is the father?"

"That's the problem, I don't know."

"What, how many men have you been with Mary?"

"I cannot say, it is all a jumble of mists and visions that drift in and out of my mind."

"Your mind is indeed troubled; I can't tell folk that, I will make something up."

"Yes please do Janet that is not the whole account."

"What there is more to tell?" Janet exclaimed with some exasperation.

Mary raised herself up and sat on the edge of the bed while Janet sat on a stool.

"You see a fine girl child in that cot yonder but the other has gone I know not where."

"Other, what do you mean, you had twins?"

"Yes Janet, I was born of twins and all seemed well, the midwife checked them and cleaned me up and made sure I was healthy and then she left. The first born is there, blond hair, blue eyes; the other had a mop of hair the colour of jet and her eyes like the darkest night."

"So where is the other child Mary, where has she gone?"

"Somewhere through the night, being tired from the birth I must have fallen asleep, when I awoke the dark twin was gone, someone must have come and snatched her away."

"Who would snatch a new-born from her mother? The sheriff should be informed."

"No Janet, let it be, I will look to this child the other is no more!"

"But she was your daughter Mary!"

"No, I do not believe that, the girl was not right, there was something amiss, the way she looked at you with those black eyes peering into your soul. I think that child was born of malevolent intention and was snatched away for some wicked enterprise. Reverend Adams was correct, evil is among us, always and forever."

"Mary, how did you know what Reverend Adams said in his sermon you were not there?"

"I don't know Janet, I know what was said but I don't know how or why."

"This is hardly believable Mary, the people of the village want answers, I cannot tell them this version, suspicion will run amok, what should I tell them?"

"I don't know Janet, I am lost to a different world, I could be dreaming it all!"

Janet left the house in a state of bewilderment and uncertainty, how could this be? She also knew well enough that the villagers would not believe whatever explanation she could come up with, it was a dilemma that would last far into the future.

CHAPTER 2

Six years had passed and Eliza Swann had begun to grow into a fine young girl, her blond locks cascaded onto her shoulders strands covering her pretty young face. However, all was not well with Eliza Swann, the people of Elersly had not forgotten the events of that night six years past. Superstition and distrust was rife in these times, it ran deeply as deep as the soul itself and the church would make sure that it would not be any other way.

Mathew Jackson was a member of one of the area's oldest families; the family held land a mile west of the village, a member of the yeoman class, his land recorded in the Doomsday Book. Nestled amidst the rugged hills of Northern England our small landowner embodies the quintessential spirit of rural life in Elizabethan England. His modest estate, comprising a humble manor house and several acres of fertile land, a testament to generations of his family's hard work and prudent management.

Mathew Jackson had risen early as usual and having had a bowl of hot porridge set off for his days tasks. His attire, though simple, is of good quality, reflecting his status as a member of the yeomanry. A woollen doublet, trousers, and a cloak protect him from the brisk northern winds, while sturdy leather boots, worn from years of toil, carry him across his fields and through the muddy lanes of his estate. Upon his head rests a felt hat, adorned with a single feather as a subtle nod to his social standing. His weathered features bear the lines of experience and resilience, a testament to the challenges of life in an era marked by uncertainty and change.

In demeanour, our landowner exudes a sense of quiet authority tempered by humility, though he holds sway over his small domain, he understands the interconnectedness of the rural community, where cooperation and mutual support are essential for survival. He is a familiar figure at the local market, where he trades goods from his land and engages in gossip with his neighbours, exchanging news and sharing in the blending of country life.

His daily routine is one of diligent labour and careful stewardship, from dawn till dusk, he oversees the work of his tenants and labourers, ensuring that crops are sown and harvested, livestock are tended to, and the estate's affairs are managed with prudence and foresight. Though the burden of responsibility weighs heavily upon him, he finds solace in the rhythms of the natural world and the satisfaction of seeing his efforts bear fruit.

Despite his modest means, our landowner possesses a keen intellect and a deep-rooted sense of pride in his ancestral heritage. He is well-versed in matters of estate management, law, and local customs, and takes great care to uphold the traditions of his forebears while adapting to the challenges of a rapidly changing world.

This being winter there was no planting or harvesting to be done, at this time of year it was all about the livestock and making sure they were well looked after. He passed the cattle shed and had a brief word with the cattleman who assured him all was in order.

He progressed past the stables where several horses were boarded and into the top field. The sun, feeble and grey, struggled to push itself through ironed and heavy clouds, as if the cold had sapped its strength. Hedgerows exploded with frost and the gorse and grasses of the moor stood still in suspended silence. Wind driven snow filled corners and rounded edges, nestling and curling like neatly folded silk, trees, icy fingers pointed skyward, waiting for better times, a witness to many seasons.

He climbed the gate and paced into the field, his sheep were hardy souls bred for these northern lands. Even though he still lost the odd one in bad weather as they would shelter from the icy winds up against the dry stone walls, sometimes they were buried. Today however, the snow was not that deep, it had been worse, much worse. He checked the walls and there were some sheep resting in the lea but there were still some missing.

Mathew Jackson carried on up the slope poking his willow staff into the frozen ground to steady his stride; he was after all not a fit young man any more. It was only when reached the top of the field that he discovered where the missing sheep were. There lying in a disorderly untidy jumble of chaos were the four sheep that were missing from the main flock, dead. It was not until he examined them that he realised they had not died of exposure to the weather but were instead butchered.

All of them had suffered a violent death by some means or other, he inspected each one in turn, all had the same injuries, savage gash to the neck. At first he thought it was a stray dog as this had happened before a few years ago, Mathew Jackson killed it. He searched around at the crimson snow looking for paw prints, he found none instead he found the small prints of a human, definite and distinct, someone had killed his sheep. You could feed a whole family with just one animal, there was no doubt but why kill them and leave them lying?

Mathew Jackson might be moderately prosperous but he could not let someone kill his livestock without retribution. Ironically Mathew Jackson was well known in the parish for helping the poor when times were difficult. He marched into the village and called at the house of Mathew Hudson, Ealdorman, who assured him he would look into it. He immediately had a poster made up and pinned it to the village board.

Later that day a knock arrived at the ealdorman's door, it was Ann Simms standing firmly in her belief that she had information concerning the loss of the sheep.

"Ah Ann, what brings you to my door this day?"

"It's about the poster you hung up earlier, I think I can help."

"Oh really Ann, well you had better come in out of the cold, now what do you know?"

"I believe I know who did this crime, there is a strong feeling in the village that a certain family is not all together well thought. Mary Swann as you know had a child and she is not wed, nobody knows who the father is and the people think her daughter Eliza is a sinful presence among us. Neither of them contributes to the community; they hide away plotting and scheming who knows what. We all believe that Eliza was responsible for these crimes."

"Ann Simms, you really are mistaken, rightly Mary Swann is not wed and never has been but she is not the first woman to be with child out of wedlock. As for Eliza, she is a six year old girl how on this earth could she have killed four sheep in such a grizzly manner?"

"We all know she is not normal, she has a malevolence about her, be warned."

"I will go and see Mary Swann, I'm sure there is nothing in this, rest your soul Ann."

Mathew Hudson, did as he promised and walked into the village to the house of Mary Swann and her daughter, he rapped on the flimsy wooden door and waited.

Mary came to the door and opened it with some caution.

"Ealdorman Hudson, what on earth brings you here today?"

"Hello Mary how do you fair we haven't seen you around much lately, are you well?"

"As well as possible, Ealdorman, is there something wrong?"

"If you would allow me to come in I will explain."

Mary opened the door fully and beckoned him inside; he sat on a simple wooden chair.

"Are you aware that some sheep belonging to Mathew Jackson have been slaughtered?"

"Well no I rarely leave the house, how would I know of such things?"

"This is a small community, word travels quickly."

"Oh yes that is very true Ealdorman, why do you think I hide myself away in this house? Can I ask you a question Ealdorman, why do you think that I could be responsible for this?"

"As a member of this community and as Ealdorman I am accountable for every person. So you were not out and about last evening, what about Eliza where was she last night?"

"She was here of course, where else do you think a six year old child would be in the night? Eliza, come in here lass, this is Ealdorman Hudson, tell him where you were last night."

"Last night mother, well I was here in my bed, where else would I be late at night?"

Ealdorman Hudson sighed, "indeed child where would you be, I can see all is well here. I will leave you in peace, Mary if you have any more trouble with the inhabitants, please tell me, that's what I'm here for, for everybody not just some, good day Mary, Eliza, keep well."

Ealdorman Hudson left the house and being a man of fair judgment was troubled by the situation. He knew fine well that Mary Swann and her daughter were more or less outcasts in the village and he knew just how superstitious and irrational the mind of the simple peasant. He considered informing the county sheriff but decided against it hoping instead that it would blow over as quickly as it started. This did little to appease Mathew Jackson whose sheep were still lying in a snow covered field and he had four short to take to market.

On Sunday morning the whole village trooped into the church as they always did without rational thought, it was just something they did on a Sunday morning, no one questioned why or their inner self as to the reasons for it. Attending church was not only a religious obligation but also a societal and legal requirement; there were several reasons why simple peasants were compelled to go to church.

Legal Mandate: The Act of Uniformity of 1559 made attendance at church services compulsory for all citizens. Failure to attend church regularly could result in fines or even imprisonment. This legal obligation applied to people of all social classes, including peasants. Religion played a significant role in the lives of people, the Church of England, established by Queen Elizabeth I, was the dominant religious institution. Many peasants held devout religious beliefs and saw attending church as a duty to God.

There were exceptions to this edict, namely Mary Swann and her daughter Eliza; they had not attended church for some time. The reason for this was that they did not want to be subject to insult and accusations from other people in the village. In the few times Mary left her house for essential reasons she was routinely ostracised and abused. Mary and her daughter stayed at home as the church bell rang out their message to the faithful.

Reverend Adams stood at the lectern and delivered his usual service, being full of warning about the evil in our midst. The congregation knew who he was referring to without directly naming them, it was of course Mary and Eliza Swann, every one of them knew and those who did not were rapidly educated of their mistakes. This was apparent when after the service several people began to throw handfuls of horse muck at the door of Mary Swann, Mary and Eliza cowered inside and waited in quiet silence.

The excrement of animals or indeed humans was not difficult to find in the village of Elersly as the whole place was one giant dung heap. Pigs, goats, chickens creatures of many different forms had free range to do basically what they wanted, where they wanted and the local population of rats had never had it so good. At times the smell was horrendous with the odour of many elements producing a thick miasma that assaulted the senses.

The population of this village were not greatly better than the livestock as cleanliness and personal hygiene were not high priorities. In the fine weather some of the villagers would take a dip in the river, this had more to do with cooling off rather than keeping clean. The water source was so polluted it was impossible to consume without the risk of falling ill, so ale was the staple drink.

CHAPTER 3

Four years had gone by in a blink, a new century had announced itself on the good people of this county and the village of Elersly, which had however, remained much the same. It was an early summer morning as Eliza Swann left the house and climbed the steep hill to the west of the village. She had now reached the age of ten years and had become a fine and intelligent young girl, she was still aware of the distrust that still lingered in the village and as a result kept herself away as much as possible.

She reached the top of the hill and sat on the grass and surveyed the view. The early morning unfolded with a gentle elegance, infused with the promise of warmth and vitality. As the sun began its ascent, it painted the sky with hues of soft pastels, blending shades of peach, pink, and lavender into a masterpiece of dawn. Birdsong filled the air, a symphony of nature. As the sun climbed higher in the sky, casting its golden rays across the landscape, the day unfurled like a tapestry woven with infinite promise.

Eliza say quietly watching life in the turning of the age, the whole scene being one of blissful obliviousness, she was calm, at peace and in harmony with all around her. It was in her state of bliss she suddenly realised that she was not alone. A young girl of about her own age was sitting next to her, she did not see her approach of even hear anything, she just appeared. Eliza looked around at this girl, long lustrous black hair cascaded around her shoulders and eyes the couloir of a crow's wing.

"Oh sorry miss I did not see you there." Eliza explained.

"You seemed to be in a world of your own."

"If only I could," Eliza replied.

The girl smiled, "It's Sunday morning you will be attending church later no doubt?"

Eliza gazed at her, she had never seen this girl before, she was not from the village.

"No I do not attend church anymore, for numerous reasons, we are not well regarded."

"Yes I know, let them go about their pointless lives, we are the different ones, the altered ones, singular in our purpose."

"Who are you I don't recognise you where are you from?" Eliza questioned.

"I am from here and there, round and about, my name is immaterial."

"You ask why I do not attend church but what about you why do you not attend?"

"My life is one of darkness and despair; I would walk always in the light, I would save myself from this torment but I cannot, it holds me in a tight embrace."

The girl stood up, "are you leaving?" Eliza asked.

"Yes Eliza I must leave, good day to you."

The girl walked away and was soon out of sight behind some gorse bushes, it was only now that Eliza realised something and shouted after her, "hey girl how do you know my name?"

Eliza returned to her house somewhat puzzled at her encounter with this strange girl, she was in some ways like herself but somehow different. She went inside the house and sat down quietly, her mother Mary noticed her disposition and came over.

Eliza, where have you been girl?"

"I went for a walk up on the hills; it was quiet and peaceful, until."

"Until what girl, you seem thoughtful, is all well?"

"Yes mother my thoughts were elsewhere, you see I met another girl up there. She was about my age but I have never seen her before, she was a stranger to me."

"What was this girl's name?"

"I don't know mother, she would not give a straight answer but she called me Eliza."

Mary Swann looked up with a start and gave her daughter a considered gaze, this was becoming stranger by the second, a strange girl on the moor and how did she know Eliza?

Sunday morning wore on and the summer air was punctured by the sound of the church bell calling people to prayer. The residents of the village began to emerge from their houses and made their solemn way to the house of the Lord. A short while later people from outlying houses and farmsteads began to appear, men, women children and the elderly and infirm being helped along the path to devoutness.

Mary Swann made use of the quiet to slip outside and collect some vegetables from the small plot at the back of the house; Eliza sat and said nothing in her contemplation.

In the church the congregation was still milling around and chattering until Reverend Adams appeared at the pulpit, all was immediately quiet. "You may sit." He announced.

The congregation did as they were told, sat quietly and waited for the reverend to begin.

"We are all blessed in the light of a summer morn and in the unceasing observation of our Lord and saviour Jesus Christ who cares for his flock as does a Shepherd. Please be upstanding and we will sing the hymn o Lord, turn not Thy face from me."

The gathering began to sing some with enthusiasm, some not so much but they tried all the same. It was only part way through when several parishioners began to notice something not quite right with Reverend Adams. He was seen to be visibly sweating although it was a warm summer's morning it was not that hot, he seemed to forget his words sometimes and was seen to sway and tremble. Several people noticed his discomfort and wondered if they should help; their caution was interrupted as the reverend suddenly fell heavily and with a dull thud next to the altar. Several people were heard to gasp and a solitary scream echoed from the rear of the church. People gathered around as Reverend Adams lay prostrate shaking and mumbling some undistinguishable words, some men carried him into the back room of the church and placed him on his bed.

"What should we do?" One man asked not knowing just what to do.

"He needs a physician!" Shouted another.

"Physicians are expensive; we are poor people we can't afford that!"

A man stepped forward, "I have an idea Blackdale Abbey have a cottage hospital where the brothers will see local people who can't afford to pay, some have medical knowledge."

Word had travelled quickly in the village and there was a sense of near panic amongst the people. A horse and cart pulled up outside of the church and Reverend Adams was carried out and place onto the back as comfortably as was possible and they set off north to the abbey, it would not be a pleasant or easy journey.

Nestled in a deep hollow of the Leam Valley, surrounded on all sides by steep hills and thick forest, Blackdale Abbey was a holy haven of tranquillity and order. It was so isolated that if you did not know of its existence, you would never know it was there, that of course was the reason for its location, tucked away from the passing eye, safe in its seclusion. The river Leam tumbled off the high, bleak moorland reckless and hurried over rounded rocks into the valley where it composed and levelled itself into a steady flow and here and there forming deep copper coloured pools. Here in the valley bottom the river would often escape its restraints and the area was littered with marshes and peat bogs, the river also formed the western boundary of the abbey.

Established in the year 1140 by Godwin of Arden the order followed the teachings of Saint Godwin of Arden and were known as White Canons because of their white robes.

The order survived attacks by Scottish bandits for almost four hundred years until 1536 when King Henry had a little dispute with Rome and dissolved the monasteries. It was 1539 before they managed to get this far north but it succumbed all the same. Religious orders were reastablished in time, which also included Godwin's teachings; the abbey was repaired and reoccupied.

The hot sun of a summer morning bleached the scene with a golden glow of radiance; grasses grew thick and verdant with the deep green hued lustre of the season as trees swayed and whispered in the soft breeze their bows heavy laden and vibrant with gentle motion. Even though this northern most part of England was far away and remote and the weather often harsh and unforgiving it was not on this day.

A horse and cart pulled to a halt in the courtyard of the abbey, the driver tied the horse to a rail while two other men jumped off the back. A young apprentice approached, "can I help you, are you expected?"

One of the men explained in an agitated manner. "We have a man in the cart, he is seriously ill; can you help him, he needs a physician, please help?"

The young apprentice ran off into the abbey and shortly later the sound of a hand bell was heard peeling through the halls of the abbey. He came back quickly and showed the men to the infirmary where people were already waiting. The men carried the reverend into the infirmary and placed him on a table. Several monks gathered round and one monk, Brother James seemed to be in charge and took the lead immediately.

"Brother Luke get some cold wet towels, quickly if you please."

Brother Luke came back in swift order with towels that he placed on the brow of the reverend and other parts of his body. "How long has he been like this?" Brother James asked.

Martin Crow one of the villagers responded, "he was giving his sermon when he buckled."

"I see I noticed his vestments, is he from your village, what is his name?"

"He is Reverend Adams; he is vicar for our parish, the village of Elersly."

Brother James continued questioning, "did he complain of any symptoms such as severe headache, delirium, rapid pulse, or did it happen quickly?"

"It happened quickly, very much so, we could see he was struggling, then he just went."

"Has anyone else in the village been ill like this recently?" Brother James pressed.

Martin Crow looked at the floor for a second as if in thought, "no, no one that I know of."

The monks had by now stripped the vestments from Reverend Adams and had placed cold wet cloths all over his skin in and attempt to control his temperature. Brother James went and consulted another monk, he came back shortly after.

Martin Crow approached him, "what is wrong with him brother, do you know?"

"No, we are not sure is the simple answer, he has all the symptoms of sudor anglicus."

"What on earth is that?" Martin asked looking somewhat puzzled.

"Oh forgive me I used the Latin name, it is known as English sweating sickness. We have not had an outbreak for many years and it is very contagious if it is sweating sickness the whole village would be ill not just one man."

"What will you do brother is there any way to help him?"

"We will keep him here and treat him as best we can, we will arrange a mixture of lavender, marjoram and sage, these things will help with his temperature."

"Will he survive?" Martin Crow asked with growing concern.

"We cannot say for sure he is essentially sweating to death! Death might occur from three to eighteen hours after the first onset of symptoms; if the patient survived for twenty four hours they would usually recover."

"My thanks Brother James, we should head back to the village and explain everything."

On returning to Elersly Martin Crow was surrounded by a crowd of villagers all keen to hear any news of their spiritual guide. Martin explained all that he could that it was a known illness that appeared from time to time and what the outcome might be. This explanation did little to appease the villages as they gossiped and muttered to one another. A man of God should not be stricken by such an illness there must be another answer.

Ann Simms pushed her way to the front of the gathering as is her habitual nature.

"There is more to this than a simple illness, poor folk die of illness, this is the work of the Devil, mark my words well, evil stalks this land, may God help us all!"

This little intervention ignited audible gasps among the populace with some noticeably sobbing as they drift off in different directions to contemplate their future. To say that business in the village was normal was something of a inaccuracy as people were not behaving normally. Jobs still had to be done, the normal trials of life like eating and surviving for another day.

It now being after five on this afternoon the people had heard nothing of the condition of the reverend and the atmosphere was charged, not only physiologically but naturally. The bright light of this summer day was changing as dark ominous clouds gathered over the hills. The sky was no longer a pale shade of azure but a forbidding mixture of dark blue, purple and deep bloodshot red, the air charged with static electricity.

The first rumble of thunder echoed in the distance, a warning of the impending commotion, a violent thunderstorm, nature's symphony of chaos and power, a tempestuous display of atmospheric fury, was drifting over with rapid advance. Suddenly, jagged streaks of lightning split the sky, illuminating the darkness with blinding brilliance. Each bolt crackles and dances across the heavens, casting fleeting shadows on the landscape below.

The clap and rumble that followed was deafening, a cacophony of crashes and growls that reverberated through the air, shaking the very ground as if the Gods of the past were angry. Torrential rain pelted down in sheets, driven by fierce winds that howl and thrash through the trees. The deluge floods roads, footways and rivers, transforming familiar paths into treacherous torrents. Hailstones, frozen missiles, battered everything in their path, leaving damage in their wake.

The River Derwent traditionally formed the western border between County Durham and Northumberland. The river takes its name from the Celtic Deerwint or river where oaks grow. Oaks still grow here but today they were twisted and broken by the fierce storm, the river corresponded with suitable energy as it raged a torrent of dirty brown liquid landscape.

As day drifted into night the storm did not relent and as the goodly monks of Blackdale Abbey tried their best to save the life of Reverend Adams. On the high hill overlooking the abbey stood a young girl, in the rain and wind, hair a tangled mass of blackness, eyes the colour of night. She stood still, motionless the breeze tugging at her black dress, she said nothing. Why was a young girl out, on her own in the early hours of a morning?

While in the village a peculiar incidence unfolded, howls were heard coming from the high moors, wails that shattered the night air with menace. Sometime later a huge black dog walked calmly into the village made its way to the house of Reverend Adams and lay down across the threshold of the door. It is and ancient superstition in these parts that if an ominous black dog known locally as the Barghest lies down across the threshold of your house, it's a sign you'll pass away soon.

Thankfully later that morning the storm abated rolling and rumbling over the distant hill and the sun of a summer morning was peeking through ready for another day. A man on horseback came riding into the village and made for the house of Ealdorman Hudson. His wife answered the door and the man delivered her a note explaining he was instructed by the abbey to convey it to the ealdorman. She took the note to her husband and handed it over.

Yesterday we received a patient into our infirmary, the man being very sick, the brothers and I tended him all night but this morning his life force left him. Reverend Adams is now in the tender arms of the Lord, may his peace be restful.

Brother James,

Blackdale Abbey.

Ealdorman Hudson called for his assistant and instructed him to have a poster drawn up and placed on the village notice board. Although most of the populace of the village were illiterate word still got around quickly. The mood in the village was that of gloom and melancholy, Reverend Adams had been their spiritual guide for decades and knew all of his flock in turn. He could at times preach fire and brimstone but he had the welfare of his parishioners at the heart of everything he did and everybody knew it to be so.

The poor people of Elersly did not have much cheer in their lives, in fact it could be said that they had none to speak of and now the man who guided them through life was gone. Things would not be the same from this time forth, change was coming if they liked it or not, it was a time of reflection and solemn discourse. Of course everything is subject to change, the weather, the time, the years and event he people, even a man of God was not immune.

CHAPTER 4

Two days later the weather set fair on this summer day, it was a time of sadness and contemplation for the good people of Elersly, it was the funeral of the reverend. The monks of Blackdale Abbey had washed and wrapped the body in a white shroud and he was placed in a wooden coffin and carried to a waiting cart. The coffin was draped in black linen shaped in the form of a cross, it set off on its final journey.

Not everyone who died during this era was important enough to receive special treatment but if you did happen to be important enough, you were remembered with a parade of sorts. Funeral processions for the deceased wealthy enough to afford it featured servants carrying banners printed with the coat of arms of the church in front of and behind the coffin. Mourners gathered along the way dressed in black, black dresses, pants, stockings, shirts, hats, shoes and even accessories such as pins, ribbons, ruffs and gloves were common, Some also wore sprigs of rosemary pinned to their clothing.

As the cortege entered Elersly the church bell began to sound out the last chime of a life of devotion. The body was transferred into the church and placed near the altar, several members of the clergy from Durham Cathedral stood in solemn silence, heads bowed. The service was mostly about God and how Reverend Adams devoted his life to his service. After the service the coffin was transferred to the back of the church where a small graveyard had been blessed as holy ground.

Several men from the village were employed to did a grave and remove the bones of local people which were placed in a charnel house nearby. Black cloth lined the grave and large candles fluttered in the summer air; Reverend Adams was lowered gently into the earth. The next few days were all about change as a new incumbent of Saint Andrew's church was due to arrive from Durham.

Two days later the villagers were called to special service, they all entered the church and took their pews. Ealdorman Hudson and his family were seated in an upstairs gallery reserved for people of means and standing in the parish. A short while later a man emerged from the dressing room near the altar dressed in his church vestments.

"Good day to you all, we are all gathered here in the house of God and in his light. I am Reverend Marshal, I will be the churches' representative in this parish. I am here for each and every one of you should you need council of support, go now, always walk in the light and you will never be alone."

The villagers left the church for some it was business as usual and went about their daily tasks. For others it was different some had never known a clergyman other than Reverend Adams. Some stayed around and gossiped as they always did others left the scene.

Eliza Swann took the chance to venture from her house and pick some herbs from the moorland above the village. It was then that she noticed a young girl standing still, gazing down on the churchyard; it was the same girl she had seen before. She ran over to where the girl was hoping to speak to her but when she arrived at the spot, the girl was gone. This was the second time she had seen this girl and she was becoming fascinated as to who she was, where she was from and she had many questions but she was gone, who knows where.

Eliza having picked some wild mint made her way down the hill and around the outskirts of the village. As she walked through some bushes she felt a tug on her smock and was violently pulled to the ground. She looked up the see four girls from the village that would not let her get up, they kept her pinned down and began to hit her with branches from a nearby tree, she screamed for help as the girls began to accuse her of all manner of things.

"You are the cause off all the misfortune Eliza Swann!"

"We all know who you are; we all know what you are!"

"Be careful, if she is as evil as they say, she might have hidden powers!"

Then for some reason the beating and abuse suddenly stopped and the four girls looked round in unison. The strange girl from on top of the hill was unexpectedly standing right in front of them. She scrutinized the girls with a stiletto stare that purveyed and air of menace and malevolence that froze the girls in a kind of stupor. The strange girl did not say anything, she did not need to, the threat was there by implication rather than words.

The four girls looked at each other, not quite knowing what to do, then in one motion they scattered into the bushes leaving nothing but muffled screams behind. Eliza lifted herself from the ground and turned around intending to thank this strange girl but she was gone, vanished without seemingly a trace of where she had gone or where she had been, nothing.

Elia went home and explained to her mother where all of the muck and scratches had come from. Mary Swann was livid as to why these renegade children could get away with such treatment to an innocent girl like Eliza. It was several days later, Eliza had been keeping her head down and not venturing far from the house. Mary Swann had gone to the house of Ealdorman Hudson and complained as to the treatment her and her daughter were receiving. This did not cut much fare with the Ealdorman as he suggested that disputes between villagers should be worked out in an agreeable manner, we must live in peace all of us.

Two days later Mary and Eliza were in their small modest house on the edge of the village eating a modest meal of vegetable pottage. It would be difficult to say that they were enjoying it as basic pottage without expensive meat or herbs was somewhat bland. Never the less pottage was all they had and hunger does not distinguish or pass judgement on the flavour, you eat what you can when you can, so they did and were grateful.

"Mother this stew is not that nice today, what is in it?"

"Eliza dear girl we are but simple folk, we eat what we can afford and thank the lord for it."

Eliza gazed at her mother in a firm manner, "why thank him, what does he do for us?"

"Eliza do not take the word of God in vein we are Godly people even if we do not attend church anymore we still have faith. I have something to tell you, how would you like to leave the village for a while, see another place but this shithole what do you think?"

"Mother Elersly is my home I was born here, why can't I walk in peace, it is not right!"

"I know it's not daughter but a lot of things could be said such, your Aunt Agnes lives in Durham City, she says you are welcome to stay with her for a while should you want to."

"Mother, they say that the Barghest was seen in the village before Reverend Adams died."

"Don't you worry yourself about such nonsense girl but you are right there is something wrong with this village, very wrong, you are best out of it my dear, go to Durham."

The next morning came and Eliza was up and about ready for the journey that she had reluctantly agreed to the day before. Her mother had arranged a ride on a cart taking wood to the city; Alfred Chase held a small farmstead on the outskirts of the village and agreed to pick Eliza up for the trip of ten miles or so to Durham City. Eliza waited with some nervousness on the road outside of the village and eventually a cart drawn by two bay horses pulled to a stop and old man looked down on her.

"Good day Eliza, climb on board."

"You know my name, we have never met."

"I don't need to meet someone to know about them; you and your mother are well known."

The cart trundled off and Eliza was able to study Alfred Chase as he steadied the horses on the uneven dirt road. An old but seemingly wise man carried the weight of years gracefully, his face etched with lines that told stories of a lifetime, eyes, though weathered by time, gleam with a spark of wisdom and his hair, once dark and vibrant, now faded into silver.

His demeanour exuded a sense of tranquillity and patience, forged through decades of experience. Despite his age, there is a vitality that emanates from him, a quiet strength that belies his frail appearance. He has weathered the storms of life and emerged not unscathed, but stronger for the trials he has faced. His wisdom is not born of books alone, but of lived experience, of joy and sorrow, triumph and defeat.

"You are going away for a while miss?"

"Yes my mother thought it wise, so I go without argument."

"It will serve your soul to and make you a woman, a fine woman, you see."

"I hope that to be so but I am not sure, my life is a muddle of disorder."

In his presence, one cannot help but feel a sense of reverence, a deep respect for the wisdom that emanates from him like a gentle aura. He is a sage, a mentor, a keeper of truths, and though his body may grow frail with age, his spirit remains resolute. Eliza had recognised these qualities soon after climbing on the cart. Those who sought his counsel found solace in his words; he possessed a rare gift for seeing to the heart of the matter, cutting through the noise and confusion to offer clarity and insight.

"You must have faith miss Eliza, there is a guide for those who have lost their way."

"Hmm, you sound wise Mr Chase."

"Wisdom comes with time and experience of life, have you lost your way Eliza?"

"I don't know Mr Chase, I might not have had a away, my life is one of confusion."

The cart trundled on southward and eventually they reached the outskirts of Durham City. It being a rather small city, as cities go it wasn't long before the cart stopped outside of the Dun Cow tavern, which dated back to the 15th century. In 995AD, Lindisfarne monks searching for a resting place for the body of St Cuthbert came across a milkmaid looking for her lost cow. She directed them to Dun Holm (Durham), and the pub is named after the historic animal.

"I have been instructed to drop you here Eliza, your aunt will be here presently, goodbye."

With that the cart clattered away over the cobbles with Alfred Chase bouncing on top. As this was the first time Eliza had visited the city it all came as a bit of a shock to her country outlook. The architecture of the city reflected its rural nature with timber-framed cottages with thatched roofs and antiquated, leaded windows. The buildings huddled closely together along narrow lanes, creating a claustrophobic atmosphere. A sturdy stone church with a tall spire dominated the skyline, its bells chiming softly throughout the day.

This was so different to Elersly she thought, the houses had windows but the cleanliness and hygiene of the place was no better. Animal dung was laying in the streets, with some possibly not the responsibility of animals and the smell was a pungent mix of many factors producing sickly, sweet aroma that caught the senses. She stood there for a while taking in the scene and the activities of the city, it was exciting in some ways, intimidating in others.

Then she saw a middle aged woman approach, slim of build with a mature head of finest grey hair tied back for safety reasons. "Hello Eliza, it's Aunt Agnes, it has been some time, Come child I will take you to my house, it's a bit of a walk but this is only a small town."

Eliza had only met Agnes a couple of times in her short life and could barely recognise her. She did look familiar and there was a resemblance to her mother but in all honesty she could have been anybody. The pair walked over Elvet Bridge and up Silver Street to the market square, the square was even more hectic.

In the central square, bustling markets sprang to life each morning, offering an array of goods from local artisans and farmers. Tradesmen plied their crafts in open-air workshops, the sound of hammering and the scent of freshly cut wood filling the air. Farmers arrive from the surrounding countryside, their carts laden with produce and livestock, eager to barter and trade with city dwellers.

The house was not that far away on the edge of town but far enough to be free of the bustle for the most part, rounding a corner there it was in front of her. Nestled within the cobblestone street stands a small house, its timbers weathered by time and adorned with creeping ivy, the structure, modest in size, exudes an aura of simplicity and warmth. The exterior is constructed of timber framing, with sturdy oak beams forming the skeleton of the house. Whitewashed walls, though faded with age, still bear traces of their original brightness, the thatched roof, golden in hue, slopes gently downwards. A single wooden door, worn smooth from years of use, serves as the entrance. Above it, a small, leaded glass window allows slivers of daylight to filter into the dim interior.

Inside, the layout is compact yet functional; a central hearth dominates the main living space, its stone facade a focal point for both cooking and warmth. Wooden furniture, crafted by skilled hands, is arranged neatly around the hearth. In one corner, a simple wooden table sits, adorned with a few earthenware plates and pewter goblets. Nearby, shelves line the walls, holding necessities such as herbs, candles, and cooking utensils.

Aunt Agnes leads Eliza up a narrow staircase to the upper level, where a small sleeping loft awaits. Here, a straw mattress rests upon a wooden frame, covered by a patchwork quilt sewn with care. "This will be your sleeping room Eliza, it's not much but it's comfortable."

"This is very good Auntie it is better than I have at home."

"Hmm my dear I think you will find a lot of things different here and importantly you will not have to endure the malice and violence of the villagers, I know you have had suffered."

"Have you no children Agnes?"

"No dear I was not blessed with such."

"So where is your husband?"

"I am a widow, my husband died some ten years since, he was a goodly man."

As the night began to creep over the land and the light faded Eliza stood at the door and gazed up at huge structure of the famous cathedral of Durham.

She was joined by Agnes, "you seem captivated Eliza, it is quite a sight isn't it?"

"Yes I have heard tales of this place but it is more than I expected."

"Tomorrow I will take you up there so you can see the full splendour."

It would be fair to say that Eliza did not sleep well that night; all was strange and unusual and as morning pierced another night all seemed better with the world. After some breakfast Agnes and Eliza set off up the narrow cobbled ascent of Saddler Street and suddenly there it was rising in front of them like some giant hulk.

Durham Cathedral stands on a rocky height bounded on the east, south, and west by a bend of the river Wear. To the north and south of the cathedral the level space is considerable, but the building occupies the whole extent of the level ground from east to west, the buttresses of the westernmost portion actually descending the face of the cliff some forty feet then the thickly wooded incline falls away briskly to the river. The position is one of the most commanding of any in England, and the view of the cathedral from the west and south-west is extremely imposing. The site has been occupied by a church from 995, the Dean of Durham, is the head of the Chapter of Durham Cathedral and the most senior priest in the Diocese of Durham.

As they approached the huge door Eliza noticed the carved metal knocker.

"Eliza, that is the sanctuary knocker, it is an important symbol of the Cathedral's governmental role. The knocker on the Cathedral's northern door, known as the Sanctuary Knocker, played an important part in the Cathedral's history. Those who 'had committed a great offence,' such as murder in self-defence or breaking out of prison, could rap the knocker, and would be given 37 days of sanctuary within which they could try to resolve with their difficulties or plan their escape.

They toured the cathedral for some time and it should be said the Eliza was in awe and wonderment at the magnificence of such a structure. They stood for a while at the tomb of Saint Bede the Venerable monk of Jarrow and then walked along the marbled floor to the grave of Saint Cuthbert. His tomb was flanked by eight large candles in silver holders, the dappled light, flickering flames casting an aura of peace and tranquillity.

Agnes gazed up at the high vaulted ceiling, "take it in Eliza this is the power of our Lord."

Eliza replied quickly, "what would the Lord know of us mere peasants; he has not been by my side in times of need, nor my poor mother, nor your husband."

Agnes was somewhat puzzled by this response but said nothing.

Eliza would adjust to life in the city gradually and would stay with her aunt for a month before returning to Elersly. The whole adventure being that of knowledge and learning that would stay with her as she contemplated the future, be it good or bad.

CHAPTER 5

The small village of Elersly was once more born of another day in the turning of the world. The morning sun lights the place like a beacon of hope and expectation. However, hope was not something the people of this village payer much heed to, as hope almost never became truth; at least the weather was fine, dry and warm. This too had its disadvantages as the smell of the place produced its own aroma, the domesticated animals contributed to the miasma and brought with it a plague of flies that inundated every corner of this hamlet.

Jane Mason finished her chores around the as any other ten year old would do, her mother having washed some clothes in a tub and Jane was tasked with ringing hand hanging to dry in the sun.

"Right girl you can go out now but don't go too far, do you hear?"

"Yes mother, of course mother!"

Jane walked into the village square and sat on the stone ring around the well. She mused on why there was a well as the water was probably no cleaner or less adulterated than the river. Before too long the other three girls in the group arrived. Mulling what to do they decided to go up into the hills to a place called Crooked Snout. As Jane Mason was the leader of the group, at least she thought she was by way of being a few months older than the other three and more intimidating, she was respected out of fear not affection.

Even though she had been ordered to stay close to the village, she ignored her mother's word of wisdom and the words of the other three girls and set off it would take half an hour to climb the steep hill up to the moor and another twenty to reach Crooked Snout. At the top of the hill they found themselves on the high open moorland, uncultivated, treeless landscape characterized by extensive expanse of grass, heather, bracken, mosses, and peat bogs, typically found in upland areas.

The vegetation on moorlands is adapted to the harsh environmental conditions, including strong winds, low temperatures, and poor soil quality. Heather, in particular, is a dominant plant species on many moors, providing a vibrant purple hue during the summer season, capturing both the harshness and the mystique of these wild places.

Further on they reached Crooked Snout, nature's grand display of cascading, tumbling and surging water, it was an awe-inspiring sight that captivated the senses, a tumultuous rush of water, plunging from a great height, creating a breath taking spectacle of power and beauty. At the summit, the river emerges, flowing gracefully before it reaches the precipice, as it nears the edge, the water gathers momentum, a relentless force ready to embrace the void below. Then, with a thunderous roar, it dives into the abyss, a mesmerizing free fall, creating a veil of mist that shrouds the surroundings.

As the water descends, it transforms into a flurry of frothy white, carving its path through rugged rocks and verdant vegetation. The air is filled with the sound of its mighty descent, a symphony of nature's raw energy echoing through the canyon. At the base, the river emerges anew, reborn from the chaos above; it resumes its journey, now enriched by the experience, carving its way through the landscape with renewed energy, its banks a haven of life drawn to the abundant nourishment and vitality the river brings.

The four girls, hot and tired sat on the grass, next to the river and viewed it with wonder, none of them had been this far from the village and it was a fine sight. Having recovered their breath, Alice Simms suggested a game of hide and seek. Jane being the most dominant and confident insisted on being first on. The other girls did as they were told and covered their eyes, Jane slipped away into the bushes.

The girls finished their count and jumped to their feet spinning around deciding which track the follow, so they all set off on different trails none of them knowing who was right. They searched for what seemed quite some time but could not find her, they regrouped at the river. They conversed with one another where they had searched and none had any clue as to where Jane was hiding. They decided between them to accept that Jane had won and they should concede defeat. Alice Simms began to shout, "Jane come out we give up!"

There was no answer, they all shouted in unison, no response came from the surrounding countryside apart from the sound of bees crickets and skylarks. They gazed at each other for some time pondering what to do, "where the hell is she?" Came an agitated question.

Jane mason ran away from her friends and into the bushes and undergrowth confident that she was much more intelligent than her friends and she would never be found. She sat and waited, she could hear the sounds of her friends down below; she climbed to the top of crooked Snout and looked down at the river below but no sign of her friends.

Then it came a voice close by but soft and composed, "Jane Mason, I see you Jane!"

Jane turned to find another girl behind her; she gazed at this girl with curiosity. Her presence a curious blend of mysteriousness and innocence, her hair, a cascade of midnight black, falling in soft waves around her shoulders, framing a delicate face. But it's her eyes that drew Jane, piercing orbs as dark as obsidian, devoid of any discernible colour, yet seemingly holding a universe of secrets within.

"My God how did you get there, I heard nothing, who are you?"

"God Jane Mason, do you believe he belongs to you?"

"No I mean it's only a saying, you look familiar, who are you?"

"I matters not who I am but I know you Jane Mason."

Jane took a step backward, "wait a minute, you're the one who stopped us beating Eliza Swann."

"You are correct Jane, for once in your life you have got something right but for you it will be the last thing, goodbye!"

With those words still reverberating through her mind she was thrust backwards by a powerful but invisible force. Her screams echoed through the gorge as if trapped in a moment in time as she tumbled and plummeted before crashing into the raging vortex. The churning mass of white water sucked her young body into its lair.

The other girls heard a scream echo in the air which produced some alarm, the searched for a few more minutes but could find nothing.

"What shall we do?" Alice Simms shouted.

They decided all that could be done was to return to the village and admit that their little adventure had turned into a nightmare. They turned as if one and made their way off the moor, down the hill and into the village. Elersly was busy with people milling around doing their daily tasks, the girls were mostly ignored, they had other things to worry about. This would not last as word spread that a girl from the village was missing.

Alice Simms returned home to find her mother resting in the sun.

"Hello Mother, where is Father?"

"He's out working in the fields, where have you been?"

"Well Mother you know how you said not to go far, well I was forced by the others."

"Forced, where have you been and how did they force you?"

"There was four of us went up to Crooked Snout, problem is only three of us came back!"

"You have been told more than once not to go up there, what do you mean only three came back, who did not return and why?"

"We were playing hide and seek, Jane mason ran off to hide, we searched everywhere but we could not find her. So we gave in and called her to come out of hiding, she didn't come."

"My God lass where is she now?"

"We don't know Mother, she is gone, vanished!"

"You stay here and don't move do you understand?"

"Yes Mother but where are you going?"

"This is serious, I must inform the ealdorman."

Ann Simms made to the house of Ealdorman Hudson as quickly as she could manage and informed him of the situation. He then informed Jane's family who were angry and distraught in equal measure. A search party was called for and a dozen men answered the appeal. They set off up onto the moors, beating the heather for any clue, the found nothing apart from the odd scared pheasant screeching disapproval. Four men stayed on the moor while the others made their way up to Crooked Snout. They searched until the light faded and they were relieved by more men with flaming torches wavering in the night sky. The men returned to the village in the early hours it being too dark to find anything torch or not.

It would be fair to say the village of Elersly did not rest easy that night. It was of course even worse for Mr and Mrs Mason as their daughter was out there alone in the darkness. As the sun lit the horizon the search resumed, the searchers joined by two hunting dogs.

Later someone rode into the village on a fine grey horse; it was the Sheriff of County Durham with four of his men. Andrew Platt as sheriff of this county was a very important and powerful man and immediately took charge of the situation. There was a notion that Jane could have fallen into the river, so four men were sent to search both banks downstream. Both upstream and down the search was becoming useless and eventually it was stopped.

The next day came and the day after and not a trace could be found of Jane Mason. Later that day John Mills was watching his flock of sheep on the moor when he realised there was one missing. He went off looking for the stray and ended up at the foot of Crooked Snout and there floating face down in the water was a body. At first the shock did not register as he was not sure at first weather it was a dead sheep. He soon realised that it was not, his stray was left to find its own way back to the flock as John Mills raced into the village shouting!

The village was immediately thrown into confusion as the news broke, a man was sent to inform the sheriff and Ealdorman Hudson took a cart and two men up to Crooked Snout. The sight that met them was one of shock and repulsion, one of the men being in a state of vomit. They gazed at the body which by this time had washed onto some rocks.

The sight was one of torment as they dragged one of their own from this resting place. It was only then that the true horror unfolded before them, the body having been in the water for a few days was nothing more stinking, bloated mass of grey and blue. The body was wrapped in cloth and transported back to the village; Ealdorman Hudson went over to the Mason household to break the news.

"Mr and Mrs Mason I bring only bad news this day, a body has been found in the river at the bottom of Crooked Snout, we believe it to be that of your daughter, Jane."

"What it cannot be, how do you know it's my Jane?"

Ealdorman Hudson rubbed his face; this was not an easy situation for him either. "We don't Mrs Mason, when a body has been in the water for some time it can make it almost unrecognisable. However, unless there is another local girl missing, it must be Jane."

Ealdorman Hudson left the Mason's to their grief and went to Saint Andrew's Church and spoke to Reverend Marshal. Ealdorman Hudson described the trauma within the village and explained the situation, "I suppose you have heard the news?"

"Yes indeed I have, I have only been pastor of this parish a short time, I hope that I am not the bringer of misfortune, the people will be asking where is their God and saviour."

"Yes reverend it is a tragedy all round, could you prepare a plot in your graveyard for this poor girl, it need only be a simple affair, is that possible reverend?"

Ealdorman Hudson, "I must ask you something first, it's a slightly delicate matter. Can you be sure this was not suicide or she cannot be buried on consecrated ground, are you sure?"

"Yes Sir it was a simple and tragic accident, no more than that."

Reverend Marshal satisfied had a plot dug at the back of the church and next morning poor Jane was lowered into the earth wrapped only in a white sheet as a coffin was too expensive. There was no great service the reverend said a prayer that was all that was required for a simple peasant girl.

Next morning Ann Simms marched through the village with purpose in mind, ignoring all around her. She arrived at the house of Mary Swann ban began to furiously bang on the door. Mary answered the door and was surprised to see Ann Simms standing rigid with anger.

"Morning Ann, what brings you here this day?"

"You know fine well Mary Swann, what more misery can this village endure? There has been nothing but sorrow since that night ten years past."

"You are deranged Ann Simms, what has any of this to do with us?"

"Where is that daughter of yours, is she blameless also?"

"Eliza is staying with her aunt in Durham and has been for some weeks, to get away from you and your pack of brutes. You must find someone else to blame for this, now be gone!"

CHAPTER 6

Five years had passed and autumn was here again, morning unveiled a landscape transformed by nature's artistic brushstrokes. As the sun rises lethargically over the horizon, its gentle rays filtering through a canopy of amber, crimson, and gold, casting a warm, ethereal glow upon the earth below. The crisp, cool air carried the faint trace of fallen leaves and the promise of another looming winter.

Dew-kissed grass sparkled like scattered diamonds, glistening in the soft morning light. The occasional rustle of leaves, carried by a gentle breeze, creating a soothing symphony, a delicate reminder of the changing season. The world seems to pause, caught between the vibrant hues of summer and the serene stillness of winter.

Silhouettes of trees stand tall and proud, their branches adorned with a mosaic of foliage in shades ranging from fiery reds to earthy browns. Squirrels scurry about, collecting provisions for the colder days ahead, while birds chirp their songs, bidding farewell to the departing warmth of summer. In the distance, the misty veil of dawn slowly dissipates, revealing rolling hills and valleys painted in a medley of autumnal colours. The landscape, once lush and green, now wears a cloak of rustic grandeur, a testament to the cyclical rhythm of nature's ever-changing tapestry.

For the people of the village of Elersly nothing much had changed, some people had reached the age of expiry and others were born into poverty and uncertainty. The son of Martha Jacobs was one of those unfortunate enough to be born into this world of pain. It had been almost five years since Edward Jacobs entered this realm and he had not fared well.

Although seemingly healthy in body, he was afflicted with some sort of mental disturbance. He could speak but only a few words and seemed to struggle to understand basic instructions. Needless to say young Edward had now become the target of people in the village, mainly the young girls who took great pleasure in mocking him with unpleasant names.

Eliza Swann although still the subject of harassment did not suffer quite as badly as she had before. She had now reached the age of fifteen and had grown into a fine young woman, with a beauty and elegance that was at odds with the rest of the village population. The local girls were somewhat jealous as the boys turned their eyes toward Eliza and not them.

Edward Jacobs was sitting on the grass flicking small stones at a wooden fence; Eliza approached and sat down beside him.

"You are Edward Jacobs are you not?"

Edward gazed at her for quite some time, "Yes, I, I I am so."

"Well I am pleased to meet you Edward, have you no chores today?"

"I am not allowed to help, father says, that I, I, cannot be, be trusted."

"Oh I see, where do you live Edward?"

Edward pointed a skeletal finger, "there."

"Oh close to home I see."

"I,I, am not allowed to go far."

"Do the children of the village pick on you Edward?"

"Yes, yes, It upsets me."

Eliza looked at him as his eyes began to water, she knew how he was feeling all too well.

"I know how it feels Edward for you see I suffered the same treatment for many years and still do. The people think me and my family a curse on the village, every turn of misfortune is laid at the door of my mother and me."

Edward stared at her, "what is y, y your name?"

"I am Eliza Swann."

Edward reacted immediately as he jumped to his feet walked off at some pace.

"Wait Edward what is wrong?"

Edward glanced back, "I have been told not to speak with you, I, I must go now."

With that he walked away leaving Eliza sitting on the grass contemplating her situation and her very future in this place, nothing had changed and nothing would.

Later that day Eliza was out picking wild berries when she was approached by Alice Simms, who possessed an expression of annoyance and, which was nothing new for her.

"You were seen talking to young Edward Jacobs this morning, you are not allowed, hear!"

"Oh truly, I speak with whomever I choose Alice Simms!"

"Let it be known that the boy is very sick, what do you know of this Eliza Swann, what dark magic have you conjured on this young boy?"

"Dark magic, what nonsense you speak Alice, if I possessed dark magic I would surly use it on you and a few more besides!"

Alice stormed off in one direction and Eliza in the other, having picked some berries, she returned home, her mother was busy washing a few cooking pots, the few they possessed.

"Hello daughter did you find any berries?"

Eliza sat on a stool and placed the basket of berries on the small, rough cut table and sighed aloud immediately attracting the attention of her mother.

"You seem troubled lass, what bothers you?"

"This morning I met a young boy called Edward Jacobs, I stopped and spoke with him a while, he has distress speaking but he tried his best, he wanted to talk to me but could not."

"I have heard of this boy Eliza, he suffers from some malady of the mind."

"I got the impression that I was one of the few people that spoke to him in pleasant manner and he was trying his best to respond until."

"Until what Eliza?"

"He asked my name and everything suddenly changed, he jumped up as if in shock and walked off as if in some sort of shock."

It was now the turn of Mary Swann to sigh aloud. "Nothing much changes around here Eliza, I do not think it ever will, we are not trusted, we are despised among the folk!"

"I was accoster by Alice Simms just now she says the boy is very ill with some sickness and of course it must be our fault as always. When I say the lad he was eating grass, I told him it was not good to do such things, I don't know what else he might have eaten. You know some medical potions, if we could help the lad, it could change things for us."

"Hmm, I do know something's there used to be a wise woman who lived in the village before she was hounded out by people who suspected her of having strange powers. She now lives in a small hut up in the high hills, she showed me how to make a potion for such ailments, I will mix it up."

Eliza walked through the village square and knocked on the door of the Jacob's family; Mrs Jacobs opened the door and stood rigid as if in fear. "Eliza Swann what do you want here?"

"I heard your boy was ailing, my mother mixed a potion, we thought it might help."

"Don't you think you have caused enough misery in this village?"

"Whatever misery befalls this village is none of our doing, take the mixture."

"It could be poison, how can I trust you?"

"You cannot know that, but if not treated your son will die anyway!"

After some discourse Eliza was allowed into the house, Edward was lying on a simple cot; he was not faring too well. He was as pale as snow, his stomach seemed to be in spasm and a milking pail was at the side of the bed acting as a receptacle for vomit.

"Give the boy this mixture at intervals overnight."

"I don't know it might kill him!"

"Mrs Jacobs see reason, he will die anyway!"

The next day came and Eliza was outside washing some clothes in a tub.

"Miss Swann." There stood Martha Jacobs, she seemed to be in some distress.

"Mrs Jacobs you seem upset, is Edward alright, how does he fare?"

"That is why I am crying, Edward is much improved, he is not completely cured but he up and about and he fares much better!"

"I am so pleased to hear that he is improving, the potion worked I see."

"Please accept the thanks of me and my family Miss Swann please pass it to your mother, we are in your debt."

Eliza and her mother hoped that this affair would change things in their favour but it would take some time if ever. They had made one ally but had their new friend also made herself enemies. This was something for future times as the days went by and winter once again licked its frigid tongue on the land it would become clearer when the sun came again and life returned.

CHAPTER 7

As another winter day unfolded with a tranquil splendour, marked by a crisp chill the landscape blanketed in a soft layer of snow, glistening under the pale, diffused light of the winter sun. The morning started with a gentle frost covering windows and tree branches, sparkling like a sea of tiny diamonds.

As the day progressed, the cold air remained sharp and the breath forms visible wisps of vapour with each exhale. Bare trees stand stark against the sky, their branches etching intricate patterns. Occasionally, the tranquillity is interrupted by the crunching sound of footsteps on snow or the distant call of a crow. The fields a pristine white, and the silence almost tangible, broken only by the rustling of leaves or the sound of a distant stream flowing under a layer of ice, the scene was one of magic, cold magic.

Five miles north of the village of Elersly lay a small hamlet, so small it did not have an official name, it had come to be known as Huntly as hundreds of years past it was a favourite hunting ground of the resident nobility. Now the local land owner had parcelled the land up into four small tenant farms, the land however, was not the best as the soil was poor and was the haunt of sheep and not much else.

John and Margaret Hopper tended to a farmstead in the small hamlet of Huntly and as the typical residents of these north lands were hard working, poor and humble folks. Life was hard and so were the people they had to be to survive, there was no help forthcoming from any quarter. On any given day John Hopper and his wife would be going about their normal duties however, this was not any given day, it was Sunday morning the Sabbath. John and Margret wrapped themselves as best they could with their meagre clothing and headed down the icy track to Elersly.

It could be said that all was not well with Margaret Hopper of late, as her state of mind had begun to wander and she had suffered strange dreams that troubled her and her husband. She was adamant that these images were not dreams or even nightmares but were real. John did not believe this and brushed it off as some malady of the mind but he knew fine well that doctors were far too expensive for his pocket, so they muddled on as best they could.

The village of Elersly was a bustle of quiet movement as the population to a man and woman and child made their way to Saint Andrews for morning mass. Margret Hopper entered and was about to be followed by her husband when he heard a voice. "John!"

He turned and there stood his old friend Harold Kerr, "Harrold how fair you old friend?"

"Oh as well as can be expected and you and Margaret?"

"I am not too bad in myself but I fear Margret is far from so!"

"Oh what ails her?"

"She is fine in body, it is her mind that is troubled and she has terrible dreams almost every night, wakes up screaming and panicking, I am at a loss Harry is she bewitched?"

"No old friend she is just having a momentary loss of balance, you will see."

The y both went into the church and sat at the pews, John sat next to his wife and spoke softly to her. "I have just seen Harrold Kerr, he fares well, Margret do you hear?"

Margret did not hear or if she did she was not saying, John tried again, once more Margret was quiet. John was somewhat disturbed by this behaviour but passed it off, until Reverend Marshal approached the lectern. At once Margret emerged from her stupor and let out an almighty scream that resonated around the church as if the church was screaming back. The congregation shocked and startled looked around in panic not knowing what was happening.

Margaret Hopper stood up and began shouting in a deep guttural voice that shook the very rafters of this old place as it had never heard of seen before. "Stay away! She shouted.

She then ran out of the church leaving the rest in stunned silence, John ran after her. Margret was in the village square pacing around feverishly. Reverend Marshal came and spoke to John in an attempt to calm him with some advice.

"John has Margret had any physical symptoms, doctors say the body was made up of four humours, blood, phlegm, yellow bile or black bile, has she had any of these?"

"No, her body is healthy; I fear her mind is diseased!"

"Take her home and see that she rests, we will pray for both of you!"

John Hopper did just that, Margret overcome with some sudden lethargy went to her bed where she slept soundly as if in some sort of torpor. The next two days she seemed to recover from what ailed her so badly and was more or less herself again. This was with great relief for John who was by now beside himself with worry. Of course as worry is banished it almost always comes back. One evening John was sitting in front of the fire place warming himself when a dreadful shriek grabbed his attention.

John ran into the bedroom not knowing what to expect, he found his wife on the bed. She was shaking and convulsing in a violent manner, John had by now been convinced the Margret was bewitched. He tried to get her to recite the Lord's Prayer, it being unsuccessful; Margaret began to foam at the mouth and could not recite the ending. The bed was now shaking before Margret sat upright staring and pointing outside.

"Did you not see him; did you not see the Devil?"

It was then that a great rumbling occurred from outside John ran out and gazed around the place, at first he saw nothing until he set his eyes on something to the side. There stood a massive black dog glaring at him with menace its eyes cutting his soul like a hot knife. John fell to his knees and began to pray as he had never done before continued to pray, the creature mercifully disappeared. As it did it was replaced by the image of a young girl with a shining complexion, he stayed on his knees before her, thanked the lord and the child vanished.

John Hopper composed himself for a minute, not quite sure if this was real or some sort of fantasy of the mind. Turning away he went to see to his wife when he was stopped by another woman, it was Sarah Armstrong from the next door farm with an expression of great concern.

"We heard frightful screams and no end of commotion, what on earth is going on here John, where is Margret is she alright?"

"She is in the house Sarah, she fares badly and I have no answers, I think her bewitched!"

"Have you been at that homemade mead again John?"

"No Sarah did you not see the dog, over there," he said pointing.

"I saw no dog John; it would be fitting to see dogs on a farm would it not?"

"Not this dog, it was massive, black as the night with glaring red eyes.

"John you should go inside and rest."

"The girl, where did she go, she just vanished!"

"Girl, I saw no girl either, I think you both should see a physician."

"We can't afford doctors or medication, we have no hope!"

"John, we have no money either to help, the only thing I can think of there is a woman lives high up in the hills, have you heard of Isabella Mosswood?"

"What you mean that old hag raven that was driven out of Elersly years back, is that her?"

"Yes John, I will admit she is a strange and unusual character but she has helped people before, those who dare to ask. Take Margret up there tomorrow, she has a small house on Split Crow Hill, it is worth a try, what else have you got?"

John Hopper went to bed that night having calmed his wife somewhat and contemplated what Sarah Armstrong had said. She was correct of course he had no other means of dealing with such matters so in the morning they wrapped up and set off into the hills. It was not that far away in terms of distance but a world away from what they knew and it was all up hill. Eventually they reached the top of Split Crow Hill and there in front of them a small cottage.

Tucked away amidst a canopy of ancient, gnarled trees, bent over by the strong winds that afflicted the high moor the house stood as a testament to the merging of nature and magic. Moss-clad stones formed its foundation, while twisted vines ensnared its walls, weaving an impenetrable barrier against the outside world. A crooked chimney protruded from the thatched roof, its smoke curling into the sky like ghostly tendrils.

It was with some unease that John and Margret Hopper approached the door, at the threshold, a weathered door, etched with arcane symbols, John banged on the door. They waited for while not knowing what the outcome of this folly would be when a noise from inside. The sound of metal scraping and an old lock turning and them it opened. There she stood in the doorway; she was a mysterious and eerie figure to behold.

She appeared to be ancient, with wrinkled, leathery skin that had been weathered by time, her face gaunt, with high cheekbones. Her eyes are a sharp and piercing green that seem to see right through you, conveying a sense of hidden knowledge and power. She was dressed in a tattered, dark-coloured robe made of course, rough fabric, long tattered grey hair tumbling over her shoulders. She looked at them for what seemed and age before she spoke.

"Who are you what brings you to my door this day?"

"Would you be Isabella Mosswood?" John asked nervously.

"I don't know yet, what do you want of me?"

"My wife has been very sick of late, she needs help, we were told that you can heal."

Isabella Mosswood looked Margret up and down, "It is a sickness of the mind I see."

The wise woman stepped back and beckoned them inside, her movements are deliberate and often slow but with an air of assurance for one so old and timeworn. They followed her inside and immediately began to take in the scene. The inside of the house is a reflection of her nature, dark, cluttered, and filled with strange objects, jars of unknown substances, and ancient books, the air is thick with the scent of herbs and incense. Several candles eliminated the place with dancing light. They gazed around in awe until their attention was taken by noise in the corner, there sat a giant raven staring at them with menace.

Isabella Mosswood motioned John and to sit on an old wooden bench, they did as said. The old woman went into a dark corner and began to gaze into a crystalline translucent orb. She began to speak in riddles or cryptic phrases, after some time she returned and stood quietly.

MRs Hopper, I have seen visions of the past, you have sinned."

Margret responded immediately, "No, we are God fearing people!"

"It was not your God that you offended but the Earth itself."

"But how could that be, I have done no wrong?"

The wise woman glared at her, "the Elder Mother is displeased, you must make amends."

"How will I do that?"

"You recently cut branches from an Elder tree without permission and you burned them!"

"Well yes I did burn some wood but I don't understand."

"You affronted the Elder Mother, damaging an Elder without permission will bring grave consequences upon the perpetrator. She is merciful; you must repeat what I say word for word. Old girl, give me some of thy wood and I will give thee some of mine when I grow into a tree."

Margret Hopper did as she was told and repeated the words and immediately she was overcome with emotion, tears began to gush from her eyes, running down her face onto the floor. She stood up and grabbed the old woman's skeletal hand, "thank you!"

In the next few days Margret was much improved, much to the relief of her husband John. She was going about her daily duties as if nothing had happened, however, while gathering wood for the fire she came across the very same elder tree that she had taken without asking.

She gazed at it for some time and wondered how a simple tree could have such power. She did however, not touch a single branch as she knew fine well that something made her sick in the mind and something made her well. Was it the strange woman in the hills or a simple coincidence? She did not know but was not prepared to risk another mistake, she held out her arms in a manner of remorse, "sorry that I offended you Elder Mother!"

She continued to pick wood that was lying around but did not touch a living tree. Tying the bundle together with a cord she swung it across her back and made for home. She did not make but a hundred yards when she was stopped in her tracks. There standing at the side of the dirt road a young woman dressed in a white smock. They gazed at each other for a while, Margret had the urge to move on but for some reason she could not. The young woman stepped forward as Margret stepped back uneasily.

Margret looked at this young woman, there's an air of otherworldliness about her, as if she exists on the periphery of truth, dancing between the realms of space and reality.

"You are Margret Hopper are you not?"

"Well yes, do I know you?"

"No I would not say so."

"You appear to know me, how so?"

"I witnessed your ailment from afar and your cure."

"Wait a moment, you were the young woman my husband saw that night, who are you?"

"I have no name, no home, not even a family, I watch over this place and its people."

"Young woman I feel anxious in your presence, do you mean me harm?"

"That rather depends on you Margret, you committed a crime against Mother Earth but you repented. I am strong and have much power but do no harm and you need not fear!"

Margret went home and told her husband of her meeting. He was somewhat surprised but there again not as the matters in this district had become more and more strange and unpredictable.

Margret sat down on a stool and rubbed her eyes as if tired from some exertion, she looked up at her husband who was observing her as he worried that she might relapse again.

"John, when she spoke, I felt something inside, I cannot explain it, was as if it touched my very soul!"

John Hopper was pacing around the room half expecting some surprise of other and was somewhat relieved when it did not appear.

"Do not fret dear wife, we live in strange times!"

CHAPTER 8

May 1618

Time went by, the days and weeks followed on as usual and winter once more blended into spring. On the high moor lark song pierced the air, everything was fresh and new, all was happy with the world. Even the supposedly cursed village of Elersly, had not been afflicted at least no more than usual.

Of course this was the ancient county of Durham and in particular the rugged North West corner. In this particular area was the village of Elersly, where nothing was normal or it seemed so at times. The spring sunshine brought light to the place but darkness was never far from creeping upon the unguarded. It was just so as word spread of strange occurrences in a village to the south of Elersly.

Once off the high moor the landscape slipped steeply into a lush green valley. A stream called the Brownie slipped past almost unnoticed until it slipped onto the main river almost unnoticed. The wooded valley was alive with a symphony of vibrant colours and sounds. The forest canopy, a delicate patchwork of newly unfurled leaves in varying shades of green, filtered the sunlight into a soft, golden glow. Light dances on the forest floor, creating shifting patterns of light and shadow.

The air is crisp and filled with the fresh, earthy scent of damp soil, delicate wildflowers, in hues of blue, white, and yellow dot the underbrush. Ferns unfurl their fronds in intricate spirals and moss carpets the ground and clings to the trunks of ancient trees. Tall, sturdy trees, oaks, maples and birches stretch their limbs skyward, their branches forming a lush canopy overhead. New growth adorns their branches, the leaves still tender and fresh, glowing with the vitality of the season. Here and there, clusters of saplings and undergrowth vie for sunlight, a testament to the valley's fertility and life.

The brownie winds through the valley, its crystal-clear water sparkling in the sunlight. The brook's gentle murmurs add a soothing rhythm to the natural orchestra. Pebbles and stones of varying shapes and colours line its banks, polished smooth by the continuous flow of water. Sitting in the midst of the forest sat the village of Greenslade, the place being much the same as the village of Elersly to the north.

Greenslade had not been adversely troubled as its neighbour to the north, apart from the usual miseries of life in this place and these times. Dirty land, dirty people and dirt poor! On the edge of the village was the little tumble down house of Jane Frizzel. The house did not have an official name but was known locally as Crooked Oak because of the twisted old tree of the same name. The house lay on a cross roads between Elersly and the hills to the north and Durham City to the south.

A farmhouse, by the name of Crooked Oak, was situated in one of the most beautiful yet notorious areas of the Valley. Jane Frizzel was one of Crooked Oaks most well-known inhabitants, known or suspected locally as being a witch. It was said she, was guilty of casting spells on men, maidens, and cattle. The farmhouse was said to be the site where witchcraft was believed to be practised, referred to locally as "Dark Arts." It has been said that Jane was tutored and trained in the dark arts of witchcraft by her mother Elizabeth and carried on the belief.

Elizabeth Frizzel had also been suspected of witchcraft but had died some years ago before the authorities could not arrest her. It is said that she is buried in an unmarked grave in a field at the back of the farmhouse near to where she lived. It is said that travellers would carry a crooked silver sixpence in their hands, when crossing the surrounding lands, to save them from an attack by witches.

And it would be so, that the sleepy village of Greenslade, would fall into the grip of darkness. The people of this hamlet had contemplated the fate of the nearby village to the north; Elersly seemed to be cursed but Greenslade seemed to be blessed, until now as things were changing.

It all started one spring morning as Mary Jones had spent the night tending to her husband Richard. He had been ill all night with a fever and could not be roused, Mary tried her best but her limited knowledge of medicine restricted her. As the sun came up that morning Mary, by now frantic with worry and frustration went out into the street and began asking people if they could help.

The people of the village had no more knowledge that she did and word quickly spread that there was some sort of pestilence. Instead of helping the unfortunate Joneses they panicked and a delegation was sent to the house. Mary Jones was bundled inside with her husband and the house was boarded up with planks of wood. Mary shouted her outrage but to no affect, as the people would not open the door until they were sure it was safe.

Later that day Richard passed away, still they kept Mary a prisoner, some people supplied her with some food and drink but would not let her out for another two days. It was declared that the cause of death was sweating sickness, although the villages did not believe this and thought something darker was at hand.

Over the next few days things began to deteriorate a s several chickens were found dead along with a new born piglet. Things got worse still as a farmer came into the village to report that his cow had died of no particular reason. This produced a great amount of discourse as to the cause of these deaths and as no practical reason could be found it was declared to be the work of the Devil.

Suspicion abounded as to the cause and one person immediately came to the minds of the populace: Jane Frizzel of Crooked Oak, she had been suspected of such practices as had her mother before but nothing could be proved. It was decided that people from the village should take turns in watching Jane Frizzel day and night, her movements and practices.

This went on for a few days and nights until one night as the sun slipped behind the hills, Roger Cole sat at the back of Crooked Oak. Sitting obscured by a bush he was not in the best of comfort and was wondering why he volunteered for this task. He did not have to wait long however, as there was suddenly movement in the half light, it was Jane Frizzel. Dressed in a black cloak she walked out into the field and pausing at a small, grass covered mound began to chant some unknown verses. Roger Cole could not hear clearly nor could he understand but lying on his stomach he observed the scene. Jane Frizzel was sprinkling some unknown substance on the ground as she chanted in an unknown language.

Having watched for some time he sneaked away and returned to Greenslade, he went to bed but did not sleep well. In the morning he decided to report his suspicions to the ealdorman and set off to his house. He arrived at the house of Mathew Hudson, Ealdorman and was allowed a meeting, his house keeper showed him in. Roger Cole was somewhat overawed not only be meeting such an important person as the Ealdorman but at the utter eminence of the house, he being a lowly peasant had not witnessed such opulence.

Roger Cole sat in a chair before Ealdorman Hudson came in.

"Roger Cole I believe, what can I do for you this fine day?"

Cole was somewhat nervous and composed himself before speaking. "Yes Sir I am he, you might not have heard but we have recently been having great upset in the village."

"You are from Greenslade I understand, pray tell of this upset."

"We have had the deaths of several animals such as chickens and a pig and a cow and one man, the villagers believe it to be dark magic at hand."

"Mr Cole, things live and things die, it is part of the life we all live, why dark magic?"

"There is a place outside of the village called Crooked Oak and there lives a woman by the name of Jane Frizzel. She has long been suspected of witchcraft as was her mother before her. Her mother died some years ago and is reportedly buried behind the house. We decide to take turns watching Jane, where she went, what she did and last night it was my turn."

"So what exactly brings you to me?"

Roger Cole continued, I observed her chanting strange verses I could not understand and she was sprinkling some sort of dust over the ground as if I some ceremony."

"I see it does sound suspicious; I will inform the sheriff, do not fret excessively."

The next morning Jane Frizzel was sitting in a wooden chair at the front of Crooked Oak, when a party of three men on horseback approached. One of the men dismounted and approached her, he being well dressed unlike the local inhabitants.

"Would you be Jane Frizzel?"

"Well yes, who are you?"

"I am Andrew Platt, sheriff of this county; I have here a warrant for your arrest."

Jane looked up in surprise, "arrest, on what grounds?"

"On the grounds of witchcraft madam, take her away to the county jail." He said to the other men, they did as they were ordered and she was whisked off to Durham City. Jane was marched through the city to the jail which was under the arch of Old Elvet Bridge. She was escorted into a cell and left there with the only light coming from a small iron barred window at one side.

"Why am I here?" She demanded to know as the jailer slammed shut the door.

"Don't you worry none, we will look after you!" He said laughing as he walked away.

Jane looked around at her new home, bare stone walls dripping with dampness, a simple cot covered with straw in one corner and a wooden bucket in another. Later that day the jailer returned with some food, a wooden cup of water and a chunk of stale bread. Again she tried to ask the jailer what was happening, she got no answer.

She drank some water and washed down some bread before lying on the cot. She did not sleep well that night; in fact she did not sleep at all as sounds of things moving in the dark disturbed her mind. The morning came as she recognised it as the light pierced the narrow slit in the wall with a golden shaft. Then shortly after the door swung open with a creak and the jailer entered. Grabbing her by the arm she was marched to another room where several men were waiting. She was stripped to the waist and sat in a chair and tied with leather straps.

"What is going on, why am I here?"

There was no answer from the men until a man in a leather mask loomed over her.

"Who are you what do you want with me?"

"Jane Frizzel you have been accused of witchcraft and the pursuit of dark arts at your home in Crooked Oak, how do you plead?"

"Plead, I have nothing to plead for, let me go!"

He produced a bible and opened it at some page, "read that passage aloud so we can hear."

"I cannot, I cannot read anything!"

So Jane Frizzel, you refuse the word of God!"

"Will you listen to me, I cannot read or write!"

He stepped forward and produced a metal spike which he stabbed into her side causing her to recoil back ward in shock, wincing from the pain, the man observed the wound.

"Well well gentlemen, observe, her skin is pierced but no blood is forthcoming. We all know what that means, witches do not bleed as the Devil protects them, you are guilty."

The next morning she was dragged still shouting her innocence in front of district judge Milford Lord. He surveyed her with some interest as she stood in front of him, struggling with the guard on either arm.

"You have been accused of witchcraft, what say you?"

"I am not guilty of witchcraft or any other crime!"

"I have been informed that you would not read from the bible or bleed when pricked."

"I have said Sir that I cannot read, I have committed no crime, you have no proof."

"Bring forth the witness."

A man was escorted into the room, she recognised him immediately, Roger Cole.

The judge gazed at him for a moment, "Roger Cole, I believe that you witnessed the accused one night at Crooked Oak, describe what you saw that night if you please."

Roger Cole hesitated for a second, he had never been in front of a judge before and to his knowledge would not know one if he saw him, he composed himself and spoke.

"There had been suspicions in my village of Greenslade that Jane Frizzel has been practicing the dark arts at her home of Crooked Oak. I witnessed her dancing in the likeness of rabbits, some in the likeness of cats and others creatures. I also observed that she had met the devil and danced with him in the moonlight."

"You are hereby found guilty of the said crime of witchcraft, take her away!"

Jane was dragged kicking and screaming from the room back to her cell, she turned to Roger Cole with a look of sheer contempt, eyes ablaze with hatred.

"You dirty rotten liar Roger Cole, I curse you and all you have to torment in this life!"

Roger Cole returned home with these very words twisting a path through his mind, what if she was a witch after all, what if this curse were to come to pass? These thoughts troubled him for some time as he regurgitated them more often than a cow eating grass.

As for Jane Frizzel, poor Jane was bundled back into her filthy flea ridden cell to wait her fate. Of course she knew just what the sentence for witchcraft was but was not prepared to contemplate it. Weather contemplated or not the reality of the situation grew by the hour as she paced the cold floor in fear and dread at her fate.

The morning came the very morning she had feared; at least it was a fine day for it. The cell door opened and two guards marched outside, her hands were tied behind her back. She was paraded through town past the local population, who were in a state of revulsion and fear. They made their way through the market square, up the steep rise of Saddler Street and into palace Green. A large had assembled to witness her fate and they watched in silence as she was steered toward a scaffold erected on the green.

There in the shadow of the mighty cathedral she climbed the few steps and gazed at the dangling rope. In this crowd was another, a young woman observing the scene quietly, she moved toward the front. A priest was in attendance and he was in the motion of giving a short service, when a heavy, dense fog appeared to rise up from the river below. It covered everything as an ashen, greyish veil that enveloped the surroundings. It created a surreal and obscured landscape, where details were muted and distant objects vanish into a white blur.

In dense fog, sounds can be muffled or misleading. The moisture-laden air absorbing some sounds and creating a still, almost silent environment, it can cause echoes, making it difficult to determine the direction of noises. The strange thing was this fog lasted but a few minutes before it dispersed almost as quickly as it appeared and once more the scene was clear. The scaffold came back into view with one difference, the priest was still there the hangman was also but Jane Frizzel was not.

Panic ensued; the sheriff reacted with some concern. "You men spread out and search everywhere she can't have gone far, I want her found!"

They searched everywhere, throughout the streets and back yards, down by the river and in the bushes and trees, they found nothing. Sometime later Jane Frizzel found herself lying on the grass on a hill just above town; she had no idea how she got there or even where she was. Her daze was soon shattered however, as the shape of a young woman appeared next to her. The woman stood there in silence, Jane was not so quiet.

"Where am I, I remember being on a scaffold and now I'm here, who are you?"

The young woman gazed down at Jane for a while her long black hair blowing in the breeze, she held out a hand. "Jane Frizzel, you must come with me now, take my hand."

CHAPTER 9

It was the day after the events in Durham, the sheriff and his men were still searching for Jane Frizzel, almost every inch of the city and its surrounding area was covered. Another posse of men were dispatched to Crooked Oak but found nothing. Eventually the search was called off much to the anger of the sheriff and other in authority, this also affected Roger Cole who gave evidence against her and was now worried of revenge coming his way.

Eliza was by now a fine young woman, a fair maid of the parish someone the people should be proud of. The young men of the village and surrounding areas, although admirers were put off by the very name, Eliza Swann!

As time went by Jane Frizzel did not return to Crooked Oak and the place was abandoned to the elements, in fact Jane was never seen again in the village or the vicinity, she had vanished. Faith and superstition are completely intermingled; they fuse and meld into one another making it difficult to discern the reality. The people of the village did not go near the house, partly because of fear of the place and the unknown elements that resided there.

Eliza Swann was out one day picking herbs and wild plants when she realised that she had walked quite a way south of her home in Elersly. She was in a deep dark forest and through the trees spirals of smoke filtered into the air, she then realised the she was just outside of Greenslade. She walked into the village passing the odd comment with local people, who as a great surprise were friendly and talkative; they did not know her here or most did not.

She decided to return home along the road as it was an easier walk than through the forest. A little way along she came to a crossroads with a small house, she then realised what this place was, Crooked Oak. She decided having heard of the incident to go and inspect the place, she approached carefully and quietly.

The old abandoned house stood in a state of weird stillness, cloaked in an impression of forgotten memories and whispers from the past. The house now ravaged by time and neglect, is a eerie silhouette against the overgrown landscape. Its weathered exterior covered in creeping ivy, tells a silent story of years gone by. The door, slightly ajar and hanging precariously on rusted hinges, creaks ominously with the slightest breeze.

Inside, the air, thick with dust and the scent of mildew, cobwebs hang like spectral drapes in the corners of rooms, and the floors groan underfoot, as if protesting the rare intrusion. Every corner of the house echoes with the faint impressions of the life once lived within its walls. It is a place where time seems to stand still, where the past lingers in every creak and whisper. The old abandoned house is a poignant reminder of impermanence, a silent monument to a bygone era, slowly succumbing to the relentless embrace of nature.

She looked around for a while before she was compelled to go to the land behind the house. There in a tangle of grasses and wild moss was a mound that seemed out of place. This she realised was the simple grave of Jane Frizzel's mother, the old witch of Crooked Oak, the stories now seemed to make sense. Eliza went back to her house and delivered the bag of herbs to her mother who put them away. Eliza sat on a stool and asked her mother to sit.

"Sit Eliza, I am busy you know?"

"Yes mother but it is important."

Eliza paused for a second before continuing, "Mother where is my father?"

"I have not mentioned your father is not here, I don't know where he is."

"But who was he, what was his name?"

"Listen Eliza, I have something to tell you, I do not know who your father is!"

"What, what do you mean you don't know?"

"I am a spinster; daughter and I have not been with a man in my entire life, not one."

"So, I am not well aware of these things but even I know you need a man to have a child."

"Eliza, I promise that I do not know how it happened, it is all a dream, and a hallucination. The thing is I felt not well for some days and then one night I gave birth to, to twins!"

"Twins mother, are you saying I have a sister?"

"Yes daughter, I am saying just that."

"So where is she, what's her name?"

"I did not name her, I did not have time."

"I am confused mother you did not have time, where is she?"

"I have no idea where she is or even if she lives, I have not seen her since the birth."

"So, she has no name and no home, what happened?"

"You were both but hours old when a strange man entered the house, he picked up the other girl and left, he said nothing, it was all like a dream, I remember very little."

Now normally calm and respectful Eliza stood up and stormed out of the house, pausing at the door she turned to her mother. "Mother this is madness, pure lunacy, I must find her!"

Eiiza left the house and walked up the hill onto the moors and walked in a state of anger and confusion. She kept walking till she came to a place called the Windsill. She sat on the edge of the sheer, granite cliff face known as the Windsill, her legs dangling over the side she looked out over the wide span of the Shield Valley.

In complete contrast to the windblown heather and gorse crouching from the elements to her rear, lower down was a spread of fertile pasture. Long grasses rippled in the breeze like a multi-hued ocean of green, and cloud-thrown shadows swept across the dale like the dark hands of some giant phantom.   She stared in awe at the silvery, shimmering slip or the river far below and off to where the shades turned to delicate pastels in the remote distance. Sarah sat in still silence taking in the panoramic view, unaware of time or trouble, and as the gentle breeze stroked her face and lifted her lustrous locks, she slipped away.

She awoke sometime later to find her head buried in the heather and her eyes startled by the blueness of spring. She sat upright and quickly realised that if she had fallen forward in her slumber instead of back, she would have decorated the jagged rocks below, instead of the heather. She gradually pulled herself around and rubber her eyes and as the light began to fade, she became aware of something out of her peripheral vision.

There sitting next to her was a young woman of her own sort of age, long black hair fluttering in the breeze, they gazed at each other for a while, Eliza a little confused.

 "Oh miss you surprised me I did not hear you approach."

"Do not fret Eliza, I move quietly and without disturbance."

"Who are you have we met before, you seem familiar?"

"Oh you know me well enough Eliza, I observe you are troubled and confused."

Eliza gazed at her she was a peculiar woman, her eyes shone like jet in the sun, then changed to the black wings of a raven, without thinking Eliza opened up to this woman.

"You observe well, I am confused, my mind is a muddle of thoughts and feelings."

"You should not fight yourself Eliza, light will turn to shadow. Concentrate on what you have inside and the outside will resolve itself, you will come to terms with the turning of the age, you will see the answers to your dreams. Remember this thing above all others, don't surround yourself with yourself."

The woman stood up and walked away slowly with a sort of elegant grace that seemed out of place for such a woman in such a place, she did not look back. Eliza watched her carefully as she paced into the distant dying light and the she was gone as if she was never there at all. Eliza realising how late it was made her way back to the village with some haste, she entered the house not knowing what would ensue between her and her mother.

"Eliza, where have you been lass?"

"I have been walking on the moors, trying to make sense of the turmoil in my head!"

"Eliza I know this is all bizarre but I have told you the truth of the matter, I know it seems impossible and it has troubled me also, ever since that night I have wondered."

"When I was up on the moors, I sat on the edge of a vertical cliff and I fell into some sort of daze. When I awoke there was another woman there, she was unusual in many ways and she spoke in riddles. I am sure that I have seen her before but I do not know where, who is she, where is she from, why would she be wandering around on the moors, it is a mystery."

"Eliza this world is full of mystery, it is everywhere, the workings of the unknown persist."

Eliza thought for a moment, "mother people in the village say that you danced with the devil and I am the spawn of evil, please say it's not true!"

"I cannot answer you dear Eliza, I had an other worldly experience, more like a dream and I remember very little but rest assured I have not danced with anyone and you are goodness!"

Eliza did not sleep well that night, the thoughts and surprises tunnelling through her brain like worms in the ground. It would be fair to say that her mother was afflicted by the same ailment as she struggled to remember what had taken place. The next morning came and Mary was up early as usual going about her daily chores. Eliza did not rise as usual lying on her cot pondering the meaning of life, the world and everything else she could think of.

Eventually she did rise and had some course bread before going into the village, on passing Saint Andrew's Church she observed several people entering for morning mass, then a familiar voice called her name, it was the young boy Edward Jacobs.

"Ah Edward you look well, you are much better I trust?"

"Y, y, yes I was given a potion, and I, I, got better."

"I know, my mother mixed that very potion for you and I can see it worked well."

"I am on my way to church; my mother is there, are you coming?"

"No Edward I think not."

"Why?"

"You see Edward when you grow older things change just as a person grows; the mind grows and begins to ask questions. I have come to realise that not all things are as they seem, I have no faith, the whole image of a church with its crucifixes, the sights and smells of a church intimidate me I am not comfortable and I would have to leave. There are no demons in hell, they are all here, remember that as you grow. "

"Mother says that I can speak to you now as long as nobody sees me."

"That is fine Edward; you don't want to be seen with someone like me do you?"

As Edward walked toward the church, Eliza walked the other way to contemplate her lot in life and her future in this village. As she would find out this would not be easy and the spiral of her life would only get more complicated and surreal, what a strange world this was.

CHAPTER 10

Autumn was slipping away once more and the needled fingers of winter threatened the realm. It was Sunday morning and the population of the village was at church, men, women, children, the old and infirm were doing their calling to the lord. They settled into their pews with the ealdorman and his family sat in the separate seats upstairs. Reverend Marshal came forth and stood in the pulpit, he stared with stern intent at each person in the congregation, he paused for a while before beginning his sermon.

"We are gathered here today in the sight of our lord, we are grateful for what we have, by his grace he allows us to live our lives and we worship him for his devotion to us. There have been several incidents of unusual behaviour in this village and those surrounding. It has been said about the place that these occurrences are the result of dark arts and witchcraft."

The congregation looked at each other somewhat surprised as their former priest Reverend Adams never mentioned such things, the listened carefully.

The reverend continued, "I say to you all that these thoughts are pure nonsense and should be put from your minds as it is an insult to your lord and saviour, go now in peace!"

The people left the church in single file, some observing the words of the reverend, some not. The harvest was in need of gathering and storing ready for winter but not today, this was the day of rest for the people, they should refrain from any sort of labour, the harvest would have to wait a while. Of course like any young children in any place the devil makes work for idle hands and two young boys were no different.

Joseph Hughes and Ralf Marr were no different, having reached the ripe age of twelve they had the attitude to match their age. The confines of the little village of Elersly were becoming more and more frustrated at the confines of their life, an adventure beckoned. They wandered around the village for a while as people dispersed on their own way.

"What are we going to do today Ralf?"

Ralf thought for a moment, "I don't know, there is nothing to do in this place."

"I have an idea, what about and adventure?"

"What sort of adventure?" Ralf replied.

"I have been told that there is a lake over the moor, a secret lake, they say that people throw dead people and babies in there, we should investigate see if it's true, are you coming?"

Ralf pondered for a while, "Are you going?"

"Yes I am, I am sick of sitting around here, I want to see things, experience life!"

"Well I can't let you go alone, come on!" Ralf replied already on his feet."

They set off up the hill and onto the high moor; they had never been as far from the village and it was exciting. The whole scene was different, unusual, the sights, the sounds and even the smell of the heather and gorse. They carried on their trek hoping that they were heading in the right direction. They walked on and were beginning to wonder if they had mad e a bad decision and adventure was not for them after all.

Then as they were on the brink of turning they both noticed a shimmer in the distance, the looked at each other in the realisation that it was indeed the secret lake, it was real and not a myth. Nestled high on the windswept moors, the secret lake is a hidden gem, known to few and visited by even fewer. Surrounded by rolling hills covered in heather and bracken, the lake is a mirror-like expanse of water, reflecting the ever-changing sky above. The air is crisp and carries the earthy scent of peat and wildflowers.

The two boys approached the lake with some apprehension as the stories were imbedded in their minds. The water of the lake is a deep, almost mystical blue, its clarity revealing smooth stones and the occasional darting fish beneath the surface, however, it is said to be bottomless in the centre. On calm days, the stillness is profound, broken only by the gentle ripple of a breeze or the distant call of a curlew. Mist often hangs over the water in the early morning, giving the area an ethereal, otherworldly feel.

Surrounding the lake, the moors stretch out in every direction, a vast, open expanse dotted with rugged outcrops and clusters of hardy trees. In the distance, the silhouettes of ancient tors rise against the horizon, adding to the sense of timelessness and isolation. The lake is a place of quiet reflection, where one can sit on the rocky shore and lose track of time, listening to the whispers of the wind and the soft lapping of the water. It is a sanctuary, a secret retreat known only to those who seek it out, a place where the soul can find peace amidst the raw beauty of nature.

The peace and beauty of nature did not touch the thoughts of Joseph Hughes and Ralf Marr as they gazed around the scene. The reputation of this place was not lost on the boys as they sat on the rugged bankside. This lake shrouded in mystery and often cloaked by the thick mist that perpetually hovered over its surface, was a place where even the bravest of souls dared not venture.

Legend has it that Blackwater was created eons ago by the fall of a meteor, which left a crater that filled with water from an underground spring. The lake's water was unusually dark, almost black, giving rise to its name. Its surface was as smooth as glass, reflecting the towering pine trees and the overcast sky, but beneath this tranquil facade lay secrets that chilled the bones of those who dared to explore them.

The locals spoke in hushed tones about the lake's eerie properties; they said that Blackwater was a gateway to another realm, a world filled with shadows and dark images that twisted the mind. According to them, on nights when the moon was full and the mist was at its thickest, one could see dark silhouettes moving just beneath the surface, as if the lake itself was alive and watching.

The two boys explored the lake, its banks and edges and as the day wore on, they felt an increasing sense of being watched. The moor seemed alive, with shadows moving just out of sight, and the eerie silence was broken only by the occasional rustle of leaves. Before they realised the light was starting to fade and a thick fog was rolling over the moor. The realisation dawned that they could become lost on this wild moorland and this weird and mystical body of water, they decided to leave.

They were just about to head for home when a voice drifted from the area of the lake, a whisper nothing more and was distorted and unclear. They turned as one and looked into the lake and in a state of shock and disbelief witnessed what looked like a figure rising from the water. It looked like a woman dressed in white and completely silent, she seemed to lock the boys in a gripping gaze before moving towards them I a menacing fashion.

The boys, their taste for adventure draining fast panicked, turned and ran hell for leather in different directions. In the confusion they were separated and in the thick mist were doing nothing more than running in circles. Sometime later back in Elersly it was now dark and the temperature was dropping rapidly.

The mother of Joseph Hughes was out in the village shouting her son's name; she was later joined by Mrs Marr who was in a state of agitation. She saw Mrs Hughes and joined her.

They both began to shout out the names of their sons but there was no answer. Another woman came running, hearing the commotion, "what is going on here, why the noise?"

Our two sons have gone missing, they should have been home long sense, they know no to stay out after dark, we are much worried about their safety!" Mrs Marr said with concern.

Other people of the village having heard the commotion congregated in the village square. One of these people being a member of Ealdorman Hudson's retinue, he asked what was happening and was told with some distress that two boys were missing. He immediately ran off to inform Ealdorman Hudson of the situation, some minutes later he came back with several other men with staves and flaming torches.

John Riddle for the ealdorman demanded to know where to start the search.

"We don't know, we have no clue where they went!" Came a collective response.

Hearing the uproar a young boy joined the crowd, "what is going on here?"

The ealdorman's deputy turned to the boy, "do you know where these boys went?"

"Are the boys Joseph Hughes and Ralf Marr?"

"Yes they are, have you seen them?" Mrs Marr questioned the lad.

"I saw them in the square this morning after mass; I heard them say they were going to a secret lake, where is this lake, I know no secret lake. Where is it?"

Mrs Marr, screamed aloud, "I know where it is, I have warned Ralf never to go there!"

John Riddle interjected, "I know of this lake it is high up on the moors, nobody goes there, it has a bad reputation, however we must put that to the side, let us get moving!"

They set off onto the moors with torches flaming the night sky and they quickly were met with thick fog. The search continued all night, torches licking the haze with an eerie silvered glow, they found no trace. As the sun lifted its lids for another day, reinforcements arrived, accompanied by a farmer with his dog. The Old English Fox Hound was let loose and immediately started sniffing the ground with interest, tail wagging furiously.

"Go on Ham, find them lad!"

The dog did as ordered and before long it was clear that he was onto a trail and then suddenly he stopped dead gazing in front at something, the farmed caught the dog up.

"What's up lad, what do you see?"

The ground was damp and in the mud, were footprints, the party inspected them.

"They are dog tracks are they not?"

"Yes but look at the size of them, they are massive, you could put three of Ham's in there!"

Ham began to bark wildly at something, it soon became apparent what he was so excited. In the mist was a shape, something dark. They moved closer with some caution as they did not know just what this was and then they did as the shape came into full view.

A huge black dog stood there in front of them an imposing and unnerving sight, in immediately evoked feelings of dread and astonishment. The creature stood much taller than most dogs, with a powerful and muscular build that suggested immense strength. Its fur being jet black, absorbing the light and adding to its ominous presence. The coat was sleek yet dense, giving the dog a ghostly, almost supernatural appearance, especially in the dim light.

Ham was still agitated even when his owner tried to calm him, the men gazed at the huge dog not knowing just what they were witnessing. The y watched the dog especially its eyes a deep, fiery red, glowing with an intensity that seemed almost otherworldly. The eyes were large and piercing, capable of instilling fear with a single gaze. They burned with an unrelenting brightness, standing out starkly against the darkness of the fur, and seem to follow you wherever you go, making it hard to shake off their presence.

The men were struck by some sort of torpor at the sight of this thing, not knowing whether to watch in awe or run like hell! The dog moved its head, broad and formidable, with a pronounced jawline that suggested a powerful biting force. The ears are pointed and alert, constantly twitching as if detecting the slightest sound.

The dog's movements are both graceful and menacing, with a silent, almost predatory grace as it prowls, then it bared its teeth, sharp, gleaming fangs, adding to its fearsome demeanour, it began to move forward with a menacing air.

This was enough for the men in the search party as ham the dog turned and bolted down the hill closely followed by the men. As far as they were concerned the search was over, and they did not stop running until they reached the village. They congregated in the village square, tired and breathless they wondered just what had happened and what on earth they had seen and experienced, other people come running at the commotion.

"What's going on did you find the boys?"

The farmer stood at the front his fox hound Ham whimpering at his feet. "We could find no trace of the boys but we found something else."

"A wild dog, massive it was and terrible in its nature, I fear the boys also came across this beast, we will go back up there later and resume the search but for now we cannot venture!"

A woman shouted aloud, "Barghest, it was the Barghest I tell you; we are all lost to hell!"

Then another voice joined the gossip this one more forceful, it was Ealdorman Hudson.

"Be quiet woman, there is enough alarm here without you. Now what happened on the moor, did you find the missing boys?"

The farmer stepped forward; he seemed to be self-appointed spokesmen for the group.

"Ealdorman Hudson, Sir we conducted a thorough search around the moor and Blackwater Lake but we could find no trace of the boys, no footprints no discarded clothing nothing!"

The ealdorman shook his head in disappointment at the news, his distress was real.

"So it seems the boys are lost somewhere on the wild moor, it gets cold at night, they will not survive long up there, what was all the commotion when I arrived?"

"We did find no trace of the missing boys but we did find something else!"

"Yes, carry on, what did you find?" The ealdorman insisted impatiently.

"Well Sir we saw a massive black dog, a huge thing unlike anything we know of. Thick black fur and burning red eyes, it appeared to have evil intent, so we ran, yes Sir we ran!"

"It's the Barghest, I tell you the Barghest, we must pray to God for our salvation!"

With this outburst the woman ran off towards Saint Andrews church in a state of panic.

Ealdorman Hudson turned to walk away, "I don't know what you saw up there but it seems you all witnessed the same thing, what it is I have no clue. When ready those of you that feel up to it continue the search, I must inform the parents."

Some brave souls did return to the moors and the lake but found nothing. In fact no trace was ever found of Joseph Hughes and Ralf Marr, no funerals were held as there were no bodies to bury. The panic in the village eventually subsided and life went on as it always did.

CHAPTER 11

It was now December and the village was hit by a severe frost that engrossed everything that lived and everything that did not, all was a freezing shade of white. Mathew Jackson was a member of one of the area's oldest families; the family held land a mile west of the village. On any normal day at this time he would be out inspecting his sheep and cattle, this morning he was marching with purpose toward the village. He made strait to the house of Ealdorman Hudson and rapped on the door.

The house keeper answered, "Yes can I assist you?"

"My name is Mathew Jackson; I would like to see the ealdorman if possible."

"I don't know Sir he is very busy, have you an appointment?"

"Just let me see him woman, tell him it's Mathew Jackson!"

She, somewhat shocked at the demand went away and came back shortly after, Mathew Jackson was shown into the house and into a room where the ealdorman was sitting at a desk.

"Ah Mathew, a pleasure to see you, it has been some time, please sit."

"Sorry to interrupt ealdorman but some time ago I lost four sheep to what looked like a wolf attack. No animal was ever found and I forgot the matter in time, this morning I went check on my flock and found another sheep dead!"

The ealdorman smiled, "Mathew, things live and they die, it is simply nature."

"Not like this ealdorman, the sheep was ripped to pieces, by something!"

"I see so what are you thinking, what could it be?"

"Recently I have been hearing stories of the two boys from the village that went missing."

"Oh yes Mathew, Joseph Hughes and Ralf Marr, they are still missing to this day!"

"On finding the dead sheep this morning I followed some faint tracks up the hill toward the moor. There had been a light snow fall overnight and this made the tracks easier to follow, they were the deepest and biggest tracks that I have ever seen. They were obviously dog prints but huge and heavy, I followed them for a good distance."

"The searchers reported seeing a massive dog on the moor; this must be the same one."

"Yes ealdorman, I followed the tracks high into the moor and eventually they reached the top of Split Crow Hill and there in front of me a small cottage, tucked away amidst a shade of ancient, twisted trees. The tracks ended here as if the creature had returned home."

"So what did you do them Mathew?" The ealdorman inquired with interest.

"I stood and watched for a while and then I realised that this was the house of the so called wise woman of Split Crow Hill, feeling uneasy at the thoughts I turned and left quickly."

The ealdorman sighed aloud, "I have heard of this woman, Isabella Mosswood I believe. She had been accused of witchcraft but it could not be proven. She was though driven out of the village by terrified people, most of them ignorant as to life and the world outside."

"Ealdorman Hudson, I do not want to trouble you without proof butt this I fear is a serious matter and if it is allowed continue unresolved it could return!"

"Hmm, I see Mathew, I have heard of someone who deals with this sort of thing. I have heard that he has been in Yorkshire, around Richmond dealing with problems there. I have heard that he was heading into Durham, I will have one of my men take a message to him and ask for help; go home now Mathew, I will deal with this matter."

Two days later on a cold but fine morning three men rode into the village, strangers to Elersly and not the usual type of local people. They immediately stood out, one of these men appeared to be in charge, tall and slim of build with, long facial features gave an uncommon appearance. He tied up his horse and looked around at the village, which was concealed in a light covering of snow.

The village of Elersly was at this time looking a touch better than normal as it was wrapped in a fine white blanket hiding its misfortune. The tall man, being somewhat better dressed than the locals was causing some interest with his knee length boots, long leather coat and expensive looking hat. He approached a young man walking past and stopped him.

"You there master, I seek the house of Ealdorman Hudson, is it near?"

"Oh yes Sir over there at the other side of the village." He said pointing the way.

The man left the other two with the horses and went to the house of Ealdorman Hudson.

The housekeeper answered, "Have you an appointment?"

"I hope so mistress, I am Isiah Blackwood!"

"Oh I see, sorry Sir, you are expected, please come in."

The housekeeper led him into a room where the ealdorman was sitting next to a blazing fire. "Ealdorman Hudson, this is the man you were expecting."

"Ah I am very pleased to meet you, please sit and warm yourself by the fire!"

"I am Isiah Blackwood, I received a message from one of your men, you have a problem?"

"Well yes Mr Blackwood we do have need of assistance, there have been a lot of difficulties in and around this village for some time, most of them unresolved, we need help."

"Your message mentioned witchcraft and dark magic, is that true?"

"Well I am not sure Mr Blackwood, we have a problem there is no doubt, whether it is dark magic as you say I know not but we need to sort it out before it gets any worse."

"Well Ealdorman Hudson, you have found the right man for your troubles, this is what I do, my profession so to speak is tracking down all who defame the word of God."

"Tell me Mr Blackwood have you dealt with many witches?"

"Yes Ealdorman Hudson, I have dealt with many, some poor specimens, some powerful!"

"If there are such dark dealings in this parish, they must be stopped!"

"Do not fear Sir if there are such things I will render them unusable. Now I have heard tales of a huge black dog in the area, is this true?"

"Yes I am afraid so, have you dealt with such things in the past?"

"Yes, I am afraid I have, it is commonly known as the Burhest and it brings with it all manner of evil and terror, this will be an extra problem. These dogs do not work alone, they will have a keeper, someone strong enough to keep the beast in check, do you have a clue? "

The ealdorman sighed aloud, "I have heard of this woman, Isabella Mosswood, I believe. She had been accused of witchcraft but it could not be proven. She was though driven out of the village by terrified people after blood. I have been informed that she now lives up on the high moor in a little cottage on Split Crow Hill."

"Very well Ealdorman Hudson, my fee for this task will be twenty Shillings if I catch her."

With that Blackwood left the house and went back to his men and horses. He could discern as he grew closer the sound of voices, raised aloud, he rounded the corner into the village square and was met with a sizable crowd of villagers. The atmosphere is charged with tension and energy, the crowd is loud, with people shouting, chanting, or even screaming. The noise was a mix of voices expressing anger and frustration.

Blackwood reached his men, what is going on here?"

"The villages know of our arrival and they want the witch caught, they are angry!"

Blackwood stood on a wooden crate and held out his arms in a sign of calm. "Please be quiet good people, my name is Blackwood and I have been called in to find the cause of these problems that affect your village, please return to you homes, leave it to me and my men!"

After a while seemingly pacified the crowd drifted away, leaving Blackwood to do his work. They mounted their horses and climbed the hill onto the moor, the moor was till and silent gripped in a frozen state of suspension. A light covering of snow littered the ground covering heather and gorse with its wintery coat. One of the men pulled his horse up and leapt from the saddle, kneeling down he checked the ground.

"What do you see?" Blackwood asked interested.

"Tracks Sir, dog tracks but bigger than I have ever seen, they are huge!"

"Alright we shall follow them."

The man on the ground walked along checking the ground carefully, the other two followed behind. Eventually they reached the top of Split Crow Hill and there in front of them a small cottage. They dismounted and secured their horses, the dog tracks led strait to the door of the house, Blackwood rapped at the door, there was no answer, he tried again, no answer.

"One of you men go round the back and check it, you follow me, we go inside now."

Blackwood pushed at the door and it opened with a groan and a scrape, they stepped inside.

"Hello, who is in here, come forward, there is nothing to be gained by hiding, come out!"

There was still no reply, all was silent, they searched the single room and found no one. The place was apparently abandoned, the contents seemingly gone with the resident. All that was left was a bowl, a dagger and an alabaster ball, outside there was the remains of a goat. Whoever lived here Isabella Mosswood or anybody else were long gone, they left no trace not even a footprint to be followed in a direction.

They carried on over the moor as far as Blackwater lake, still and serene in its white frame, they found nothing, no trace of witches, nor anything else to speak of. One of the men dismounted and began to walk around the edge of the lake looking for any sign of a clue. Then he noticed something that he was not expecting, up ahead the figure of a woman in white watching them and by her side a huge black dog.

He pointed and shouted aloud, "look Sir over there!"

Blackwood turned his horse around in the direction and witnessed the very same sight. He stared at the woman and the dog as they stood stagnant and motionless against the horizon. The other man remounted his horse, "should we detain her Sir?"

"I do not think so, I believe that dog to be the legendary Barghest, the thing is indeed real!"

"What should we do now?"

Blackwood looked at him with distress and disappointment in his eyes. "We will return to the Ealdorman and explain what we discovered, his fears are all too real, there is evil in the air here. We could try to halt it but we cannot get even close, whoever or whatever this malevolence is I fear it is too powerful for mortal men, may God preserve them all!"

They left the moor and returned to the village with disturbed by the vision of the woman and dog, whispered rumours of strange occurrences lost in her wake. But to those who truly see her, she's only a shadowy mystery waiting to be unravelled.

CHAPTER 12

The village of Elersly was the same as always, winter had once more slipped into spring; the snow with its stinging voice had cleared, the people coming to terms with the turning of the age. The troubles of this place were still in flux as the world rotated, Eliza was by now not only a beautiful young woman but highly intelligent. There were not many books in circulation at this time, as most people could not read them anyway.

However Eliza collected all that she could get her hands on and although she had no teaching learner to read to a good standard by studying and tutoring herself. Sometimes pamphlets would find their way into the village and Ealdorman Hudson would have them pinned to the notice board, Eliza would stand and read them, she was doing just that this day.

An old woman came past, "you are Eliza Swann are you not?"

"Yes I am."

"I have always been distrustful of you and your mother but after you cured young Edward you have enhanced your reputation somewhat, not that I still don't trust you, understand."

"Well, I am grateful for that, I think!"

The old woman bent and twisted with age pointed a finger at the pamphlet. "What does it say, is it good news of bad, bad seems to be the general rule in these parts?"

Eliza read the pamphlet and the turned to the old woman. "It says that King James is touring around the country, he wants to see his entire realm in turn."

The old woman laughed aloud, "I'll wager he does not come to this shit hole, who would?"

She them hobbled away mumbling to herself something about royalty and taxes.

Ealdorman Hudson was a man in the eye of a storm as he was in charge of the village of Elersly and it' surrounding areas, the people of this place were his responsibility and he knew it. His mind was troubled constantly by the misfortune that blighted this place and its residents. Although he was disbeliever in all things dark and mysterious, witches, warlocks and other nefarious manifestations, he was beginning to question everything.

Leaving his house he headed to Saint Andrew's Church and was received by Reverend Marshal in his chambers, he welcomed his esteemed visitor and they sat to talk.

"Good morning Ealdorman, what brings you here this fine day?"

"Well Reverend Marshal, my mind is troubled, why have this village and its people been so severely troubled these past years, is this the will of God to punish these poor people?"

Reverend Marshal looked at him sensitively, "I sense your faith is in question Ealdorman?"

"I have an open mind on all things but the constant difficulties we have suffered have caused me to wonder about all things, are we being punished for some unfaithfulness?"

"Please be assured Ealdorman Hudson, the lord is with us at all times but on occasion he will test the faith of his flock. It is my work to make sure they do not lose faith, you may question your loyalty but he will judge all who lapse, I am sure you will not Ealdorman!"

Ealdorman Hudson left the church no better off than when he entered his mind a buzz of thoughts and worries. Passing the village square he say someone reading the notice board.

"Ah you are Eliza Swann are you not?"

"Yes Ealdorman Hudson, I was just reading these pamphlets."

"I honestly do not know why I have them posted, the people can't read them!"

"I find them interesting to see what is happening in the world, Eliza replied.

"I see that you can understand them, how did you learn to read miss?"

"I am self-thought Sir; I have ambition to better myself, in some way."

"That is a fine endeavour, Miss Swann, tell me do you and your mother still have trouble?"

"Not as much but we are still branded as suspicious and not to be trusted."

The ealdorman shook his head, "Yes indeed the power of rumour and superstition, it seems to have no bounds. There has been a man in the village trying to root out the cause of all this misfortune, Blackwood, his name but he could not find the cause so he did not get paid."

"What exactly was he looking for?"

"Witches, Miss Swann, witches, demons and all manner of darkness, he found nothing. They did see a massive black dog on the moor that scared their horses but nothing of proof."

"Ah the Barghest, tell me was there a young woman with the dog?"

"Why yes they did report seeing her but how do you know this?"

"I don't know Sir, I see things in my mind, I always have I cannot explain."

"Listen Miss Swann, I have a friend out on the coast, he is a sea captain. He spends a lot of time transporting cargo, so he does not spend a lot of tome at home. He is looking for a housekeeper to look after his cottage when he is away; I think you would be perfect for it."

"Well Ealdorman I am not used to receiving such offers but it would get me out of Elersly, how long will it last?""

"Just a couple of weeks, his sister, a widow is coming to take it on. The wage will not be great but it will certainly help, think on it?"

"I will indeed Sir, I will discuss it with my mother and let you know!"

Mary Swann on hearing the news was excited that her daughter would finally get a break in life and if the ealdorman was vouching for his friend all the better, she agreed Eliza should go. Eliza returned to the house of Ealdorman Hudson rather quicker than he was expecting and accepted the offer with grace and gratitude.

So Eliza was destined for a trip into the unknown, Carlton Bay being no more than ten miles from Elersly and it being a fine morning she would walk the path over the moors to the east, it would not take long. It was so that she arrived at the edge of the moor and there below was Carlton bay, she stood and looked around for a while, this was all new to her.

The village was remarkably unremarkable, fairly typical of this part of the coast. The wind swept heather clad moors plunged sharply and suddenly away at an alarming angle to the sea several hundred feet below. A collection of small cottages clung to the hillside as if they had no right to defy gravity in such a way, the weathered, grey stonework contrasting softly with the reddish brown of the roof tiles.

The morning was crisp and a cold breeze blew in off the sea, carrying its fresh aroma that lifted the senses. A long stairway of wooden steps had been installed from the edge of the moor down to the sheltered cove. The whole village was surrounded by sheer, jagged cliffs, which gave some lea from the prevailing winds.

The cottage was situated near the bottom of the hill, with an impressive view across the bay. It was small but tidy. Equally, her room held little space, but was comfortable. Captain Harrison had left earlier in the morning, and after clearing up and doing a few chores. The captain seemed to be a keen reader, as there was huge collection of books on every subject, several of which Eliza would read in an attempt to relieve her monotony. This was after all a tiny fishing village, even smaller than her home village of Elersly but cleaner and quieter.

The next few days passed slowly, Eliza made busy tidying the cottage and making good the scene. She was it could be said that she was not feeling comfortable in her new surroundings. There was a note on a table from the captain detailing that he would not be back for at least a week and there were supplies left for her. Eliza was feeling homesick and the lure of the filthy village of Elersly drew her back. She knew no one here, although the locals knew of her.

One morning having done her chores she decided to leave the house and take a walk around the place. To the right was the small harbour and to the left the long rise of wooden steps leading up to the path and the moors. She climbed the steps and continued upward, the briny air and pungent smell of the kelp beds were diminishing, being replaced by another aroma. A few steps further she realised what that was. An elderly man was leaning on the doorframe of his cottage, the discharge from his clay pipe drifting off in the breeze.

"Morning, Miss. Taking in the air, are we?"

"Yes, I thought I might take a walk; it's a fine day."

He smiled, revealing his disintegrating teeth, some of which had long since departed that particular harbour, his features as weathered as the local stone.

"How's that old sea dog treating you?"

"Oh the Captain is away for a few days."

"Don't you be too long out, miss, there's a storm brewing, I can feel it, smell it."

"I won't be too long; just clearing the cobwebs."

Sarah recognised that although these people were rough and ready and could be prone to lapses of dignity, they would forget petty differences and go to the aid of a fellow villager who was in trouble, be it at sea or otherwise. On reaching the top, she sat on the last step or for some the first step and looked out to sea. She could see some of the cobbles, a sort of large, open sided rowing boat common in this area out at a distance, bobbing on the cold greyness of the North Sea.

She wondered how men could put their faith in such a small vessel, but then remembered from her education that just such vessels had brought the dreaded Norseman to these shores. Her eyes were drawn to the black clad figures of the fishwives on the harbour wall. What a simple, thankless life these people lead, she thought, as the cormorants dived and the shearwaters shrieked and wheeled about the cliff sides.

Just along the pathway stood an old church, Saint Stevens, she observed several simple graves in the church yard and wondered just how many locals were beneath the earth here. Then a voice came from behind. "Good morning to you." the gentle voice from behind said.

He stood there tall and straight in his black cassock, arms firmly clasped behind his back. His features gave an impression of sternness, but his smile was nothing but benign.

"I'm sorry my dear, I did not mean to startle you. I am Edmund Teach and I have the responsibility of delivering the word of the Lord to the people of this parish, be they good, bad, or indifferent. We do not get many strangers in these parts. Are you from along the coast perhaps?"

"No Sir, I am staying in the village for a while."

"Oh, you are Captain Harrison's young housekeeper; all the way from Elersly no less, it must be strange coming to a wind blasted place such as this?"

Reverend Teach smiled as he nodded. "I have passed through your village on a number of occasions as I did my training and indeed I was ordained in the splendour of Durham Cathedral, this world of ours is shrinking I think."

Eliza looked around. "This is an old church is it not?"

"Yes, indeed it is, we have documents and chronicles up in Durham that state that a church has stood on this very spot since the year six eighty four. It has been plundered by Viking raiders and almost burnt down fifty years ago. However, as you can see we are still here scattering the good word of the Lord."

"Oh, the Lord; I remember him," she said somewhat mockingly.

He gazed at her in a confused manner. "If you have no faith, maybe I can help you find it."

"No, Sir, I doubt it, you see, it is not that I have no faith, I have simply lost it. I was brought up in a Christian home, we were devout in faith my mother and me, where was the good Lord, when we needed him, was absent. He turned his back on us in our time of want; now I have turned my back on him."

He sighed. "Sometimes we are tested, sometimes painfully so."

"Then tell me, Sir, have you been tested?"

"Yes I have. I have questioned my faith at times, but we must fight it."

Sarah shook her head. "The faith of my family was not in question. Why should it be tested?"

"My dear girl, I can see that you have had difficulties in your short life, but you must be strong."

Eliza stared into his blue eyes intently and boldly. "Oh I am strong, Sir, I can assure you of that. I should be getting back now; it was nice to meet you."

He walked with her as she crossed the path, his words followed.

"If you need reassurance, or just want to talk, I am always here."

"Thank you," she said, turning back to see his willowy frame against the greying sky, his hair billowing in the gathering wind.

Sarah made her way back down the hill. Arriving at the cottage was something of a relief, as the sky by now was a menacing darkness, and rain spots churned among the wind. Out across the bay, on that gloomy grey carpet, and in the distance white horses danced ever closer. She busied herself about the house for a while but soon became bored, she pondered what the local Reverend had said and questioned her response to him, did she really mean what she said about losing her faith or was it a mere passing thought?

Wiping the condensation from the small front window, she stared out. The bay was a maelstrom of churning water, pitching the cobbles at their moorings like a pack of terrified horses straining to be loose. Huge waves cracked against the sea wall, sending plumes of white, fizzing spray into the evening sky. Rain lashed at the window, as if seeking shelter, as the savage wind howled eerily, rattling the timbers of the old house.

Then in the midst of the rage came a noise, a bell tolling its tone wavering in the wind, E;iza went outside and saw people running around in alarm.

A man came past she stopped him, "what's going on?"

"There is a ship on the rocks!" He replied anguish on his features.

nThe ship, an imposing silhouette against the stormy backdrop, struggled amidst the tumultuous sea. It's once proud sails now hanging in tatters, whipped mercilessly by the howling wind. The rigging, normally taut and orderly, dangled chaotically, swaying with each fierce gust. Waves, dark and fizzing, lifted like monstrous walls, crashing against the hull with deafening roars. Each impact, sending a shudder through the vessel, a testament to the relentless power of nature.

The sky above is a churning mass of grey clouds, illuminated sporadically by jagged forks of lightning. Thunder rumbles ominously, adding to the cacophony of nature's fury. Rain lashes down in sheets, reducing visibility to mere feet and drenching everything in a cold, relentless deluge.

On the deck, sailors scrambled desperately, their figures barely visible through the storm's fury. Commands are shouted, but the wind snatches the words away, rendering communication a near impossibility. The ship tilts perilously, leaning to one side as it grinds against unseen rocks beneath. The sound of wood splintering and the groans of the hull under stress fill the air, a disheartening symphony of impending disaster.

The ship's lanterns, normally bright beacons of hope, flicker weakly, their light swallowed by the darkness. The sea, an unforgiving maelstrom, shows no mercy as it pummels the vessel. The once steadfast ship, now at the mercy of the elements, seems like a fragile toy amidst the chaos, battling valiantly but futilely against the storm's overwhelming might.

The next morning Eliza had seen and heard enough, she packed her few things in her sack and left the house. The villagers were down in the harbour, the night's storm having subsided, Reverend Teach was there praying for the lost souls of the sea, a Siren came to them in the night and whispered their names.

She climbed the steps up from the village, at the top she looked back at the scene, waves lapping calmly at the harbour wall. The skeletal frame of the ship unclothed and stripped against the grey sea. She pondered for a while and wondered, why did misery and misfortune follow her every step? Was she indeed burdened with some sort of jinx, had an evil curse been fostered upon her shoulders?

Back in Elersly she confided in her mother, who could not answer her questions to and reasonable degree. Eliza had thought for some time that there was something wrong but could not resolve what it was, was she really losing her faith or did she never have it?

CHAPTER 13

It was now high summer in the north lands and in the biggest town in the region Newcastle the temperature was climbing. This town was much the same as the other towns around only much bigger. The same problems were present here as anywhere else, poor people struggling to survive while some at the top lived lives of relative indulgence. Poor housing, bad sanitation resulted in disease and pestilence that was ever present.

It was a Sunday morning when in this town a very special visitor arrived, the gates of the city were flung wide open to welcome the guest. king James, on his way towards Scotland, came to Newcastle upon Tyne, where he was met upon the Sand Hill by the mayor, aldermen, and sheriff. After an oration made by the town-clerk, the King was presented by the mayor, in the name of the whole corporation, with a great standing bowl, to the value of a hundred jacobuses, and a hundred marks in gold.

The mayor, carrying the sword before him, accompanied by his brethren, on their foot-cloths. On Sunday, evening his majesty, with all his nobles, dined with the mayor, when it pleased the king to be served by the mayor and aldermen. One of those distinguished people attending was Henry Alderson, merchant and alderman of Newcastle-upon-Tyne.

The Aldersons established themselves as Newcastle merchants in the 1520s, trading in both of the main Tyneside commodities, cloth and coal. They served on the corporation for much of the sixteenth century, and were returned as MPs for the borough regularly from 1529. Anderson's father, Henry, made his fortune during the vast expansion of the coal trade under Elizabeth, being a party to the Grand Lease of the lucrative Wickham and Gateshead mines in 1583 and a founder member of the Newcastle Hostmen.

The king stayed in Newcastle for two weeks before leaving on his way to Scotland.in return for the hospitality he received, he gave a gift to the people of Newcastle. A three part book named Daemonologie in 1597 on how to identify, prosecute and protect against accused witches. As the religious and political authority of Scotland and England as well, James I and VI gave sanction to the persecution of accused witches, laying the foundations for the procedures of the witch trials.

Witchcraft was defined, in his eyes, as having the power to cure or cast diseases, weaken the nature of men and make them vulnerable for women, more than the ordinary course of nature would permit. He believed that this power was given to them by serving the Devil as the master.

The King's book had been read by all the notable people of the city, those that could read and the content of this book and its meaning had not been lost on these men. Suspicion about the nature of witchcraft and the Devil's work were ingrained in the minds of the people. Reading this book only elevated the sense of dread even further.

A few days later another man entered town with two others, he made his way to the Ealdorman Alderson's house. He was met at the door by one of the ealdorman's men and was allowed in.

"Ealdorman Sir, a gentleman would like to see you if it is convenient?"

"Yes send him in."

A man walked in, tall, well dressed with his knee length boots, long leather coat and expensive looking hat.

"Come in Sir, please take a seat, how can I help?"

 My name is Isiah Blackwood, I track down and destroy witches, do you have a problem?"

"Hmm, I have heard this name before; tell me are you good at your trade?"

"Yes Sir I am very good, if you have a problem I will resolve it!"

"As you say, we have had incidents at times and sometimes people take matters into their own hands, this will not do, the sheriff and I are the law, not the people."

"You need a professional to deal with this; if you employ me I will rid this town of evil."

"You make a good case Mr Blackwood; firstly I will have to discuss this matter with the Sheriff and the Mayor. I will call them to a meeting tonight and I will contact you in the morning. I am sure you will have much work to do here, we must rid ourselves of this!"

"What methods do you use, to determine whether a person is a witch or not?"

"Ealdorman Alderson, let me assure you I have a deal of experience in these matters, sometimes I can identify a witch be looking at them carefully, some are clear to see.

"What you can tell a witch by just looking upon them?"

"Sometimes but I have other methods, Ducking or 'ludicium aquae,' adapted from a trial by ordeal using water. The suspect would either be placed in a sack or have their arms and legs tied, then thrown in a deep body of water. If they floated, they were using their magic to stay afloat and would be taken out and executed. If they sank, they were innocent."

"Anything else you have used?"

"I have a number of methods, Prayer test. The accused would have to recite a particular prayer or passage from the Bible. Failure to do so would see them guilty."

"But Mr Blackwood, most people in this town cannot read the bible or anything else!"

"Then there are other methods, such as finding a Devil's Mark. This could be any kind of strange mole or skin lesion that could be anywhere on the body. This was apparently a marker of the covenant between the witch and the Devil. If found, a bodkin would be used to pierce these spots, as they were insensitive and usually didn't bleed."

"You make a good case Mr Blackwood; firstly I will have to discuss this matter with the Sheriff and the Mayor. I will call them to a meeting tonight and I will contact you in the morning. I am sure you will have much work to do here, we must rid ourselves of this!"

Later that day a meeting was called in the town hall, some of the distinguished people in attendance were Henry Alderson, merchant and Ealdorman of Newcastle-upon-Tyne along with the Sheriff of Northumberland and the Mayor.

"Welcome gentlemen, as you know we have had problems in this city for some time with dark dealings. A man came to see me by the name of Blackwood; he deals in this sort of matter. He has assured me that he can rid this place of such malign influence but he will want to be paid in accordance with his profession."

The Mayor leaned forward, "how much will he want?"

"Twenty Shillings per witch convicted," replied the Ealdorman.

"What, that I think is a King's ransom!"

It was now the turn of the Sheriff of Northumberland. "It is agreed that it is a lot of money but if we want to get rid of the evil in this city, we must pay up, we have little choice."

"Very well gentle men do we have agreement on this matter?" Ealdorman Alderson said.

The other two men nodded in agreement and the deal was settled. The next morning Ealdorman Alderson, informed Isiah Blackwood of his employment. He immediately set about his progress in settling the matter at hand. His first task was to visit to the city printer, and have posters displayed around town.

ANY PERSON OF GOOD CHARACTER IN THE CITY OF NEWCASTLE-UPON-TYNE IS THEREFORE OBLIGED TO REPORT TO THE AUTHORITIES AND PERSON SUSPECTED OF WITCHCRAFT OR UNHOLY DEALINGS WITH THE DEVIL FAMILIARS.

The city bellman was summoned and instructed to walk through the city ringing his bell and instructing any person with suspicions to come forth and speak. The good people of Newcastle-upon-Tyne on hearing this were immediately attentive and were already plotting to hand in certain people. Over the next two days twenty people were arrested, nineteen women and a single man on charges of witchcraft and flung into the county jail.

Of the people arrested they were mostly old and broken-down some confused and disorientated, some simple minded and some were only guilty of being disliked. This would play little part in the proceedings as money was at stake and Isiah Blackwood was intent on getting rich. Over the next two days the suspects were led one by one to the town hall where they were interrogated by Isiah Blackwood, having already been tested of the Devil's marks.

Of the twenty five were found not guilty and set free, the next fourteen were summarily found guilty, now there was only one suspect left, Catherine Poll. She was marched into the room by two sturdy men and stood in front of the desk. Isiah Blackwood regarded her with distrust and a sense of revulsion in his dark eyes, he motioned her forward.

"Has she been examined?"

"Yes Sir, she has several marks of the Devil about her body, none bled when pricked."

"I see, what is your name?"

"My name is Catherine Poll!"

"You know why you have been brought before me today?"

"Yes I do, I have been falsely accused of something I did not do."

"You have been accused of dark magic, namely the casting of spells on the people of this city, how do you plead to these charges?"

"I plead Sir not guilty, why would I otherwise, I have done no wrong!"

"How old are you Catherine Poll?"

"Old, why would my age be relevant, I am twenty one year's next month!"

"Because you have had many years to learn you trade, a craft so powerful it would take many years to master and much practice, how do you plead?"

"I am not guilty, to any and all charges, this trial is rigged and you will all pay for this!"

"Very well Catherine Poll, this court finds you guilty of the heinous crime of witchcraft and the denial of our Lord and saviour, take her away and lock her up securely!"

The men dragged her away but not without a response from her. "I know you Isiah Blackwood, I see you and your brutes, you will pay dearly for this crime. Let it be known that I Catherine Poll, a citizen of this city of Newcastle-upon-Tyne. I hereby curse you and all your family and friends thereof to a life of pain and misery from this day forward."

The next day horses and carts were assembled outside of the jail and the accused; hands tied behind with coarse rope were loaded onto the carts and set off westward out of the city to an area of open land known as the Town Moor. Here a scaffold had been erected especially for the job in hand, namely death of their fellow citizens by hanging. They were dragged of the carts and lined up; Isiah Blackwood ordered them to be counted. It was at this point that they realise that there were only fortune, there was one missing.

"Are they all accounted for?" Blackwood inquired.

"It seems there are only fourteen, one is missing!"

"What how can this be, is she still at the jail?"

"No Sir I was assured by the jailer that they were all accounted for!"

"Then where is she, what is her name?"

The guard went back to the line-up and returned a short time later. "We believe it to be someone named Catherine Poll!"

Isiah Blackwood's face immediately drained of colour and he was obviously in some distress, he called for one of his assistants and confronted him in an aggressive manner.

"Where has this woman gone how could she escape, I want answers do you hear me?"

We honestly don't know how it could be possible Sir; she just seems to have vanished!"

"You know who this missing woman is, the very same witch that cursed us all at the trial."

"My God Sir, do you mean that Catherine Poll could have been the only true witch among them? If it be so, what lies ahead for us, have we been cursed, what should we do now?"

"Our task here is not done, there are thirteen witches and one wizard waiting to be dispatched, see to it without delay, we will deal with curses later."

And so it was on this open field the scaffold creaked with the flailing, twisting bodies of the people of this town, guilty of not they swung in the breeze like rag dolls, task complete. The bodies were taken down and wrapped in cloth, then loaded onto carts and transported to the city. All of them were buried in an unmarked mass grave at St. Andrew's Church in the City Centre, on Newgate Street, without ceremony or service, no one attended.

After the internment the church yard was quiet, curiously so and in the silence two women stood in some sort of respect watching the grave site. One of these women, tall, slim and in possession of the darkest eyes ever seen, long black hair wafting in the breeze. The other woman younger and smaller in stature looked up at the other. "Where am I, who are you?"

"It matters not who I am, what matters is that you are here and not in the ground like these unfortunate souls."

"But I don't understand the last I remember I was in a jail cell, what happened to me?"

The tall woman pointed at the ground. "There are fourteen bodies in this patch of earth that should not be, they were innocent and you Catherine Poll are the only true witch among them."

"But why, are you some sort of guardian angel?"

"A dark angel perhaps, you have a gift, knowledge, it will be needed in time. Your life will no longer be the same, you belong to us now, come with me Catherine, there is much to do."

CHAPTER 14

It was a cold and frosted morning when Martin Howe arose from his bunk. He was by trade a hunter if such matters could be called a trade in the real sense. He sustained himself with meat of varying types, deer, rabbit, pheasant and grouse on the high moor. He would also supply fresh meat at the village.

He left his small, ramshackle house to the north east of Elersly on the road to Newcastle, if it could be called a road. However, it was a great improvement on the other byways of the area, a gift left by the Roman Legion. He left his small, ramshackle house to the north east of Elersly on the road to Newcastle and walked up onto the moor with his trusty bow and a quiver of homemade arrows of willow and pheasant feathers.

It was however, for the unfortunate Martin Howe a day when there were few birds to be seen and even les in bow shot range. He paced around in growing frustration before settling on a large stone to rest his legs. It was then that he noticed in the snow tracks, a deer, probably a Roe by the size of them. They led away across the moor and down a steep slope into a valley; he followed then checking the prints frequently.

The valley was heavily wooded with thick tree of varying forms all struggling for their share of the light. Bushes and thick ferns hampered his progress to a degree but the thought of some fresh venison for supper spurred him on. Eventually the undergrowth cleared and opened up into a small clearing. The deer tracks were no more, replaced by something different and more alarming; these tracks were clearly made by some sort of canine but of a massive size.

Wolves had not been seen in the area for many years having been hunted out, further more these were bigger than any normal wolf. He walked a little further until he came to a solid sheer rock face which was at least two hundred feet in height almost up to the moor itself. At the front of the cliff was a narrow gash in the rock, about ten feet high and the width of three men abreast.

The tracks led inside, he followed and peeked his head into the void, it was dark and seemed to go far into the hillside. It was at this point that his nerve deserted him in rapid fashion and he turned and left in rather more haste than he arrived. He did not go straight home and there would be no venison for supper as he scrambled through the bushes and onto the moor and down the hill into Elersly.

His destination was the house of Ealdorman Hudson, he was allowed in.

"Good day to you Sir, you are Martin Howe the hunter are you not, have you meat to sell?"

"Yes Ealdorman Hudson I am Martin Howe and I am a hunter but this morning I was up on the moor looking for game birds when I noticed some deer tracks. I followed them and they led into a deep ravine, there instead of deer tracks they were that of a dog, a massive dog!"

"What a dog you say, could it have been a wolf?"

"No most definitely, there are no wolves in this area, it was not a wolf!"

"So what happened then Martin?" Hudson asked becoming more uneasy by the minute.

"The tracks led into a cave, I was afraid to follow the beast; I believe it was the Barghest!"

"Very well martin I will look into it, I don't want to get the sheriff involved just yet."

The next day a poster was pinned to the board in the village.

I HAVE BEEN INFORMED THAT A GIANT DOG THAT HAS BEEN SEEN IN THE AREA FOR SOME TIME HAS BEEN TRACKED DOWN TO A CAVE ON THE OTHER SIDE OF THE MOOR. THERE IS A REWARD REWARD FOR ANY MAN THAT KILLS THE BEAST.

EALDORMAN HUDSON.

A crowd gathered in the village square to discuss the matter, when a woman barged her way to the front, Alice Simms strutted forward as she is prone to doing, arms folded.

"Well is there a man among you with the guts for this work?"

"But Alice it's the Barghest, are you insane woman?"

A man stepped forward holding a pike with a serious looking iron tip, a big man with a big beard. "I am John Slade, I might be insane but I need the money!"

He took the job and with the blessing of Reverend Marshal in his thoughts he set of on his quest. He walked up onto the moor and over to the other side, he eventually came to the ravine, this must be it, he thought. Climbing down the slope, through the trees he was not at all sure what lay ahead of him and he was not at all sure why he was even there, as the doubts of the human mind raged. He came upon the clearing and looked out of the bushes, there was nothing much to see, apart from the breeze in the trees and wavering ferns.

He stepped into the clearing pike at the ready and approached the cave entrance; he paused for a moment as the apprehension and no little an unbelievable tension gripped him as he neared the gash in the cliff. The questions came, what was he thinking of accepting this mission, was he really so poor to be in a situation of this magnitude?

He did not have long to ponder these matters as his mind was made up as anxieties turned quickly into stark naked fear! The sky darkened abruptly as a massive shadow swept across the blue sky. A giant raven, feathers black and eyes gleaming with a malevolent intelligence, swooped down with a chilling, ear-piercing shriek that echoed through the valley.

Sharp, talon-like claws gleamed menacingly as it descended upon its target with frightening speed and precision. The air is filled with the sound of flapping wings, a terrifying mix of feathers and fury. John Slade ran, arms flailing as he tried to escape, in his panic he fell over and tried to cover his face and head.

The raven's attack is swift and brutal as it swooped downward, bill snapping and claws extended, aiming for anything that moves. The bird's movements are both graceful and deadly, a predator fully in control of its domain. Its beak, strong enough to crush bones, strikes with the force of a battering ram, its claws ripped and tear with savage efficiency.

As quickly as it came, the giant raven lifts off, soaring back into the sky, leaving behind a scene of chaos and destruction. The ground is littered with debris, and the air is thick with dust and the lingering scent of fear. The raven's dark silhouette fades into the distance, a harbinger of nightmares and a reminder of the fragile line between humanity and the wild unknown.

As for John Slade, he lay on the grass, dust in his mouth and nose for what seemed an age. After sometime having been quiet, no screeching, no wings he dared to look up. His relief was intense, he could still be in danger, he pulled himself to his feet and stumbled into the bushes where he fell to his knees, and began to contemplate just what had happened.

It was at this point that he realised that he was in pain and bleeding heavily. Blood was pouring from his hands and his head, running down his face in a warm stream. He knew that he did not have the strength to climb back up to the moor; his only choice was to go east and hope he could make it to the main road to Newcastle. His journey was not easy as he was becoming weaker by the minute but he stumbled on, he had to. Eventually he emerged from the trees and there it was the old Roman road, he fell onto it in a state of collapse.

John Slade did not know how long he was lying on the road side and neither did anybody else. Eventually a cart came along driven by Alfred Chase owner of a small farmstead on the outskirts of the Elersly. He pulled up the horse and climbed down to take a better look.

"My God, fellow, what happened here, was it robbers?"

John relieved that some help had arrived looked up at him, "no, I have nothing to rob."

Alfred Chase helped him up and bundled him into his cart, "you need help mister, hold on!"

John Slade was lying in the back of the cart, "where are we going Sir?"

"The closest place is Blackdale Abbey, I will take you there, they will help you."

The horse and cart trotted into the courtyard of the abbey and several brothers were quickly alerted that there was something wrong, one of them came over to inquire what was happening. On seeing the state of John Slade he shouted to another brother to fetch Brother James, he went running of at affair pace. Brother James came out and assessed the situation.

"Take him into the medicine room, quickly!"

Two brothers helped him into the Abbey; the surgical room was not too far fortunately.

Brother James turned to Alfred Chase, "what happened to this man?"

"I do not know brother; I just found him on the side of the road and brought him here."

Brother James went into the room where others had taken most of John's clothes off and laid him on a table. Brother James examined him carefully; he had several deep wounds to his head, the drying blood tangling his hair. What looked like stab wounds on his hands and three gashes running down his back. John was treated for his wounds at the abbey for several days before being deemed well enough to leave. He thanked the brothers warmly for saving him, he then returned to Elersly.

He went to the house of Ealdorman Hudson; the ealdorman was surprised to see him return.

"Well John, I see you made it back but with some discomfort, what happened?"

"I am not really sure Sir; I approached the cave ready to destroy the giant dog, when I was attacked by a giant bird. The brothers of Blackdale Abbey tended me, I am a blessed."

"John, you are indeed blessed, what sort of bird could have done this damage to you?"

"I am not sure, it was massive and black, it looked like a giant raven."

"A raven you say, the great black bird of legend, a bird associated with death, because of its habit of eating carrion, including dead human flesh, it has been confined for years to England's mountains and moorlands, you were indeed fortunate. Even though you did not succeed in you mission, you deserve a reward for your efforts, please take this with gratitude."

It must be said that John Slade did not venture anywhere near the cave again and advised any other foolhardy soul to do the same. In time his physical wounds healed, but his mind would be terrorised endlessly with dark thoughts and night terrors.

Ealdorman Hudson held a meeting with the High Sheriff of Durham and other notable people. The people were restless they wanted to know why a small village like Elersly and the surrounding areas could suffer so much misery. Giant birds attacking people, the strange woman that kept appearing at times of grief and of course the Barghest, had been seen a few times, by several people, it was indeed real.

Reverend Marshal did his best to calm the people in his sermons but the feeling was there and growing that the whole district was cursed by some witchery or the work of satanic forces. Where the words of the convicted witch Jane Frizzel of Crooked Oak coming to pass? Despite the attempts by Reverend Marshal to calm the situation wicked whispers would spiral around like a wasp's nest that had been disturbed.

What had happened to Jane Frizzel, where was she was she dead or alive watching and planning her revenge, no one knew the truth and no one would, that was for other people. The atmosphere in and around the village was one of suspicion and distrust, no person could be trusted and no person would be.

CHAPTER 15

Nestled in a deep hollow of the Leam Valley, surrounded on all sides by steep hills and thick forest, Blackdale Abbey stood solid as it had for hundreds of years. Things here had not changed; even King Henry's reformation and destruction of the monasteries had not reached here in this isolated place. The day of a monk was regulated by regular prayer services in the abbey church.

These services took place every three hours, day and night. When the services were over, monks would be occupied with all the tasks associated with maintaining a self-sustaining community. Abbeys grew their own food, did all their own building, and in some cases, grew quite prosperous doing so, largely on the basis of raising sheep and selling the wool.

That was no different today as the monks were busy at their tasks, then a loud bell rang out around the courtyard and the monks immediately stopped their work and made their way to the abbey church for prayers of the Eucharis. After the service they assembled in the dining room for lunch, this would be a simple vegetable dish, porridge and pulses were served. Meat from four-legged animals was exclusively reserved for the sick. Only fish and poultry were allowed, additionally, each monk received one pound of dark rye bread and a half pint of wine mixed with water.

They sat quietly as the abbot praised God for the meal, he carried on speaking.

"We brothers are all aware of the man John Slade who was brought to us with severe wounds caused by some unknown creature. He is I am informed healing well, thanks to the work of Brother James and the others in the infirmary. It is said to have happened in a clearing of the forest next to a cave, it is also said to be a place of unholy practice, we can only hope that this evil does not threaten our order, be vigilant in your prayers!"

That night the abbey was at rest, the monks in their cells mostly asleep as they were early risers for prayer. One monk, a young novice, Brother Benjamin was not asleep; his mind was troubled by the words of the abbot. If indeed there was a cave that was breeding evil, it must be stopped for the sake of all people and their very souls. It was just so that Brother Benjamin in his troubled mind and insecure youth he decided to examine this place of blackness.

In his robe and sandals he sneaked out of the dormitory and went to the abbey church where he filled a small bottle with holy water. He then took a iron axe from the garden storeroom and a flaming torch to guide him, set off on his quest. His young mind was playing tricks with his nerves but he knew that if he could find this cave and rid the land of evil he would be a hero, spoken of in history.

He walked out of the courtyard and headed westward, the moon, full and luminous, casts a silvery glow over the landscape, making the snow-covered ground glisten like a sea of diamonds. The cold air was crisp and still, with a sharpness that invigorated his senses. Trees, stripped, stand in stark silhouette against the moonlit sky, branches etched in delicate, intricate patterns, stars glimmer overhead, their light intensified by the clarity of the winter air, creating a celestial canopy. Snow crunches underfoot, the only sound in the hushed silence, adding to the sense of isolation. Breath left his body as grey ghosts looking for a home.

Brother Benjamin even though he was of youthful energy was feeling tired and a little breathless, it could be fatigue or fear, he was not sure. Having found the right place he left the road and entered the forest, trees pointing skyward like skeletal fingers, bushes laden with snow and then he was there in the clearing. The full moon illuminated the space reflecting off the snow in a silvered radiance. He went forward cautiously and slowly, eyes shifting and darting, he stepped inside.

The cave was hidden deep within the forest, its entrance a gaping orifice of darkness that seemed to swallow all light. Jagged rocks framed the opening, resembling the teeth of some ancient, long-forgotten beast. The air around the cave was thick with an eerie stillness, as if the very forest held its breath in fear of what lay within. He stepped inside, the temperature drops noticeably, and a damp, musty smell enveloped him, his torch flickered in the stagnant air casting weird shadows on the walls.

The walls are slick with moisture, glistening faintly, and the air is heavy with the scent of earth and decay. Stalactites hang from the ceiling like ancient, stone fangs, dripping water that echoes ominously as it hits the ground. Stalagmites rise from the floor, creating grotesque, misshapen figures that seem to shift and move in the peripheral vision.

As he moved deeper into the cave, the light faded into an oppressive darkness, swallowing all but the constricted glow of his torch. Strange, rustling noises and distant, unidentifiable sounds reverberate through the tunnels, adding to the sense of foreboding. Occasionally, he caught glimpses of small, skittering creatures, bats, spiders, and other unknown denizens of this subterranean world.

The path narrowed and twisted, leading him deeper into the bowels of the earth. Ancient cave paintings and cryptic symbols adorned the walls, telling stories of long-forgotten rituals and unspeakable horrors. The deeper he ventured, the more he felt an inexplicable, growing dread, as if the cave itself was alive, watching, and waiting, he grabbed the simple wooden crucifix around his neck and clutched it tightly, was this the gateway to hell?

At the heart of the cave, he came upon a vast, echoing chamber, the air heavy and still, the silence almost deafening. In the centre of the room, a massive dark pit its depths immeasurable. The edges are lined with peculiar, shimmering fungi that radiate a faint, spectral glow, casting an unnatural, pale light on the scene. Despite the overwhelming sense of dread, an inexplicable pull drew him further in, deeper into the heart of the cave, where the true source of its dark power awaited discovery.

Every instinct urged him to turn back, to flee this place of ancient darkness and unknown fears, but something compelled him to stay, to uncover the secrets that lie hidden in the shadows of this mysterious cavern. Every sound was amplified, the dripping of water echoing like distant footsteps, and the occasional rustle or squeak hinting at unseen creatures lurking in the darkness. The path twisted and turned, narrow passages giving way to vast, echoing chambers filled with an oppressive silence that weighed heavily on the spirit. Whispers seemed to float through the air, unintelligible and haunting, as if the cave itself was trying to communicate its ancient secrets. The sense of being watched inescapable, eyes seeming to peer out from the inky blackness, their owners just out of sight.

It was then that Brother Benjamin began to realise that he was a long way into this warren and if he was not careful he could become lost, especially as his torch was beginning to fade. He decided to think again, he after all done a duty to the area and the world, no one could expect more, he turned and made his way back to the entrance just as his torch died.

Brother Benjamin returned to the abbey which was still and tranquil in its darkness, he slipped quietly inside and down the corridor to the dormitory. He was just about to climb on his bunk when the Brother Mark in the next bunk awoke. "Brother Benjamin what are you doing, is it time to get up already?"

"No, Mark it is nothing, go back to sleep."

It had to be said the Benjamin did not sleep at all with the thoughts of his adventure freshly turned in his head. So not much more than an hour later he rose from his bunk red eyed and tired as the bell went for Morning Prayer. The abbot gazed around at the brothers and it was not long before his eyes landed on Benjamin.

Brother Benjamin, you look tired, and your clothing is unclean, see me after prayers."

After prayers Benjamin attended the abbot's chambers with a degree of nervousness.

"Well Benjamin, you were a pitiful sight at prayers, explain yourself?"

"Brother Abbot, I have a confession to make, last night I left the abbey and went looking for the cave where John Slade was attacked, I thought that I might help resolve the situation."

"Did you now, you know it is expressly forbidden to leave this place without permission?"

"Yes brother I have been foolish, I have disrespected you!"

"Yes Brother Benjamin I agree you have been foolish, you have broken the abbey's rules and with that comes punishment. I accept your plea that you thought to do a good deed, so I will be lenient, I could have you whipped or even put in the prison. However, you are young and not at full grasp of the ways of the world, so you will do penance by doing the most unclean and ungodly tasks in the abbey until I deem it to be justified."

Benjamin left the room suitable chastised and knowing it could have been a deal worse.

The abbot sat back in his chair and smiled, "foolish child, he will learn in time."

Benjamin spent the next few days doing things reserved for as punishments, he cleaned the latrines, mucked out the horses and the pigs until he was sick to death. One morning he was tasked with cleaning the shrine of saint Godwin of Arden at the far end of the abbey.

Next morning came the Leam Valley was still, held in a shivered silver shroud of chilled mist, the abbey's ancient stones definite and defiant amongst the swirling grey wrapping its very foundations. Ice toped puddles littered the grounds and the multitude of multi-hued leaves, frost folded into dead brown, swept into neat piles.

The brethren of this place had been about their purpose long before the feeble sun, attending morning offices and dealing with the daily duties of a, working, self-sufficient sanctuary. Now after seven, it was a time for a break in the busy bustle of life and for the brothers` time for food.

The refectory was a whirl of white habits, collecting their food and taking their place at one of the simple wooden benches, where they sat patiently waiting for the instruction to begin even though they were hungry, discipline was stronger. Brother James, the Prior of Blackdale Abbey and as such second only to the abbot himself would supervise proceedings.

James sat at the head of the largest bench, with several smaller versions which were mostly used for the novices lined up in ordered manner, James tapped on the bench with his hand and what little noise there was in the hall ceased instantly and all was quiet.

He looked around at those in attendance, "We are gathered here on this morning in the sight of God to take nourishment, to give thanks for our blessing and to remember the code that we follow: Subdue the flesh, so far as your health permits, by fasting and abstinence from food and drink.

"When you come to the table, listen until you leave to what is the custom to read, without disturbance or strife. Let not your mouths alone take nourishment but let your hearts too hunger for the words of God. Self-restraint and denial are of course righteous virtues and indeed our own brother abbot has chosen to abstain from sustenance this day. However, I realise that young men require such things and we have novices to consider, but before all else, dear brothers, love God and then your neighbour, because these are the chief commandments given to us, you may begin."

The ambience of the hall changed at once into one of activity and movement, simple wooden spoons clattered off rough wooden bowls as the meagre serving of plain porridge was quickly dispatched. After the meal, each was given a task to carry out, from brushing leaves or attending the gardens, fish ponds and grounds, to cleaning chores.

Brother James stood up and called for attention, "has anybody seen Brother Benjamin this morning, is he sick?"

Brother Paul answered, "Last time I saw him he was on his way to clean the shrine."

The Prior shook his head, Paul go and check on him, the boy is immature."

Brother Paul lamp in one hand made his way down the narrow, constricted passage and into the small room at the eastern most side of the abbey, where he entered quietly before kneeling at the foot of the shrine where he offered a short prayer.

He opened his eyes and gazed for a short while at the shrine. The room was quite small to be the final resting place of such a venerated man as Saint Godwin, but it reflected in death what he was in life, devout, saintly and with a truthful austerity and humbleness that was said to radiate from every pore of his being.

In the centre of the room, a simple bronze plaque set into the sandstone flags of the floor read simply: "Godwin" and was lit by four large candles placed at the corners of the grave, held high on candlesticks of silver. At the head of the grave, a plain wooden altar covered in an embroidered cloth of red and gold and on the alter the cross of Arden, behind that a thick drape of deep purple covered the wall, the scene was on of serenity and peace.

 The flagstones which in certain places had worn away by the footfalls of many a pilgrim and now held a saintly shin,e which shimmered in the dappled candle light. The sense of things was different; a silent stillness filled the air. The shrine was always a place of quiet reflection but this was somehow changed. It was not until he approached the altar that the cause of his disquiet became apparent.

In a dark dimly lit corner was a white cassock, crumpled and perverted in an untidy manner. He looked closer and realised that the robe was not only in disarray but it was also red in places, shining a lamp near he realised that there was also a body entangled in the weave, it was brother Benjamin. Blood had pumped out onto the cold stone floor like a warm red blanket, holy blood spilled in this sacred place of God. Brother Paul knelt by the body gazing upon the body of Benjamin lying on his front, eyes agape stilled in silence as if in shock, a grey, blue staining his once brown eyes, his face a ghastly pallor of his past life.

The face of Brother Paul fared no better as the shock of such a discovery was not what he expected within these hallowed walls. Yes people die; brothers no matter how devout grow old as is the way of things and at some point in time they leave this mortal world for a better place. Brother Paul up stiff and transfixed a rigid statue of humanity as if frozen in time and place. He stood there for some time regarding the scene until reality came upon him with a wasp like sting of certainty. He turned in one motion and ran from the room, along the passageway to the office of the abbot where he crashed through the door and stood silent in a state of panic.

The Abbot was sitting at his desk, equally surprised and unimpressed by this young man standing before him. "What are you doing barging into my office, what is this about?"

"So sorry Brother Abbot but, I have found Brother Benjamin, in the shrine of Saint Godwin!"

"So how does that concern me, is he unwell?"

Brother Benjamin hesitated for a moment, "no brother, he`s dead!"

CHAPTER 16

The next day at the house of John Slade came a knock; John opened it to find one of Ealdorman Hudson's men. "Mr Slade the ealdorman would like to see you, will you come?"

"What is this about, am I in some sort of trouble?"

"No Sir, he merely wants to speak with you."

"Alright, I will come with you."

John was escorted to Elersly where he entered the home of Ealdorman Hudson.

"Ah John how are you, have your wounds healed sufficiently?"

"I am still in some pain Sir but it gets better by the day, you wanted to see me?"

"The day you went up to treat cave and were attacked, well one of the monks from Blackdale Abbey thought he would try and resolve the situation."

"Was he attacked as well?"

"Not at the scene but yesterday he was found dead in the abbey!"

"My God, is no one safe in this place?"

"It would appear not John, the Sheriff has been informed and he is sending his best man to help, his name is Daniel, Matthews. He is some sort of expert at investigating crimes, would you speak to him and tell him what you know?"

"Yes Sir, I would gladly if it would help!"

Later that morning the investigator, arrived in the village, he was a nondescript sort of man, short in stature; he was taken to the ealdorman's house where he was introduced to Ealdorman Hudson.

"Good morning Ealdorman Hudson, I am Daniel, Matthews, the sheriff sent me."

"You are some sort of expert I am informed, I think that you might want to go to Blackdale Abbey. The funeral of the young monk is this afternoon; the abbot will consult with you. I have arranged one of my men to accompany you as you are a stranger in these parts."

"Thank you ealdorman I will make my way there promptly."

The two men rode over the moor and down into the Leam Valley where hidden among the tall trees was Blackdale Abbey. They were guided to the Abbots room and were welcomed into the abbey.

"Brother Abbot this is the man you are expecting."

"Good day Sir, I am Daniel, Matthews, I have been sent by the Sheriff of County Durham."

"Ah please come in, have a seat, what is it you do exactly Mr Matthews?"

"I investigate crimes for the sheriff, crimes that are difficult to solve are passed on to me to deal with, I work mostly alone and I have developed my own methods over the years."

"One of our young novices, Brother Benjamin was found dead in the shrine of Saint Godwin, he did not die of natural causes. I suggest you go and see Brother James in the infirmary, he dealt with the situation, it should help, the funeral will take place later."

"Thank you Abbot I will do that now."

Daniel, Matthews was escorted to the infirmary where Brother James was working on the sick, mostly monks with a few local people in attendance.

"Brother James this is Daniel, Matthews sent by the sheriff."

"Ah welcome, how can I help you?"

"Yes Brother James I am told you are in charge of the sick here, tell me how did Brother Benjamin die, he was young and healthy, the abbot thinks he was murdered, how so?"

"I examined him closely expecting to have sarcomas to some illness until I saw the gaping wound on his neck, he bled to death, I would say it was caused by a long thin knife."

"What, who would kill a monk?"

"Well he broke the rules and went to investigate the same cave that a local hunter was attacked, he thought he could do something that an experienced, grown man could not."

"I see, tell me where on the body was this wound, precisely?"

"On the left side of his neck, it was about that long."

"Thank you Brother James, I have been invited to attend the funeral, good day to you."

Daniel, Matthews returned to the abbot, and they left and walked to the abbey church. The body placed on a pedestal in an open pine box in front of the abbey church's altar. Two monks take turns keeping prayerful watch beside the body. This centuries-old tradition of keeping Vigil throughout the hours preceding the funeral is a beautiful embodiment of the spiritual bond that unites all monks.

The abbot paused just inside of the door. "This Mr Matthews is what we call the School of Charity, the brothers have kept vigil all night, taking turns so Brother Benjamin was never left alone. We are now ready for the service, you are welcome to witness the ceremony but I would ask you to stay detached?"

"Yes Brother Abbot of course I will stay at the rear."

Daniel Mathews watched as the monks arrived singing the entrance hymn, the entire community was led into the church by a monk carrying the processional cross. The funeral began with the traditional Mass for the Dead, presided over by the Abbot, clothed in white vestments to symbolize the resurrection of Christ. When the Mass, was over the abbot stepped forward to bless the body with incense and sprinkle it with holy water. While this is taking place, the rest of the monastic community sings a hymn which affirms the Christian's belief in the power of Resurrection. The Abbot raised his arms out wide and spoke.

"And I will raise him up and I will raise him up and I will raise him up on the last day."

He then stood aside as six monks came forward to carry the pedestal from the church. With the Paschal Candle to guide them, the procession moved forward through the chapter room and out the door of the Abbey to the cemetery. During the final procession, the great abbey bells rang at solemn intervals until everyone has gathered at the grave site.

Daniel Mathews remained in the background as he observed the service. The bier was carefully placed atop four straps that have been laid across the grave; next to the grave is a mound of fresh dirt and several shovels. Standing at the head of the grave, the abbot prayed while blessing both the body and the grave one last time with holy water and incense. A white cloth was placed over the body and then the body was carefully lowered into the grave while the community sang Psalm 138.

When the body was lowered all the way to the bottom of the grave, the straps were pulled back, the brothers stepped aside as the Abbot threw the first handfuls of dirt onto the body. The shovels were then handed from brother to brother in order for the entire community to take a turn at filling in the grave.

Before leaving the cemetery the Abbot invited all present to join him in praying the Lord's Prayer prior to concluding the burial by singing once again, the words of the Resurrection Song "And I will Raise Him Up." At the conclusion of the song, the burial has come to an end. There is no procession back to the church, and no reception.

On top of the abbey stood an ancient cross in the design of Saint Godwin's Pectoral cross that guided him to this secluded place all those centuries ago. On top pf this cross sat something else, cast against the sapphire shades of a winter sky, a huge black shape watching the proceedings below, eyes focused, great talons gripped the top of the cross as a giant raven surveyed all. On the hill overlooking the graveyard were two more onlookers, a woman in a white robe, black hair wafting in the breeze and at her feet a huge black dog sat quietly, the barguest!

Daniel Mathews thanked the abbot and left to return to Elersly where he informed the ealdorman of his visit to the abbey. The ealdorman graciously offered Daniel Mathews a room at his house for as long as needed and he gratefully accepted. The ealdorman, his wife and Daniel Mathews dined together that night and discussed the death of the monk as well as other matters that had arisen in the area and most importantly what could be done.

The next morning came fine and not unpleasant for the season, Daniel Mathews decided to take a walk around the village. Of course he being a stranger in the hamlet stood out strait away and was approached by several people wanting to know who he was and why he was here. He explained that he was looking for reasons behind the unfortunate reputation of this village and surrounding area, he needed help of which there was little.

He visited Saint Andrew's Church and spoke to Reverent Marshal.

"Reverend, would you say that you have a witchcraft problem in your parish?"

"I am a man of God Sir I resist such thoughts but it is peculiar that so many bad things happen here. Several people have been accused in the past most recently a woman by the name of Jane Frizzel, she lived in a farmhouse, by the name of Crooked Oak."

"What happened?" Daniel asked.

"Jane Frizzel was one of Crooked Oaks most well-known inhabitants, known or suspected locally as being a witch. It was said she, was guilty of casting spells on men, maidens, and cattle. The farmhouse was said to be the site where witchcraft was believed to be practised, referred to locally as "Dark Arts." It has been said that Jane was tutored and trained in the dark arts of witchcraft by her mother Elizabeth and carried on the belief."

"What became of her?"

"She was arrested, there were witnesses prepared to give evidence against her and she was found guilty. She put in jail awaiting her sentence but before the hanging took place she somehow disappeared, just vanished. No one could explain how or why but she was gone and has never been seen since, whether dead or alive none can say."

"Now Reverend these tales about giant birds and dogs have you seen them?"

"No I have not but there are a few people around who have and they firmly believe it!"

"Elersly, reverend is like most villages in this county full of people that are uneducated and subject to wild rumour and superstitions could they have imagined these things?"

Reverend Marshal shuffled in his chair and considered for a while. "Yes I am sure there will be some of that, people in these places do not understand much more than keeping themselves alive. They have now idea of the world outside of their immediate area, so yes."

"One more thing Reverend, have there been any rumours in the village itself?"

"One assertion that refuses to go away is that of a woman, Mary Swann and her daughter Eliza. She gave birth some years ago without being wed and without it seems a man at all, so they say. The pair have been subjected to abuse ever since, I am sure it is all hogwash but they keep themselves out of the light as much as possible."

"Very well Sir thank you for your time, good day to you."

He wandered around the village for a while and spoke to a few locals; he asked one woman if she knew Mary Swann and her daughter. He received several answers none of them pleasant and some decidedly disgusting, he stopped one woman and asked where they lived. The woman said nothing but pointed a finger in the direction, her name was Ann Simms.

Eliza was in the house reflecting on things quietly, "What troubles you daughter?"

"Troubles mother, I have many, many questions unanswered, why am I disturbed in the night by things that come to me in dreams? I see things that come to pass, I see giant dogs and a woman about my age, she speaks to me as if she wants me to join with her for some reason. I have seen her and spoken with her but is she real or a dream, I cannot say, am I insane mother, why is this happening?"

"You are indeed a special woman, but you are my daughter, we are one."

Eliza left the house and walked into the village square, there she saw a man a stranger in the village. Somehow he seemed familiar as if she had seen him before was he in one of her dreams? She walked closer and as he turned their eyes met, he seemed gaze at her for so long but probably not that long, he removed his hat and bowed graciously.

"You are a stranger here are you not Sir?"

"Yes I am my name is Daniel Mathews at your service."

Eliza paused for a moment she was not used to being addressed in such a polite manner.

"Have you business here Mr Mathews?"

"I have indeed, I work for the sheriff of this county and I have been called upon to aid the ealdorman with the problems that persist in this area, tell me, what is your name?"

"I am Eliza Swann."

"Ah, Eliza Swann, daughter of Mary Swann."

"I don't know you; do you know my mother Sir?"

"I do not know her or yourself but I know of you both, you have somewhat of a reputation."

"Well I cannot argue with that, we have been abused so much over the years!"

"Tell me Eliza is any of this true?"

"No Sir none of it, it is all nonsense and rumour!"

"I see, then you have no need to worry."

Eliza went back home and told her mother of her meeting with this man. As the day went into night Eliza thought about this meeting and its meaning, she knew his name but what was his purpose? Her mind was troubled as it had been for some time, she could not understand.

CHAPTER 17

Next day Martin Howe the hunter was up on the moor looking for game but was not having the most productive of days. He had been hunting and tracking in this area for many years and had become proficient at tracking various animals from the size of the tracks to their depth in the soil. He then came across some deer tracks and for a second thought about following them but remembered the last time he did that and as the prints were heading in the direction of the ravine, remembering what happened the last time he entered the ravine, he decided he would have better judgement this time.

The morning was cold and a thick mist enveloped the high ground, damp and clinging, it swirled like clouds in a breeze. The next he knew he was standing on the banks of Blackwater Lake, the lake of the dead as it was sometimes known as people seemed to go missing around its shores. The lake was deep and black even at the edges and seemed to be always covered in a dense fog the confused the senses.

Martin Howe was just about to give up his search for food and turn for home when from in the mist he heard a faint cry, like that of a young child. He looked around but could not decide where the sound had come from or even if he had imagined it. He managed to spot his own footprints and followed them off the moor and into the village where he reported it to the ealdorman. It would be fair to say that Ealdorman Hudson was weary of this behaviour and was sitting head in hands when Daniel Mathews entered the room.

"You look troubled Ealdorman, what ails you?"

"Oh you perceive me well Daniel, I have just had a visit from Martin Howe, he is a hunter in these parts and supplies us with meat when he can, he came to me with another tale."

"What sort of tale?" Daniel inquired with some interest.

"He said he was out hunting earlier this morning up on the moor next to Blackwater Lake when he heard strange noises, wails of a child, he was scared and thought he should inform me of it. He is the same man I have told you of before, the one who tracked a deer into a valley and found the cave where he saw the huge tracks of a dog."

"I see ealdorman; I intend to visit some of these locations today, I will need my guide."

"Yes of course Daniel, I will send for him promptly!"

Eliza left the house and walked into the centre of the village to fetch water from the well. Having done that she made her way back home and as she drew closer to the small cottage she became aware of something on the wooden door. She placed her pail of water on the ground and examined it, there was a design carved into the wood of the door. A design she had not seen before and had no meaning to her, she felt it with her fingers as the groves etched into the dark, weathered wood of the door.

She opened the door and shouted inside. "Mother come here quickly!"

Mary Swann did just that and came outside, "why the shouting Eliza what is wrong?"

"Look, look at the door that was not there last night, what is it, what does it mean?"

"My God Eliza, this is not good, I know this sign, I have seen it before."

"What is it mother?"

"It is what they call the witch's knot it is a sign of protection used in folk magic."

"But what does it stand for?"

"This symbol represents a kind of magic known as knot magic that witches have practiced for centuries. People used this symbol as a charm against witchcraft by carving it into the doors of their homes. It's a powerful symbol of protection since it represents the binding of witches and their magic."

"So the people really suspect that we are witches, what can we do?"

"At the moment we just stay low and hope it passes, if not we will have to think again!"

"I realise now, when I was out I saw a man in the village, a stranger, we spoke briefly and he had a pendant round his neck and it was that same symbol, do you think he did this?"

"I don't know Eliza, let's go inside, it's cold."

Mark Laws was waiting outside as Daniel Mathews came out, "Good day Mark."

"Good day Daniel where are we going today?"

"Firstly I would like to visit the house of Jane Frizzel, Crooked Oak I believe."

"Of course it's a few miles south of here, not too far."

They set off along the road towards Durham City; Crooked Oak was on the way. the two men arrived and began looking around the house, the place was by now in a dismal state.

"Well Mark, I would say judging by the state of the place Jane Frizzel left on a hurry!"

Mark looked at him, "yes Daniel she was arrested!"

Daniel Mathews began moving things around, not that there was much to move.

"What are you looking for Daniel?"

"Anything Mark any clue that she was practicing witchcraft here."

They searched the building and were not getting far until Mark moved a wicker basket.

"Daniel, over here what is this?"

Daniel dropped somethings he was inspecting and went over to mark. "What is it Mark?"

"I moved this basket and say this on the wall, what is it, do you know?"

"Oh I know what this is alright, this mark is what we know as a pentagram and it's upside down with two points on top symbolizing matter's domination over spirit. Many people often associate an inverted pentagram with black magic and the Devil."

"So the rumours were right she was practising Black Magic here!"

"Yes Mark it would seem so, no one would have a symbol like that in their house."

"My God, I thought this was all superstition and gossip but it is all true!"

"Yes mark, tell me what happened when this woman was arrested?"

"She was flung in jail and stood trial; she was convicted of witchcraft and dark arts."

"Then she was hanged I assume?"

"That is the strangest thing of all, on the day of the execution the guards went to get her from her cell and, and she was not there, she had simple vanished, not to be seen again!"

"This situation is worse than I thought Mark, if she diapered, most witches do not have the ability to vanish or change shape, these things are learned through time and practice. I suspect that she has a more powerful protector, a teacher wise in the ways of these things."

"So what now Daniel, where do we go next?"

"I would like to see the house of another suspect, Isabella Mosswood, is it far?"

"It is a few miles north of here on the moor."

"Then let us make haste."

The men mounted their horses and rode north climbing in altitude as they went and were soon on the bleak wind swept moor. As the trotted across the heather clad ground Daniel Mathews pulled his coat up around his neck, being from the city he had not experienced somewhere as isolated and desolate before. They proceeded up a steep slope and eventually they reached the top of Split Crow Hill and there in front of them a small cottage.

"Is this it Mark?"

"Yes Sir, this is where Isabella Mosswood lived."

They dismounted and began to look around; just like Crooked Oak the house was in a state of disarray, things were lying around in no particular order, dishevelled and disordered.

"It would seem that our Isabella Mosswood left with some haste as well, what happened to her Mark, she did not vanish also?"

"Having been mentioned that she could be a witch and involved with evil matters, the authorities' came to arrest her for interrogation but…"

"Don't tell me Mark, she was gone!"

"Well yes but how did you know that Daniel?"

"Look around what do you see?"

"Well nothing much just a lot of rubbish!"

"Well, Mark I have done this occupation for many years and I can identify clues that others cannot. Look on the table over there the fleshless skulls of various animals, I can see a deer, rabbit, fox and what seems to be a cat, they are all items which would have."

Daniel went over to a shelf where several small wooden bowls were placed; he picked each one of them up and examined the contents, sniffing them at the same time.

"What is in those bowl Daniel" Mark inquired.

"There are a mixture of herbs and roots commonly used in rituals, I think we have another witch on our hands, more over they have a protector, someone most powerful and dangerous, it is getting late I would like to see this cave before dark, is it far?"

"Not too far it is over that way in a valley."

The men set off and were soon at the top of the slope leading into the ravine, as it was steep and strewn with rocks the horsed were not too happy about chancing it, they were left behind and the two men scrambled down the steep slope. Having reached the bottom they made their way through the trees and bushes to the open glade.

Instantly Daniel saw something, there tracks in the snow, he bent down for a better look.

"Look here Mark; these tracks are that of a dog but not any dog I have seen, look they lead into the cave over there. This dog could be witches familiar and they could be hiding in that cave, it could well be a coven, we need more help, this is too much for two people."

Daniel Mathews returned to Elersly and informed Ealdorman Hudson of what he had found. It was not good news as the ealdorman understood the serious nature of situation. Daniel Mathews decided to return to Durham and inform the sheriff of his investigations and explain that the undertaking should not progress without a group of the sheriff's men, armed.

Daniel Mathews left the house and was unhitching his horse when he was approached by a woman; he turned to find Eliza Swann standing rigid and resolute.

"That pendant you wear, that same design was carved into our door, what does it mean?"

"That design miss is a protection from evil, does it bother you, do you fear it?"

CHAPTER 18

Spring had arrived in Elersly not that you might realise as it was still cold and sometimes frosty overnight, spring has a habit of coming late to these parts. Strangely nothing much had happened in the village for a couple of months, no dramas, no unusual deaths and no sigh of the terrible events that had beset this area.

Eliza Swann was going about her business as usual, still somewhat troubled by the symbol carved into the door of her house. She tried to rub it off and even tried to fill in the cracks with various substances but it was still there for all to see. The mood in the village had in the past months changed somewhat from the doom laden disposition to one of a brighter outlook. Things were changing little by little as the memory of things past began to fade. It was Elersly's time in the sun however, nothing much changes and the sunny days do not last.

Ten miles north in Newcastle the city was a mass of movement, people going about their business as always. This city was no different to others the rich merchants lived in relative comfort, at least compared to the common folk with neat houses on the outer sides of the city, quiet and semi-rural. For the others that were confined to the inner parts of the city it was not so pleasant.

Houses were poor and dilapidated, some appearing to have already given up and were leaning on each other. The streets were no better, cramped and restricted they did not see much of the sun as they were too close together. 'Filth running in open ditches in the streets, fly-blown meat and stinking fish, contaminated and adulterated ale, polluted well water, unspeakable latrines, diseases, were experienced indiscriminately by all social classes.

Down on the docks it was just as bad, even worse in places, especially the coal staithes where coal brought from the mines of Durham and Northumberland to Newcastle where it was distributed around the country and abroad. Keel men were used to link the mines upstream to the colliers at the quayside, Newcastle coal was cheaper than land-borne coal elsewhere in the country.

A collection of quays, staithes, and landings were overlooked by dark faced warehouses with bricks stained black by years of ingrained coal dust; ropes dangled and swayed. Tucked away in a narrow street, just off the dockside, cobbles and shadowy alleys surrounded the office. In daylight, it was a bustle of humanity and industry; at night it was distorted into another entity.

The hours of darkness would consume the dockside, sucking out its basic decency, leaving only depravity and corrupted souls to flounder in their own mess. Numerous inns and taverns supplied strong ale and rum to the sailors and keel-men that frequented the neighbourhood. Ladies of ill virtue haunted the streets like stalking herons in search of prey. Drunkenness, violence, and other forms of base behaviour were commonplace.

The view over the River Tyne was on of an industrial landscape of workshops, shipyards, and dry-docks; the sounds of heavy chains and the striking of iron filled the air. The river was home to all manner of waste, manufactured and natural, dumped into its current to be carried down to the sea at Tynemouth. As rivers go this was a poor example: no bank side reeds and bushes, no fish gliding through the streaming weed. In fact, it was an open, moving sewer and its stench would drive a saint to sin.

As the day had progressed the sky had darkened and had almost banished the sun from her position. The rain, which had started benignly enough a few hours earlier, was now torrential, piercing the sky like liquid bullets. Rivulets of water ran down walls and dripped from eaves; gutters changed into shallow streams, like tributaries seeking out the main river. People, hunched and stooped, moved with purpose in pursuit of their tasks, not lingering for long.

It was in this turmoil of nature's misery that a ship approached the estuary and sailed slowly up stream and docked at the coal staithes. It was a Dutch flagged merchant ship form Amsterdam come to collect a cargo of coal. The crew now with some time to kill disembarked the ship and made directly for the more down beat areas of the city dock land, where the ale would flow gleefully, amongst other things.

Most of the sailors never made it past the first tavern, "The Mallard." This was a place with a reputation for bawdiness and drunkenness, in all its forms. Inside the main area where patrons gathered was typically large with a central hearth providing warmth and light. The room would be filled with wooden benches, often worn and stained from years of use. A large open fireplace or hearth served as the heart of the tavern, used for both heating and cooking.

Lighting was provided by tallow candles, oil lamps, or the fire itself, creating a dim, smoky atmosphere. Bar or counter a simple wooden counter where the tavern keeper or servants dispensed ale, wine, and sometimes spirits. Barrels of ale or casks of wine would be visible behind the counter. Patrons, a mix of locals and travellers including farmers, merchants, sailors, craftsmen and taverns were places where news and gossip were exchanged.

However the sailors were not the only creatures to leave the ship that wet and dreary night, as several black rats decided to do the same and mix with the local in this fine city. As the spring wore on things were changing in Newcastle, people were falling sick, of course disease was no strangers to this place, dysentery being rife in the filthy conditions.

Not far from the docks in a street of tumbledown cottages in the filthy, poverty-stricken Sandhill area of the Quayside, Fredric Hall was feeling the effects of some disorder. Several days before he was feeling unwell with a stomach ache and noticed blood in his excrement, the next day it was also in his urine. The day after that he became even worse, vomiting and fever gripped his body causing him to shake uncontrollably. Within a day he became steadily worse as great black boils appeared in his armpits, oozing puss and blood. Within hours he was dead, the Black Death had arrived in Newcastle.

Unfortunately for the people of this city the plague spread among the populace like the fires of hell. Nobody knew the cause and not one person knew the cure, the medics thought the pestilence was the result of bad air, miasma so mixtures of herbs were everywhere to combat the foul smell that emanated from every part of the city.

A meeting was called in the Moot Hall, the Mayor of Newcastle, the Sheriff of Northumberland, the Ealdorman and some high ranking traders and merchants. They discussed the cause and what cause of action to take. It was suspected that merchant ships from the Netherlands and Flanders had brought the disease to this city and there would be a temporary sanction on such vessels.

An order was issued for all persons to lock themselves indoors and not to venture out. The city was locked down and the streets deserted apart from the rats, the cats and the odd stray dog. The bodies however, were piling up and needed to be dealt with, there not being the space or time for proper burials the bodies were placed in plague pit around the city. Saint Nicholas' Church, also plague pits at the town's three other parish churches – Saint John's at the bottom of Westgate Road, Saint Andrew's on Newgate Street and the old All Saints church on lower Pilgrim Street. Land was also put aside on the Town Moor as an overflow.

In the village of Elersly word had quickly spread of the tragic events in Newcastle, Ealdorman Hudson decreed that no commerce be undertaken between the village and Newcastle. This did not go down well with the local farmers who supplied meat, milk and wool to the city and would now have their income ruined.

At Saint Andrews church Reverend Marshal was in a state of extreme piety.

"You may be seated, we have all heard about the dreadful nature of the pestilence that has befallen our brethren in Newcastle. They say the plague was brought be Dutch sailors, I say that this is the work of god! He is not pleased with the folk of that city and this is his punishment! We do not want the same fate to befall us here in our village, so you must be even more devoted than normal, pray, pray to god for your salvation, pray like never before!"

It was now several weeks later and spring had flowed seamlessly into summer. The people of Elersly were beginning to resurface as news came that the epidemic in Newcastle was easing and fewer people were falling sick with this devilish disease. Eliza decided to venture out and walk up onto the moor thinking there could be no illness up there in the clean air. She walked for some time between the clumps of heather and the odd gorse bush and sat for a while on a rock overlooking the valley.

"Good morning Eliza!"

Eliza turned in shock and there once again was the young woman she had met before.

"Oh you gave me a shock, how did you come up on me without a sound?"

"Oh I have my ways Eliza, are you not locked down still in the village?"

"They say the pestilence is easing and I thought it would be safe up here."

"You are right the people are beginning to re-emerge from their burrows."

"Reverend Marshal says it is a punishment from god for immoral practises."

"Ha, well he would say that, come with me I would show you something of his god!"

They walked awhile over the moor until they reached the edge where it looked down onto the main road between Newcastle and Durham City. Down below Eliza could see a column of men about twenty strong stripped to the waist, they seemed to be lashing themselves with some sort of whips, as they grew closer she could see blood running down their backs and collecting on their clothing, she put her hands over her face and turned to the other woman.

"What is going on here who are these people why are the beating themselves bloody?"

"These fools are known as Flagellants, they believe the plague came because god was angry, so they whip themselves. Some upper-class men joined processions of flagellants that travelled from town to town and engaged in public displays of penance and punishment: They beat themselves and one another with heavy leather straps studded with sharp pieces of metal while the townspeople looked on."

Eliza gazed at them as they walked slowly by, this is madness!"

"Is this what you god demands Eliza, is your god not kind and compassionate?"

"I, I am not sure any more, why would god want this?"

"Understand this Eliza their god has abandoned them and he will abandon you, you are not one of them, you belong with us, one day you will come to us willingly."

Eliza went home and was sitting outside in the sun when her mother came out.

"Eliza where have you been all this time, do you wish us all dead?"

"Oh don't fuss mother, the plague is almost over in Newcastle so they say and we did not get it here in Elersly, it being confined to the city and its constricted nature, it is past now."

"So, Eliza Swann, where exactly have you been?"

"I went for a walk up on the moor, it being fresh and quiet up there and it was just so."

"You did not meet any other person up there?"

"No mother, well there was one woman."

"What woman?!

"I don't know her name but I have met her a few times before, she is peculiar, almost like some sort of wraith. She speaks in perforated words but they have truth to them and I sometimes see her in my visions, she comes to me in the night, in dreams she lives."

CHAPTER 19

Edinburgh

Summer 1621

Edinburgh like other cities of this time was much the same; rich people lived a life of relative comfort while everybody else did not. Some years ago Edinburgh was recognised as the right and proper capital of Scotland and its influence grew with it. Edinburgh was famous for making wool cloth and nearby was the port of Leith which was Edinburgh's harbour exports were rawhides and wool. Cattle and sheep were sold at a market in Cowgate. They were then butchered in the town; grain and hay were sold in the Grassmarket.

From the King's Palace in the east the city rises higher and higher to the west and consists mainly of one broad and very fine street. The rest of the side streets and alleys are badly built and occupied by very poorest people of the city. Its length from east to west is in the region of a mile while the width of the city from north to south is narrow. The castle, on the rocky outcrop at the top of the hill, being the most prominent aspect and dominated the scene.

As the population grey there was a need for space, so it was decided to build upward instead of outward. The Royal Mile while being a fine street, on either side was not so good as a series of confined closes were spread along the length. One of these closes was named Mary King's Close as it was reported that Mary Queen of Scots was held captive here.

Mary King's Close is actually a cluster of several closes, connected by small alleys and walkways; it is very much a labyrinthine warren. The houses at the top of the tenement were the best and brightest of all and were home to successful merchants, lawyers and even doctors. The people who lived in the lowest houses were everyone from tradesmen to the very poorest; the houses were dark and lacked sanitation.

The corridors were lighted with oil lamps with fish oil, the smell being one of overpowering revulsion. People threw their buckets filled with urine and faeces down the street, the rooms cramped and shared with the whole family, there was no privacy. The cramped, reeking streets and rooms were bad enough but one also had to be cautious at all times, as danger lurked around dark corners and in the shadows aplenty.

Murderers, rapists, and thieves were also living in the close but there were other dangers, Workshops, like the tanner's, used horse urine in the leather making process, which was a danger to health. Mary King's Close was also located next to the Old North Loch, a deeply contaminated bog used for dumping rubbish. A toxic gas arose from the swamp, piercing the walls of the close. This gas could cause deliriums and formed an eerie green light, which was frequently mistaken for spectral phantoms.

It was into this subterranean city of the dammed that three men entered from the High Street. the paced down the cobbled path past houses on either side the darkness, shouts and the odd scream echoing around the narrow passages as if they were trapped. Near the bottom they turned into a small room, one candle lit the scene wavering of the damp walls, the low ceiling giving the feeling that they were in fact in a box rather than a room. They sat on the floor and discussed the urgent matter at hand, the reason they were here. They were all landowners and farmers from the hills outside of the city and had connections everywhere.

Alan Borthwick, set the tone, "Right gentlemen we all know why we are here so let us proceed with urgency and get the hell out of this stinking cavern!"

"So what is the plan Alan?" James Lockhart inquired.

"I have been informed by my spies in England, there is plague in Newcastle, they will be at their weakest, now is the time, it is our chance to take the whole city."

Robert Hay interrupted, they might be low but the city will still be well defended!"

"That is true but the soldiers will also be sick and struggle to live never mind fight."

"How many men do we have?" Lockhart questioned.

Alan Borthwick was beginning to get animated. "We have many strong and capable men from around the city and more waiting in Dunbar, we have the numbers!"

Robert Hay was pondering, "I don't know Alan it is a big risk, if we fail we are dead!"

James Lockhart was considering another plan. "May I suggest another proposal; we pass Newcastle and attack Durham City instead?"

"The whole point of Newcastle is there is plenty of booty, what is there in Durham?"

James Lockhart continued, "I have been to Durham, the guard is much lighter than Newcastle and easier to win the city. As for booty, there are several churches in and around the city and the cathedral is full of gold and silver."

Robert Hay, looked around, "I agree with James, Durham will be much easier!"

"Alright, we should vote on it." Alan Borthwick turned to the men in turn.

Robert, how say you?"

"I say Durham!"

"James, what about you?"

"I also vote for Durham!"

"Well I seem to be out voted, Durham it is, go now and gather your men, we make haste! The cruel plague of the English was because of the revenging hand of God, and I swear by the foul death of England, the English are overwhelmed by the terrible vengeance of God!"

Over the next week preparations were made and men at arms began to gather about ten miles north of the English border. Plans were made solid in camp before they set off southward and it was not long before they crossed the Cheviot Hills into Northumberland.

The small villages were ill equipped to fend off such a massive raid and people were killed mercilessly for trying. Some Scots abandoned their cause and instead stole cattle and horses and made back across the border. In England word spread quickly of the coming invasion and preparations were hastily made.

In Newcastle a meeting was called between the Mayor, the Ealdorman and the High Sheriff of Northumberland.

The Major began, "well gentlemen we have all heard the news, what are we to do?"

Both the Ealdorman and the Mayor turned to the Sheriff as he was in charge of security.

"What is the plan sheriff, do we have a plan?"

The Sheriff was not best pleased with this tone and answered with some distain.

"Yes we do have a plan, I have ordered all outlying farms to enter the city and bring as much food as they can muster, we must out last any siege. I have also ordered the city gates to be closed and entry forbidden unless authorised by me. One more thing I have sent a rider to Durham to ask for reinforcements, any one they can spare will help."

"Anything more?" The mayor questioned.

"One more, I have sent spies out to scout the land to keep an eye on where the Scots are."

"Very well gentlemen I suppose all we can do is wait." The Ealdorman said despondently.

The city of Newcastle was in something of a chaotic scene as people scrambled around storing food and drink and wondering what might happen in the next few days. Soldiers were running around preparing the city for attack, the blacksmith had all of a sudden become a very busy fellow. Swords, axes and pikes were in need of repair and sharpening, tunics mending and as many new arrows crafted as was possible, bodkin tipped if possible.

The mood was much the same around the area even in the remote and secluded Blackdale Abbey. Although tucked away in a valley and surrounded by Hampston Forest, measures were still being taken. The abbot called a meeting of elder brothers, when assembled he stood before them in a solemn manner and head bowed began to speak.

"Dear brethren, I have been informed that, a large force of Scots have crossed the border and are heading for Newcastle. We are of course a peaceful religious order; we cannot hope to defend ourselves. We are in a good position here in the valley hidden amongst the trees, we must hope that they do not realise our location."

"What can we do Brother Abbot?"

"Firstly from now until I say so there will be no ringing of bells for any reason, not for meals, not for prayer, until I say. Next Brother James go to the shrine of Saint Godwin, take his pectoral cross and hide it in the safe place we decided in case of emergency. All we can do now dear brothers are to wait and pray for salvation."

In the village of Elersly, a man rode into the village in great haste, jumping off his sweating, gasping horse he made strait to the ealdorman's house. Ealdorman Hudson was in his study when the door opened swiftly, "Ealdorman Hudson Sir a messenger to see you!"

A man entered, taking his hat of having had more on his mind at that time.

"You have a message I understand?"

"Yes Sir, I bring a message and a warning from the Ealdorman of Newcastle!"

"A warning you say, what about?"

"A Scottish army has crossed the border and is camped north of Newcastle; they expect an attack at any moment. They have already burned and looted several villages to the north, people have been slain, be warned Ealdorman Hudson, you must leave, find safety!"

"Thank you and the officers of Newcastle for the information but I will be staying here!"

"Very well Sir I will report back."

Ealdorman Hudson called a meeting in the village square, people stood around wondering what was happening and of course gossiping and whispering things that had no truth. Hearing the bell, Eliza and her mother made their way to the square and stood at the side of the crowd but close enough to hear.

Ealdorman Hudson waved his arms to quiet the gathering and paused for a moment.

"I have just been informed by messenger that a large raiding party of Scots has crossed the border and are now north of Newcastle. I have sent word to Durham for some protection, whether it comes, I no not. They might pass by this village, Lord protect us we have little to steal. Those who can pack your things and head west, I am told it will be safe there until the danger has passed.

"And what of you Ealdorman Hudson, where will you be?" A voice echoed around.

I can assure you that I will be here among you at your service."

The people of Newcastle were in state of fear and foreboding as the thoughts of an invasion was imminent. They knew that the soldiers stationed here were not enough to hold back a full assault. Days past, people stored what food they had in secret places as that was their only form of wealth. Soldiers maned the city walls, nervous and ever vigilant day and night.

The Mayor and Ealdorman were in the Mayor's office discussing the situation.

The mayor was shuffling uncomfortably in his chair, "It's been days now, why don't they attack, why do they wait, are they trying to starve us out?"

"I do not know the answer to that, it appears strange, they know we are weakened."

The door opened and in walked the High Sheriff of Northumberland, he sat down.

"Good day gentlemen, I know what you are thinking, why haven't they attacked by now? I have news; one of my scouts has just reported that the Scots and their army have moved on."

"Moved, moved where?" The Ealdorman inquired.

"They have been seen to the south of the city on the road to Durham. My spies have reported that the Scots think it too risky as they believe the plague to be still in the city."

The Mayor joined in, "Durham has fewer soldiers than we do, I fear they are lost!"

"Yes indeed and we cannot help them," The Sheriff replied.

Eliza Swan was up on the moor when she heard a sound, so unfamiliar coming from the road to Durham; she decided to find a spot where she could look down onto the road from high up. There it became immediately apparent what was the cause of the noise. There on the road a column of soldiers, men at arms and baggage carts, the line stretched back as far as she could see, this was the Scottish army, thousands of them!

She ran as fast as she could back to the village and warned Ealdorman Hudson. He ordered there to be complete silence and all fires extinguished. Although the village of Elersly was hidden from the road by trees and foliage, the people took to their houses and hoped the army passed by of considered this little hamlet not worth the effort. Eliza and her mother did the same and waited in silence.

After some time the people remerged from hiding and several men went to the road and to their relief the army had long passed. All that was left were a great deal damage to the already poor condition of the dirt road, boot prints and wheel ruts everywhere.

People were beginning to gather in the village square, Eliza was also present. Ealdorman Hudson came out of his house and gathered people around a wooden plinth.

"Everybody, it seems that we have been spared the wrath of an invading army, we are blessed, that the plan worked and we appear to be safe. That is in a large way due to that woman there." He said pointing to Eliza.

Eliza became uneasy as all eyes turned to her.

Alice Simms shouted out loud and pointed, "Ealdorman Hudson, she is a witch!"

"Be quiet woman, Eliza Swann warned me of the approaching army, she saved us all!"

There was a noticeable change in atmosphere and there were even some kind words directed at her, of course not all were kind but it was a surprise none the less.

Of course it did not take long for the populace of Durham City to realise what was coming their way. The combination of plague and fear of a Scottish invasion caused such unrest within Durham itself that there were disturbances on the streets. The fear was well founded, as the Scots were quick to take advantage of their English neighbours' distress.

Not only was Durham an important religious site but also a defensive one. Situated high on a hill and protected by the river on three sides, Durham was important in defence against the Scots invading English lands. The Cathedral and Castle were built together by the community of Benedictine monks who wanted a monumental shrine for Saint Cuthbert and a place to live for the Bishop of Durham.

On hearing the news the great and the good of city folk gathered their belongings and fled onto the promontory, some made for the relative safety of the castle, some for the cathedral. The Bishop and the Dean ordered the great door and any other means of entrance to be sealed shut. Lookouts were place on the tower roof facing in all directions, they waited.

It did not take long for the army to form up on the hill overlooking Durham City. Alan Borthwick, James Lockhart and Robert Hay were at the front of the massed ranks, sitting astride their horses they surveyed the scene below and regarded each other closely.

Alan Borthwick waved a hand, "look gentlemen, it is ours for the taking!"

On the signal the ranks moved forward and as the closed in they began the traditional Scottish Charge. They did not have much to overcome as the city was poorly defended and the few soldiers were easily beaten. Within a few hours the deal was done and the city pacified and the Scots began to rob and pillage everything of value, anyone who resisted was killed in a ruthless manner.

James Lockhart led a party up to the castle and cathedral but without heavy siege engines they could not brake in. they would stay in the city for several days drunk on wine, mead and ale they caused havoc among the population. Eventually the decided there was nothing much left to steal and left the city. Having had so much success they decided to move further south to see what could be taken in the North of Yorkshire.

They made their way south and camped for the night around the town of Auckland. The camp site was in a shallow depression with trees around away from any road. Alan Borthwick, James Lockhart Robert Hay and Robert Hay, the plotters of this raid sat around a fire drinking what was left of the ale and laughing aloud.

"Drink up lads, fine hosts the English!" Borthwick joked.

"Aye fine indeed!" James Lockhart replied, ale running down his chin.

"Tomorrow we head south to Yorkshire and see what we can find there!" Hay laughed.

Tomorrow came and the camp was begging to rise along with the sun, soldiers were stretching and groaning as the thought of another days march. James Lockhart wandered into the middle of camp and stood next to the still smouldering fire from the night before.

Lockhart parted his arms wide when with a hiss a piece of piercing iron parted his ribs. In his shock he grabbed the arrow shaft with both hands before his strength faded and he fell to the floor, unconscious. Alerted by his misfortune the camp roused and rallied to his side, it was then that a single arrow turned into a shower as the sky filled with wood and iron. The camp was subjected to a cascade as arrows fell in all directions, unable to find cover; the Scottish soldiers were falling in scores.

The Scots fell in all being hit from all directions, fell in all directions as arrows pierced their bodies, in the chest, in the back in the head. With the unmistakable thud the arrows sliced through vital organs, liver, kidney, stomach splitting violence! Panic gripped the camp as soldiers ran in every direction looking for safety, most finding none as they ran into the trees and into the face of English soldiers who cut them down with flashing, slashing steel. Some would be lucky and find a way out of the carnage but not many, as for Alan Borthwick, and Robert Hay they managed to escape on horseback to the north.

Hearing of the Scots advance toward Yorkshire, the Sheriff of York send part of his Northern Army to intercept them and it worked as the remnants of the Scottish invasion was well and truly smashed. Cavalry pursued the fleeing soldiers, cutting them down from behind mercilessly. Captain Warren rode his horse into the camp and dismounting scanned the scene. The battlefield, once teeming with the energy of combat, is left strewn with the dead and dying. The air is thick with the smell of blood, sweat, and smoke. Survivors tend to the wounded, and the grim task of burying the dead begins. Any surviving Scots were taken prisoner and transported to Durham City and flung into filthy jails to await their fate.

Alan Borthwick, and Robert Hay, two of the ringleaders of this little adventure fled northwards as fast as their horses could manage. All they had to show was two tired horses, no army, no booty, no gold just the desperate hopes of a long lost quest lying in the dirt. The landscape would be forever scarred by the clash, a silent witness to the vicious reality of brutal warfare.

Alan Borthwick hardly had time to readjust his life into a normal rhythm when a visitor arrived at his door. James Allen stood at the door searing with indignation, he was shown in, Alan Borthwick was not surprised to see him, as he was expecting a visit. James Allen, being one of the financial backers of the operation and he wanted answers.

"I have heard some news Alan, how did the raid go?"

"Well James old friend, we heard that Newcastle had plague, so we went to Durham instead, we plundered shops, houses and even the cathedral, we got much gold and silver."

"So where is it, where is the gold Alan Borthwick, where is my share?"

"James, my fiend we were ambushed by part of the English army we were outnumbered and surprised. It was a massacre. We managed to escape but many did not. The gold was left behind we had no choice, gold is not much use when you are dead, is lost all of it!"

"A foolish venture Borthwick, foolish indeed and more fool me for backing you."

"Well James not every venture works out, sometimes they do not, as with this one. We can gather our men and resources and try again at some point, what do you think?"

James Allen stood up rapidly and glared at Borthwick, with some menace. "You are as mad as you look Alan Borthwick, you will receive no more backing from me for your adventures, stick to farming Alan and leave raiding to those who know how to raid, good day to you Sir!"

Alan Borthwick watched as he stormed out of the room, he knew James Allen was right but it was a mere stroke of bad luck that they failed, at least that is how Alan Borthwick saw it. He was however; glad to see him leave as he was not in the best of humour. He had been suffering from a severe headache all day and was now overcome with episodes of dizziness. He informed his wife of his ailment and retired to his bed, rest could cure most things.

Later that day Borthwick's wife checked on him assuming it was no more than a chill entered the room. Alan was lying in bed in some daze or other, squirming about, sweating and fevered. His pillow was wet with fluid; she placed cold cloths on his head and body in an attempt to cool him down and did so throughout the night.

When the morning came Alan was worse, he had begun coughing and bringing up blood and sputum, she also noticed the large puss filled bulges under his arms and around his body. She did not know what it was of how to treat it for that matter but she would find out in due time as would the people of this city. Alan Borthwick at least brought something back from his raid on Durham, the plague!

Two days later Alan Borthwick succumbed to his illness and passed away in his sleep. He was however, not the only one by any means as the illness gripped the city. People were dying in their scores and it prompted the Mayor to write a letter to be sent to other towns as a warning not to venture near Edinburg.

Letter

'In 1621, there has occurred a great pestilence and mortality of men in the kingdom of Scotland. The fine city of Edinburg has been decimated, so great a plague has never been heard of from the beginning of the world to the present day, or been recorded in books. For this plague vented its spite at God's command. The harm was done by an unusual and unique form of death. Those who fell sick of a kind of gross swelling of the flesh lasted for barely two days. This sickness befell people everywhere, but especially the middling and lower classes, rarely the great. It generated such horror that children did not dare to visit their dying parents.

The pestilence raged in the city and the church yards ran out of space for graves, it was decided that bodies would be taken outside of the city walls and placed in mass graves. As Alan Borthwick was being laid to rest on his farm, the very place where he and his collaborators had hatched their disastrous plan to raid into England was in a state pf panic.

In Mary King's Close among the filth and depravity and overcrowding within the city walls, the plague spread like and oil stain. The close was riven with disease and the pestilence spread quickly and mercilessly in the confined space. People were so afraid of any person escaping from the close they began to erect make shift barriers to keep them inside. Over three hundred infected residents were sealed within the Close. The sealed in victims were not left to die on their own. They were given food and ale each day and Plague Doctor George Grey was left with them for care. He wore a long, leather coat and birdlike beak filled with herbs to protect him against miasma. Grey saved many lives by cutting away the boils and burning the flesh!

The only conspirator to survive was Robert Hay, who by some means managed to escape the English ambush but also escape the plague. He vowed to his wife and family never to undertake such folly again and he did not!

CHAPTER 20

In the village of Elersly Eliza walked into the village square where she had received a message from Ealdorman Hudson, she arrived at the house and was shown in.

"Ah Miss Swann, please come in, have a seat won't you."

"You wanted to see me Sir, is there a problem?"

"No Miss Swann not at all, I have invited you here the thank you in person for what you did, you saved this village and you have the appreciation of all of us, we thank you."

"Well Ealdorman Hudson, maybe you should tell the rest of the village that!"

"I know you and your mother have not had an easy time of it but you have my backing!"

Eliza had nothing more to say and left the house, she walked through the square and past saint Andrew's church where she was stopped by a voice from the side.

"Miss, over here!"

Reverend Marshal was standing in the doorway, "Eliza isn't it?"

"Yes Eliza Swann, daughter of Mary."

"Ealdorman Hudson told me of you warning about the Scots army; you saved a lot of people here in the village. I do not see you at the services, nor your mother, why is that?"

"I am sorry Reverend Marshal but I have strange feeling about being in churches."

"Oh why is that?"

"I don't know, I cannot explain, I fear it and it worries me!"

"You should not fear the Lord he is there to protect you!"

"He has not done much in the way of protection; I do not feel protected by anyone!"

"Where is your faith Miss Swann? Sometimes we are tested, we must be strong!"

"Oh I am strong Reverend, I have to be, God seems to be looking the other way!"

Eliza looked him in the eyes with a stare of comprehension and walked away.

"Miss Swann remember walk always in the light!" Reverend Marshal cried with torment.

Eliza went home and paced around the room for a while before sitting on a bench.

"You are quiet Elisa what ails you, what did Ealdorman Hudson want of you?"

"He wanted to thank me in person for saving the village, some good that will do!"

"At least he acknowledged your efforts Eliza, which is something at least."

"I also met Reverend Marshal; he questioned why we do not attend church."

"What did you tell him?"

"I told him the truth, I do not like being in church, I feel uncomfortable."

"He might take that as a sign that you have no faith."

"Well, mother he can take it as he pleases, to be honest I lost my faith a long time ago!"

"I hear you daughter but we must not invite trouble."

"Yes I know keep your head down, lie low, what of your faith mother?"

"I am much the same I was never destined for such things; I have spent my life in the shadows in the realms of darkness and solitude."

Eliza exhaled loudly, "I had another dream last night?"

"What, not the same thing again?"

"Yes that woman I keep seeing came to me in my dream. I saw her rise out of a deep dark lake, like some Siren she spoke to me in whispers."

Mary Swann paced over and stood next to her daughter, "This is important, what did she say Eliza?"

"She says the same thing that I have the sight that I have a gift, a power and people will fear me because of it. What gift do I have, what power do I possess, I ask you that, what does it mean? I have also had forewarnings of things not yet passed but I cannot understand them!"

"I am sure that you will understand them in time, anything else?"

Yes I keep seeing a giant black bird; it comes to me in my dreams, a raven!"

"A raven, which is important, throughout history, the raven has been regarded as a symbol of evil and death, they are carrion eaters and scavenge the dead, they symbolize bad luck, darkness, and evil. The raven has been considered a bird of death, the mention of the raven conjures up images of filthiness and death, with the bird feeding on the dead and decaying."

"But what does it mean mother, why do I dream so, why a raven and not a sparrow?"

"A lone raven flying above one's house is often taken as a sign that death is at one's doorstep, it is a sign of terror for most people but not all!"

"There is something else mother; lately I have an urge to do harm, not only to property but people also. This compulsion consumes me at times, I felt the same thing when I spoke to Reverend Marshal earlier, I wanted to hurt him and I do not know why!"

Her mother sighed aloud, "Eliza don't surround yourself with yourself, concentrate on what you have inside and the outside will resolve itself and you will see the answers to your dreams."

It was now the turn of Eliza to sigh out loud as she gazed at her mother. "One day when the sun was asleep a Siren came to me and sang my name, now my life is dark. The silence speaks to me in a dream, night time, life time, the darkness never fades!"

Why don't you go and visit Aunt Agnes in the town for a while, see how she is?"

"Yes mother, I think I might!"

Eliza went to Durham City the next morning not knowing just what she would find there, was her Aunt alright, was she still alive?

The city of Durham, had suffered badly not only from the failed Scottish raid but the pestilence that followed. Violence broke out in the city, firstly in Elvet and there was soon a general flight of all who could leave, those having the means and will to do so. Seeing the turmoil the mayor and ealdorman had booths and huts made upon the moors outside Durham for the benefit of the poor but they died off rapidly, so that, poor Durham this year was almost undone.

The gaol did not escape, and twenty-four prisoners were carried out for burial from it. In addition to these 400 died in Elvet, 100 in St. Nicholas, 200 in St. Margaret's, 60 in St. Giles', 60 in the North Bailey; and Durham was not alone in the disaster, for the disease spread to many of the towns and villages in the neighbourhood.

It was with some nervousness that she arrived in Durham and made her way to her Aunt's house. The small cottage was apparently untouched as it was tucked away from the main city. She rapped on the door with some uneasiness as she did not know what she might find. Shortly after came the sound of metal scraping as bolts were drawn back and the door opened revealing a pair of eyes peering out.

"Hello what business do you have with an old woman?"

"Aunt Agnes it's me Eliza!"

"Eliza what a surprise, come on in!" Agnes slammed the door behind her and hugged her tightly before sitting her down in a chair, clasping her hands together.

"Tell me Eliza how have you been and how is your mother?"

"Mother is well enough and I am, fine in body."

"You sound unsure; you have matured into a fine young woman, you will have prosperous future ahead, what on earth could trouble you?"

"Oh it is nothing to worry about but I have been having strange feelings lately and recurring dreams which I do not understand, it will right itself I am sure, so Aunt what news of you?"

"Well dear, I was not bothered too much By the Scottish raiders, there being many younger and prettier women in town than an old crone like me. As for the pestilence, I just waited it out in my little cottage, tucked away in this corner of the city out of the main streets. This pestilence will long be remembered for its appalling mortality, nor did the gloom it elicited lift for some years, it may be said to have disorganized the city and neighbourhood."

Eliza would spend the next few days in the city wandering its streets and watching as the city went about the business of living and surviving. The town had of course altered its appearance and lay out many times through history, but the old town especially in the area of the market place had changed little for centuries with narrow cobbled alleyways leading through a collection of tumbledown, timber fronted buildings, medieval streets, steep sided and constricted.

Shops of all descriptions lined the streets, cobblers, tailors and butchers, meat freshly killed and hanging on hooks, blood running into the gutters along with all manner of other revolting mess. Rats ran about the place seemingly without fear of capture spreading their disease ridden fleas on to every living thing.

On her last night in the city she was consumed by fear as she woke in the early hours of the morning with a jolt, eyes wide open and sweating profusely she sat bolt upright!

Aunt Agnes came over to see what the matter was, "are you alright Eliza?"

"Oh yes I just had another of my dreams."

"What about?"

"I dreamt that there was a fire in a village somewhere, it was so real."

"Never mind you are going home today, see your mother."

"Yes I will, I think I will go outside for some air."

"Be careful out there, you do not know who is prowling about."

"Yes I will do that."

Later that morning Eliza boarded a coach and set off on the Newcastle road northwards to her home village. She had enjoyed her few days in the city but was glad to get away from the bustle and thoughtless nature of urban life and back to the quiet of the countryside.

CHAPTER 21

Summer was now drifting into autumn once more in the turning of the age and the people of the village of Elersly and surrounding areas were busy reaping the harvest and making general provisions for winter, which would sneak upon them with a sharp tongue. Eliza was up on the moor as she often did embracing the cooling air she wandered for a while. She made her way over the moor to a place where she could look down at the fields of crops and the peasants busily gathering them in. She sat for a while and watched them work, the cultivation of wheat, barley, rye, and oats was fundamental to survival. Baked into bread, it was the staple of their diet. Malted, it was the basis of ales which they drank abundantly, as thatch, it provided their shelter. As the spiral appeared in the crop, was it a corn devil, the catcher of rye of simple nature, who knows such things?

Then as if from nowhere, the strange young woman of her dreams appeared next to her.

"Good day Eliza."

"You again, I did not see you come, where did you come from?"

"I have been here all the time Eliza, I am always here, I see you watching these peasants toiling and sweating, just to survive, have you never thought of a different path?"

"Well I suppose I have, I have been confused of late I do not know where my path lies."

"You will learn Eliza Swann; it will become clear in time."

"Who are you why do I see you in my dreams, are you some sort of angel?"

"Ah Eliza you would know secrets you are not ready for, I sit on the shoulders of angels but there are no white feathered wings only horns and tusks my guardians in this world, my angels are fallen and dark. I also dream as did my ancestors, they dreamt of me! "

"Why do you follow me so, for what purpose?"

"Because you Eliza Swann are in my charge, a duty I must fulfil."

"What is your name, do you have a name?"

"Very well it is time you knew, my name is Gaia, I am named after an ancient god."

Then she was gone, somewhere, Eliza went back to the village and into the house.

"Mother, you know about these things, who was Gaia an old god or something?"

"She is Goddess of the earth, one of the earliest elemental deities, having been created at the beginning of time, all of creation is descended from Gaia, the great mother of all things, where did you here that name Eliza?"

"Oh it matters not mother, let it pass!"

Two days later Eliza was again up on the moor picking blackberries, she sat down on the same rock as always for a moment of rest when she heard a noise, it being like the snapping of branches and then came the odour, the unmistakable of burning. She looked around not sure where the smell and sound were coming from, she set off back across the moor and as she reached the path down into the village she realised the awful truth!

In the flickering light of an autumn morn, the village lay quiet as if the populace had not yet realised what was happening. The thatched roof of the blacksmiths shop was firmly alight as flames licked at the morning sky as if trying to escape some fate or other. The flames leaped onto the dry straw of the roof and in moments, the flames caught, hungrily devouring the thatch, sparks racing from house to house.

The fire spread with alarming speed, a ferocious beast consuming wood and straw with a crackling roar. Smoke billowed thick and acrid, cloaking the village in a choking shroud. Villagers awoke to the chaos, their shouts of alarm piercing the early morning calm. Men, women, and children poured into the streets, their faces lit by the hellish glow of the inferno. Some fought to save their homes, forming desperate bucket brigades to douse the flames, but the primitive tools and scarce water supply rendered their efforts nearly futile. Others scrambled to rescue livestock and gather belongings, their lives reduced to frantic moments of salvaging what they could.

Amidst the tumult, the village church bell tolled a mournful warning, its sound carrying over the din of crackling wood and the cries of the distressed. Shadows danced grotesquely in the firelight, and the air was filled with the pungent scent of burning thatch and timber. The fire's roar drowned out all but the most urgent cries. Flames licked the sky, casting an ominous glow visible for miles around. As the fire raged, roofs collapsed in showers of sparks, and beams buckled under the intense heat, sending plumes of embers skyward like a swarm of fireflies.

The villagers were largely at the mercy of the flame, a blessed shift in the wind or a timely rainstorm was their best hope. But until then, the fire would continue its relentless march, leaving in its wake a charred landscape of smouldering ruins and a community forever scarred by the devastating power of nature unleashed. Eventually the blaze died down and in the wake four houses were left in a smoking heap of charred wood and the remnants of daily life, scorched pots and cooking vessels blackened and bent.

Eilza watched in amazement from on high at the devastation below, it was only then that she realised that she had seen this all before in her dream. The village on fire in her dream was her own home of Elersly, she ran home as fast as she could to check on her mother. Mary Swann was standing in the doorway of their house when she arrived.

"Mother! Mother, I had a dream that this was going to happen, what is wrong with me?"

"Shush girl come inside we do not want to raise suspicions!"

And of course suspicion was present as always, it mattered not that the fire started in the blacksmith's shop, to these naive and simple people it was the work of an angry god and evil was once again among them.

The next morning the embers of the fire were still smouldering under the charred beams, wisps of smoke rising into the autumn air. Eliza left the house to survey the damage, people were milling about and it seemed like the whole village was engaged in some form of enterprise. There were as always exceptions as several of the women were in deep discussion as to what the cause was. One of these women was Ann Simms who when noticing Eliza began to whisper to her neighbours, hands over her mouth, the others turned and looked.

Eliza walked past them without a glance in their direction but could hear the murmur as rumour and gossip filtered the air. Mercifully no person was seriously injured in the blaze; Eliza walked on and saw an old woman sitting on an old stool, her house a pile of burned and blackened chaos and disorder. At her feet the old faithful dog that had laid at her doorstep for many a year had not the strength or possibly the will to escape. It lay not three feet from her owner, fur burned off, ears charred and face charred, eyes open with a deathly tone of grey.

"Mrs Waggot, is that your dog?" Eliza questioned her in a compassionate manner.

"Yes that's old Peg, my faithful old Peg, dead and I fear I will follow soon after!"

"Do not fret Mrs Waggot, where will you live now?"

"Reverend Marshal has said that anyone who lost their home can live in the church."

"But what of your house, you cannot live there forever?"

"Ealdorman Hudson has said that the people of the village will rally around and rebuild the burned houses and he will apply to the Chancellor of Durham for funds, some hope there!"

"You do not seem to have much faith in the authorities."

"When you have lived as long as me, you become aware that nothing will change. No help will come, the people at the top will get richer and we will stay poor, we are alone as usual!"

"Your house was close to the blacksmith's shop, is that where it started?"

Mrs Waggot looked up at the smoke rising, "Aye they say it was, but others will be blamed, I have no doubt, the simple minded folk will say it is the work of evil, they always do."

Eliza gazed at the old woman, "I see you have burned your hand, my mother could mix a potion that might heal it or at least help with the pain?"

"No my dear, do not worry about an old woman like me, I have had worse!"

"Very well, I will be off then, good fortune to you Mrs Waggot!"

As she walked away Mrs Waggot shouted. "What is your name, are you that Swann girl?"

"Yes I am Eliza Swann, daughter of Mary Swann!"

Mrs Waggot looked at her intensely, "I have heard tales about you and your mother."

"Oh, what manner of tales?"

"Mostly bad but now I have met you I can say they are not true, go in peace Eliza!"

Ealdorman Hudson sat in his study, regarding the other two men across the table, Reverend Marshal was in silence and next to him the Sheriff of County Durham, they looked at each other for some time, each waiting for the other to speak, Ealdorman Hudson broke the hush.

"Well gentlemen we are once more sitting here considering another disaster in our midst."

"Yes indeed Ealdorman Hudson, we are, the question is what we do about it"

Ealdorman Hudson, placed his hands on the table. "The blaze we are sure started in the blacksmith's shop, a loose spark from his forge was all it took, we have thatched rooves."

The sheriff agreed with his knowledge. "What do you think Reverend Marshal?"

"The mood in the village is not good the people think it is a punishment from god, they think that we are harbouring evil in this place and they demand something be done!"

"What can we do, we cannot fight evil, the people are gullible idiots!"

"You are indeed correct Ealdorman Hudson but that will not solve the problem!"

The sheriff interrupted, "hold forth gentlemen, I would bring in a man to rid this village of its nightmare, he is expert at dealing with such things."

Ealdorman Hudson sat forward, "who is this man, what is his name?"

"His name is Isiah Blackwood, he is an expert witch finder."

Ealdorman Hudson clasped his hands over his face. "No, not him again I have met him the man is a fool, not only that he is a fraud, is there no other way?"

"As the reverend said, the people wasn't action, his presence will at least show we are doing something, it could calm them down if nothing else. I hear he has convicted some witches in Cumbria and more in Northumberland, we have nothing to lose!"

Ealdorman Hudson sighed aloud, "very well, you may contact this fellow!"

Two days later Isiah Blackwood arrived in the village and went directly to the house of Ealdorman Hudson. He was of course looking for clues as to who might be responsible for the misery of this place and its people, but had few clues from Hudson. As he left the house he was approached by a woman who waved him over from a secluded spot near a bush.

"Are you the witch hunter?"

"Yes I have been employed by Ealdorman Hudson to root out this evil, have you news?"

"I have at the edge of the village is a house, two women live there they are both suspected of dark magic. Sadness and despair has followed us ever since that night all those years back. Mary and her daughter Eliza are the ones who are to blame, start your job there!"

Mary and Eliza were in tier house when a knock came at the door, Eliza answered.

"Hello, can I help you?"

"Good day, Miss Eliza, do you remember me?"

"I am not sure; you are from the village though, are you not?"

"I am Mrs Jacobs, mother of Edward Jacobs."

"Oh yes I remember young Edward, how is he?"

"He is doing very well, thanks to you and your mother that potion saved him and I am so grateful. Why I have come is that you might have heard there is an investigator in the village. his name is Isiah Blackwood, and I have been informed that someone in the village have pointed the finger at you and your mother as being guilty for all of the fear in the village."

"Well there is nothing new in that, we have been subject to that for years!"

"Yes I know but this is different, I think he will come for you and it will not be good!"

"My god how far has this to go, we have done nothing wrong, why us?"

"I don't know Eliza but I and my son owe you a debt, so I have given you a warning!"

"That is good of you Mrs Jacobs but what can we do?"

"I do not know Eliza but you are in danger here, leave please, go anywhere!"

Eliza went back inside and sat on a stool in a state of anguish.

"Who was that as the door Eliza?"

"It was Mrs Jacobs; remember you made a potion to treat her son Edward?"

"Oh yes I remember them, what did she want?"

"She came to warn us."

"Warn us, whatever for?"

"There is a man in the village, Isiah Blackwood, some sort of witch hunter!"

"What has that to do with us?"

"Because, mother, he coming for us, we have been accused!"

"Jesus, what can we do, who accused us?"

"Mrs Jacobs says it was Ann Simms that pointed to us!"

"We must leave and quickly we have little time, Eliza you must go to Durham and stay with your Aunt Agnes until this is over, pack a few things and go!"

"What about you mother, are you not coming with me?"

"No dear daughter I do not want to put you two in any more danger, there is an old hut up on the moor, it will be safe there for now, I will stay till it calms down!"

Eliza did just that packed few things in a sack and skirted around the village onto the main read and headed south towards Durham City, it being a walk of about tem miles but one she made without question or looking back. Mary Swann also left the house and trekked up onto the moor. It was not too far of a journey but the terrain being steep and uneven caused some discomfort and no little distress to Mary as she was be this time becoming quite aged. Although she knew of many potions and cures for sickness, there was none for getting old.

Eventually she reached the shaded hollow in the moor near the top of Split Crow Hill. There was the small cottage, the same small cottage that was once home to the wise woman and suspected witch, Isabella Mosswood. The door was hanging of and the place was in a state of dereliction but it was dry and sheltered and it would do for now, it would have to.

Eliza was of course welcomed at her aunt's house and had stayed for a week already, she had heard nothing from her mother and this was becoming more concerning by the day. Eliza sat one night as she watched the fire diminishing in the hearth and by the light of the flickering candles the shadows danced in their lonely corners and shape shifted silence.

It was then she noticed another shape near the door, tall and black even blacker than the shadows, a shape in human form malevolent and unnerving, was she dreaming again or heaven forbid awake. She closed his eyes for a few seconds then pointed a nervous glance at this thing, but to her immense relief it was gone vanished into the dark night. Two days later on a cold autumn night the dream changed into reality or she thought it had at least a resemblance of it. She woke to find a tall black figure at the foot of the bed; she began to scream but could not manage a sound.

In the morning her thoughts still troubled, the events of the night would not leave her bothered mind. Was all of this real or was she losing her sanity, was it a premonition or a message from another plane? In some dream of nothingness, a hushed vacuum in the fabric of life, surreal and strange, why was she troubled in this way?

CHAPTER 22

It had now been about ten days since the left Elersly and she was concerned about her mother, so she decided to return quietly and as unobtrusive as possible. The day was cold but bright as she walked north on the main road, nearing the village she left the road and skirted around the back to her house. The warning from Mrs Jacobs was indeed true as the door was smashed in and the inside ransacked, her mother gone, had she escaped in time?

Her mother did not have much in the way of possessions but what was left was smashed and destroyed. Eliza began to search among the rubbish looking for anything, she knew not what. Then she remembered that her mother has a place, a secret place where she kept important items. She went outside and around the back of the house and pulled a small metal box from under the floor. She them collected anything she could from the house that could be useful and climbed up onto the moor.

Once more as she had done for years she sat on her favourite rock and opened the metal box, what on earth could be in here? She opened it with care and looked inside. There were several items, strange and unusual, a black feather, the bare skull of a rat or something, a small metal cup and a black candle, some parchments folded neatly. She was somewhat puzzled as to what this meant, what did it mean, what were these strange items for?

She continued waking over the moor and up Split Crow Hill and there hidden by some twisted, wind bent trees, a small cottage. This must be the place her mother was on about; she made her way to the front door and carefully pushed it open. She was in some ways expecting the place to be in a state of disorder but was surprised to see it was quite orderly. Someone had clearly been living here. There was not much in the way of furniture a simple stool and a makeshift bed in the corner, she did not expect much else as furniture was expensive, especially up here in the middle of nowhere. There was she was happy to see a brick fireplace with burned wood still in the hearth, cold and grey.

However, her mother was nowhere to be seen, it was plain that she was living here at some point but where could she have gone? Eliza decided that her mother must have found a better place and for now this would have to be home as she did not dare return to the village. She set about collecting wood for a fire and food she could muster, mostly berries. Later that night she sat on her stool beside the fire and unfolded the parchments she had found in the box. They were full of deigned and symbols of which she had not seen before and script seemingly showing how to interpret them. She was now feeling tired, it had been a long and interesting day, she curled up on the simple bed made of bracken and ferns, she fell asleep.

She awoke having slept very well considering the circumstances, she went outside into a fresh but bright morning, there was a distinct chill in the air, winter was on its way once more. She knew that if she was to be here over the winter months on this bleak hill she would have to make as much provision as possible. She filled an old pot with water from the butt outside and collected some nettles which she brewed into a sort of tea, hot and soothing.

Searching around the house she noticed a piece of cloth folded neatly and picking it up it felt heavy, something was inside. Unfolding it she found a book, a very old book it seemed from its design and the worn and faded cover. She sat down and opened it up; she discovered that just like the parchments the book was full of designs and script in a language she could not understand. Then she saw that the ciphers had translations into English, she read out loud some of the symbols and their descriptions. A pentagram, the pentagram is a five-pointed star; the five points of the star represent the five elements, air, water, fire, earth, and spirit, with the spirit being at the top.

Inverted Pentagram, when inverted, it signifies a reversal of the natural order of things, resulting in evil and distortion. In its inverted position, the pentagram is the hieroglyphic sign of Baphomet, known as the black magic goat or the Sabbatic Goat, used in occultism and Satanism. The symbol depicts a goat with its head at the centre and the horns the two points of the star piercing the heavens. In Christianity, this sign represents the rejection of the dominance of Christianity over society. The veneration of Baphomet was known to be undertaken by the Knights Templar.

Eliza placed the book down in a hasty motion as if it was hot. What was this all about, why did her mother have parchments with the same designs, this was dark magic, was her mother involved with such things, was she even a witch? Over time she began to translate the transcript and realised that some of the symbols mixed with lines of text formed into what Eliza realised were some sort of curses.

She was reluctant to consider these things but was gripped with a curiosity as to how they would work and how to use them. Over the weeks she delved deeper into the book and became aware of the signs and symbols and how to use them. She had a diving urge to try some of them but put it off for long enough, whether through lack of her own confidence or fear that it might go wrong. Eventually as time went by she became more and more embittered as to how she and her mother had been treated. The urge for revenge was beginning to be overwhelming, as the thoughts of sending vengeance it the direction of certain people was by now gripping her thoughts.

She decided to act, collecting certain materials she fashioned a crude doll of candle wax. She sat on the floor inside of the house and lit the black candle; summon demons to enhance the power of the ritual.

"What next?" She wondered gazing at the book, get Black fabric and cut two large crosses. She put the doll on a cross, then cover the doll with the second cross. After that she wrapped the doll with black thread nine times, and said aloud, "AN ALU BAR ANABA."

She then read more of the text and found the next section of the curse.

"I call down the Wrath of hell upon you. By this Blasphemy I curse you. In the name of evil. I curse you In the name of all which is unholy."

She flicked the page.

"I damn thee for betraying me, I damn thee for disgracing me, I damn thee for the pain thou hath caused, so shall my will be done and so it will be."

Now to use it, she waited all day until nightfall, and waited again until three in the next morning. She took her doll and slipped off the moor in the light of the full moon and into the village. Elersly was quiet not a thing moved except for some rats and a hunting cat, a dog awoke at here presence but a look from Eliza was enough to calm it. She carried on through the village, slowly and silently she knew where she was going well enough and around the corner she was there, the house of Ann Simms.

She quietly dug a small hole under the house and placed the doll in it before covering it up.

"You have cursed me and my mother for long enough Ann Simms, now I curse you!"

She sneaked out of the village and up onto the moor, it being after four in the morning and she was ready for her bed, tired but happy at her work.

Two days later, winter had arrived with its icy talons grabbing the earth. There had been a series of severe frosts and freezing temperatures. The ground was a thick mass of iced and stiff and rigid, everything was solid. The land was in a deep state of frigid silence, the earth seemed to glitter like a field of shimmering diamonds, icicles hung from roof tops like the teeth of some long forgotten dragon.

Ann Simms was not feeling well, her body was not the problem but her mind was in some sort of turmoil. She was experiencing episodes of blurred thinking and confusion, forgetting things, misplacing things and in a general state of muddle. Ann Simms was becoming more and more unpredictable, wandering from her house in the early hour of the morning. One early morning her husband caught her in the house acting strangely.

"Ann it's four o'clock in the morning, what are you doing?"

Ann turned around with a flaming torch in her hand and a wild gaze in her eyes.

"This house must be destroyed, it is evil, I must burn it!"

Her husband grabbed her arm and wrestled the torch from her grasp, Ann ran from the house screaming. This even at this time in the morning caused quite a stir as several people came from their houses in response to the unearthly clamour. Some women managed to grab her and take her back to the house and calm her down, her husband was not doing well either.

"What on earth is wrong with your wife, is she sick?"

"Oh she is sick alright but not in body, she says she must burn our house down!"

"Whatever for, do you think she has some malady of the mind?"

"I do not know, she also keeps saying that she has to go up onto the moor for some reason."

The women managed to pacify her and she was placed in her bed and watched until she fell asleep, seemingly exhausted from her nocturnal ramblings. The villagers left and returned to their night time pursuits, namely sleeping. Her husband also in a state of drained despair, he lay down and was quickly asleep.

Eliza stepped out of her hut high up on the moor, she did not exactly know why she was outside in the freezing cold but she was compelled, something was going to happen and she knew it. For some strange reason she was not feeling the cold as she waited, then from out of the moon lit night a figure appeared walking slowly but with purpose, toward her. Eliza gazed at her before she realised it was Ann Simms, out alone on the cold moor.

Eliza was filled with a strange sort of pleasure as she realised that the ceremony she carried out days ago had to her utter amazement worked. Ann seemed to be in some sort of trance, staring ahead but without seeing, eyes focussed and with some kind of glaze about them.

"Good morning Ann, you have come here for a reason, that being I have summoned you. You have been the jinx of my life for so long, now it is my turn to plague you and your family. You must go onto the very top of the moor and there you will lay down in the soft frostiness and sleep, sleep a thousand dreams, go now and obey my wishes!"

Ann's husband awoke at six of the morning and immediately saw that Ann was not there. He searched the house and outside but could find no trace. A man walked by carrying some fire wood, he saw the state of distress and asked what was going on.

"It's my wife she has not been well lately and she is missing!"

The woodman pointed to some marks in the frost, "look footsteps, small that of a woman, bare feet on a day like this it is madness! Do not fret good fellow, I will see the ealdorman and organise a search party."

He did that and Ealdorman Hudson gathered some men and set out to follow the footprints. They were clear to see in the frost and led out of the village and up toward the moor. It was still dark at this point the light just beginning to rise above the hills to the east. They searched the moor for hours but could find nothing and as the light of day began to illuminate the scene, they had hoped that the trail would be easier to follow. However, the footprints clear up to then were now beginning to fade and not much further on disappeared altogether.

They continued their search but the trail was gone, not knowing which direction to follow it was decided to call off the search for the time being and hope that Ann returned on her own and in good health, she did not! Her husband along with the rest of the village knew fine well that Ann could not survive out in these conditions for very long and unless she was sheltering in a house or somewhere she was probably dead. She could have slipped and injured herself; she could have tumbled over a cliff but whatever the circumstance she would not return.

CHAPTER 23

The freezing temperatures of the past few days had eased somewhat but with good reason as Mother Nature had other plans. A stiff wind had risen in the north and thick clouds were gathering ominously on the horizon. Dense and heavy, dark blue, grey and flecks of purple they drifted across the valley and began to climb the rise onto the moor, like some great cloak of colour. Then without a sound it came slowly at first, then as the world seemed like it was covered in some giant blanket the snow started.

The wind became stronger by the hour and the snow was coming sideways pelting the side of the hut with icy daggers. Eliza watched the as the raw power of nature displayed an awesome sight, she was warm in the hut with a good fire blasting out lifesaving heat. It was not much better down in the village as life came to a halt. All was quiet, not a single thing moved as the snow piled up against walls and covered rooves with its soft but frozen down, it was as if the world had stood still.

The next morning the storm had mostly passed toward the south and the people of the village were beginning to venture out once more, winter or not there was work to attend to. The sun, feeble and grey, struggled to push itself through steeled and heavy clouds, as if the cold had sapped its strength. Hedgerows exploded with frost and the gorse and grasses of the moor stood still in suspended silence. Wind driven snow filled corners and rounded edges, nestling and curling like neatly folded silk, trees, icy fingers pointed skyward, waiting for better times, a witness to many seasons. The houses were dark and solid, walls silver studded, icicles dangling from the roof like the teeth of some great reptile. Frosted flakes of moisture fell slowly, merging quietly, laying a carpet of sparkling diamonds; snow clung to the road into the village, turned by heavy wheels, casting shadows of grey and blue.

Martin Howe arose from his bunk and collecting his bow and arrows; he left his small, ramshackle house to the north east of Elersly on the road to Newcastle and made his way up onto the moor to hunt for some meat of any type. The moor was smothered in snow from the day before but he ploughed on, he had a mission to feed himself. He walked for quite some time without seeing any game and eventually he found himself on the very top of the moor at a place known locally as the Pike. Here now that she storm had passed he could see for many a mile over the whitewashed valley and to the north smoke rising into the still winter air as far away as Newcastle.

The morning was cold and even though he had been walking in the foot dragging snow he was now feeling the effects of the season, he decided to turn back and give up his hunt for the day and try again tomorrow. Walking along the ridge overlooking the valley he noticed something in the snow, he stopped and inspected it. It looked like a hand or limb of some sort, possibly a sheep caught up in the storm and died of frost. If so it could still be fresh frozen and edible, a bit of mutton would be a fine meal and last for more days, he might even have some to sell. These thoughts percolated through his mind as he began to clear the snow away first with his boot, then with his hands.

It was not much longer that his excavating was halted suddenly and with icy snap of reality as he realised it was not a buried sheep at all but a buried human! He fell to his knees as the reality of the situation took hold, what he had seen was a hand and now a wrist, he dug further and revealed a shoulder. He paused for a minute not sure whether to dig any more but after a while to calm himself, he carried on. Moving more snow away he began to see hair, light brown and matted twisted and tangled in its frozen state. Moving more snow he revealed the face of a woman, contorted by the cold or something else, eyes open wide, glazed and grey with a touch of blue, the last thing she saw in this world.

By now Martin was feeling the cold very much, on his knees and hands frozen from digging he could not uncover the whole body without help. He left the scene and trudged down into Elersly where he made his way to the house of Ealdorman Hudson. He was escorted into the ealdorman's study where he found Hudson at his desk.

"Good day Ealdorman Hudson, I am Martin Howe I live just outside of the village."

"Oh yes Martin I remember you coming here before, have you a problem?"

"Well I have not but I suspect someone else will soon enough."

"Oh how so have you a dispute with a neighbour?"

"No Sir you don't understand, while I was out hunting on the moor I came across a body, that of a woman. I dug it out as much as I could but I t will take more than my fragile hands, could you send some men up there to retrieve the poor soul?"

My God Martin, we have been searching for a missing woman for some time, I will get help, will you show them where to look, it would save time?"

"Yes of course Ealdorman Hudson, I will wait outside for the party to gather."

Martin Howe left the house and it wasn't long before there was activity around the house with the sound of horses and movement. Then from around the side of the house there appeared two men, suitably dressed for the conditions with a stout looking cart pulled by one horse, which was not suitably dressed and did not seem to be too happy at being taken from its relatively warm stable into the cold.

"Are you Martin Howe?" One of the men asked.

"Yes I am, are you two my helpers?"

"Yes we are." They both replied in a unified fashion.

The clambered aboard the cart and with a cry of displeasure and a flow of grey ghosts from its nostrils the horse set off. The covering of snow in the village had been disturbed somewhat by the movement of carts and feet and losing its frosted nature. This condition however, was not the same as the cart began to climb the old dirt track up onto the moor. The lack of traffic meant that the snow was still quite hard packed and frosted. The horse in its reluctant state was struggling to make progress and the passengers were forced to leave the cart on occasions to pull and push the animal forward. Eventually they reached the top of the rise and the wide open moor came into view they carried on with travel easier on everyone.

"Is it much further Mr Howe?" One of the men questioned.

 Martin Howe stretching out an arm pointed a finger ahead. "See that rise ahead, it there."

They reached the place shortly after and jumped off the cart into the crunching snow and ice. They were prepared as they had brought a couple of shovels to aid their task. They wasted no time and began to clear away the snow and ice that had trapped this woman in the arms of winter's breath. It took a while to extricate the body, they lifted it stiff and still, frozen in time, they bundled it onto the back of the cart.

"Are you coming back to the village with us Mr Howe?"

"No, I live outside of the village in that direction, but thank you, for your help."

The two men, the cart and the reluctant horse set of back down the path to the village, it being somewhat easier than going up. On arrival they were instructed to carry the body into Saint Andrews Church, which they did. Reverend Marshal and Ealdorman Hudson were waiting, the body wrapped in a white shroud was beginning to defrost and a distinct odour was beginning to discharge its aroma. Ealdorman Hudson pulled back the cloth to reveal the face, grey, twisted and contorted but with still the features of a woman. "Who are you?"

Reverend Marshal looked, "I know this woman, it is Ann Simms."

"What, the missing woman from the village?"

"Yes indeed Ealdorman Hudson, I am sure it is her, a member of my parish, now with the Lord, he will watch over her now as before."

Reverend Marshal sighed aloud, "What away to meet your end on a lonely, cold moor!"

Ealdorman Hudson agreed with his sentiments, "My question is why was she up there in the first place, I must go and break the news to her husband, a task I do not want."

News of the death of Ann Simms flowed through the village of Elersly like a gushing stream and before too long it was common news among the people. As usual in this place gossip filled the air, the vast majority wrong but who cared about the truth? A service was held in Saint Andrews Church and prayers were said for the departed soul of Ann Simms and her husband, who did not attend, preferring to be alone in his grief.

Two days later as the ground defrosted enough to dig a grave, a funeral was held. It was a simple affair at the back of the church as she was laid to rest in her white shroud. Reverend Marshal said a prayer as she was lowered down and the people of the village watched on, some in the church yard, some on the walls and some on the hill behind the church.

Up on the church roof another looked down on the proceedings, a great raven, eyes aglow, a radiant beam of yellow. A black feathered fiend on the house of God, it watched the solemn procession as the crowd of mourners left the church yard and with a screech and a spread of its great wings flew away to who knows where. The silence of the scene interrupted as people looked skyward and wondered what it was they had witnessed a raven on the house of the holy, the bringer of death on the house of the Lord!

There was, watching and observing every move another, a man, tall, well dressed that stood out from the crowd without trying, Isiah Blackwood! He too saw the raven and knew fine well the meaning of it, he had witnessed such things before on his mission to free the world of evil and make a tidy sum of monies in the process, he was of course doing God's work.

As the day went on Isiah Blackwood and his two assistants began to inspect the village, every corner and crook, every angle and curve. One of his assistants had on a strong leash a large dog, a type of mastiff with long shaggy fur and a muzzle full of teeth! They searched the village and after a while they came across the house of Ann Simms. The dog was extremely interested in something as soon as they arrived, straining at the leash, front legs off the ground.

"What is it boy, what do you smell?"

The dog lurched forward and began to claw at the snow and then the soil at the base of the house, until it started barking furiously at something half buried in the cold, damp earth. The man pulled the dog away with no little strength, while the other man grabbed something and pulled it out of the hole. He handed it to Isiah Blackwood, he gazed at it with the knowledge of past times, he knew well enough what it was. He unwrapped it with care, the black cloth falling away to reveal a wax doll, he dropped it back onto the earth with a look of disgust in his eyes and took a step back, mouth agape, eyes wide, a sign, a sign of evil in this village.

His assistant did as he was told, they continued their search and eventually they arrived at an abandoned house on the edge of the village, the house of Mary and Eliza Swann. They searched it thoroughly looking for something anything that could prove once and for all that the suspicions were correct. Once again the dog was agitated over something scratching at the floor in a corner. A simple woven mat covered the ground; the assistant pulled it away and pointed to the floor.

"Look boss, look at this!"

And there carved into the surface an inverted pentangle and Septagram, the men went back to the house of Ealdorman Hudson. Hudson was in his study when Blackwood entered.

"Ah Blackwood, what news of your search, you found nothing I assume?"

"On the contrary I found much and it is of a debauched and corrupt nature!"

"How so, what did you find?"

Blackwood pulled the wax doll from his bag and placed it on the table.

"What on earth is this?"   Hudson demanded.

"This Ealdorman is a mark of evil, it was found at the house of Ann Simms, whose funeral is still in the mind, she had been cursed Sir, you have evil in this village and I will find it!"

Blackwood pulled out a book, and old book and placed it on the table, he opened it and pointed at some symbols. "Look at these designs Ealdorman Hudson."

"What are they?"

"They are symbols of Devil worship, this one is a pentagram, it is displayed upside down."

"What does that mean?" The ealdorman questioned.

"The pentagram has been used for centuries as a symbol of protection and good luck. The five points on the star represent the four elements, earth, air, fire, and water along with a fifth element that unites them all, spirit. However, when it is it is displayed upside down it means it is a sign of the Devil being worshipped of even invited into the village."

He then pointed to another symbol. "This one is the Septagram, it is considered one of the most powerful symbols of Witchcraft as it can be used as a gateway to other realms!"

"You are correct Mr Blackwood, this would account for all the misery and darkness that has befallen our community, we must find the cause at all cost, you have my blessing!"

Isiah Blackwood continued to make enquiries around the village, while up on the moor, tucked away in her little shack Eliza was wondering whether to venture out for some food. She opened the door and stepped outside and there standing in front of her was that mysterious woman looking straight at her with piercing but calm eyes.

"Good day Eliza!"

"Oh it is you Gaia, I did not see you arrive, do you need something?"

"I need you Eliza Swann; I see you have already begun to practice magic, the magic you were born to, as am I. What is more it worked, well done you learn fast, though the spell you used was of a very basic nature, you performed it well!"

"But how did you know about that, I told no body?"

"I know many things Eliza, you also will in time, there is much to learn, spells and curses of much greater power than you can manage at this time."

"Magic, spells, what do you know of such things, what command do you possess?"

"I have many things that will become apparent during your training; Primal Spirits are the greatest and most powerful of nature spirits and are pure manifestations of the aspects of nature. They can only manifest in areas of extremely powerful primal magic, and most often as the result of a summoning by a group such as ours.

"I was just going to find some food."

"Yes I know Eliza but you will not be in need of food any more, the death in the village which you conjured has caused quite a stir, you must come with me now, you are not safe."

"Where are we going Gaia?"

"You will know soon enough, come this way."

Eliza did not question any further as she knew she would not receive a straight answer. Gaia had the habit of talking in a strange manner, more like riddles than sentences. She walked over the moor and down a steep slope into a ravine surrounded by trees and bushes. In the clearing stood a rock face, high and wide with a narrow crack in its façade. They stepped inside and Eliza was amazed by the very size of the cavern, its high ceiling reverberating sounds and voices to the extreme.

"What is this place Gaia, where am I?"

"This is our secret base in this area, nobody comes here, they dare not, you are safe here!"

Gaia left and Eliza began to look around, the whole place was massive with tunnels leading off in various directions. In one corner red drapes covered something; she pulled them back to reveal a living area. Spacious, the floor being carpeted, a luxury she had never known, in one corner a table and chair, in the other a bed. The whole place was lit by oil lamps which gave a golden, yellow glow to the room. On the table were items of food, meat, fruit and a jug red liquid she assumed to be wine, though she had never tasted any. She dipped a finger into in and placed it on her tongue, it was indeed wine, she thought.

Gaia came back a little later, "how is your room, is it to your liking Eliza?"

"Oh yes it is fine, much better than that draughty shack on the moor, in fact much better than my house in the village, is that wine in that jug?"

"Yes it is, drink it but be cautious it is strong and can cause a mighty head ache!"

"Gaia, are there other people staying here, why me?"

"Because Eliza, you are with us now, your old life is over and yes there are others here, you will meet them in time. Now eat and drink, I must go I have much work to complete!"

"Eliza did as she was told and ate some meat and bread washed down with red wine and as she found out Gaia was indeed correct as it distorted her senses somewhat. She lay back on the bed, it was comfortable and for the inside of a cave comfortably warm, she quickly fell asleep and dreamed the dreams of past and future.

CHAPTER 24

The winter with all of its power and displeasure was rapidly giving way and spring was rising around the county. It was still cold at night and sometimes in the day but things were on the up and the people of Elersly knew it. However, Mother Nature was not a forgiving soul and she knew just when to hit people with another show of force. The rain had started late last night and was by mid-morning belting the village with its liquid force.

Isiah Blackwood had been staying in the village, determined to find the source of the dark energy that had plagued the village for so long. However, his leads had dried up and his search was caught and stagnant, he received a letter delivered by a boy and passed on by the housekeeper, he opened it. It was from the sheriff of the county asking for his assistance, he went to see Ealdorman Hudson.

"Good morning Ealdorman, I have just received a letter from the sheriff, there seems to some sort of disturbance in a village south of here, Greenslade, do you know it?"

"Well yes of course it is a mere five or six miles distant, what manner of disturbance?"

"It seems they have a problem with the dark arts being practiced, they need my help."

"Well you might as well go; all is quiet here, well for now at least."

"Thank you Ealdorman, if anything were to happen I am only a ride away."

"Go with my blessing and rid that village of its torment, as we have suffered it!"

Isiah Blackwood and his men mounted their horses and set of south. They seemed to be moving away from the rain at least for now. They trotted down the main road, once off the high moor the landscape slipped steeply into a lush green valley. A stream called the Brownie slipped past almost unnoticed until it slipped onto the main river almost unnoticed. Greenslade was a very quiet backwoods village not so troubled by the weather of its neighbour to the higher ground to the north.

Isiah Blackwood was instructed to arrive at the house of John Cable who being part of the sheriff's personnel. He found the house fairly quickly and was invited in; his two assistants took shelter in a barn. John Cable bade him welcome and insisted he wait out the storm here. Outside a wild wind unfolded with a dramatic intensity that grasps the senses. Over the hills to the north, the sky transformed into a churning mass of dark, ominous clouds creeping ever closer that seem to swallow the daylight.

The wind begins as a whisper, rustling through the trees and tugging at leaves but it quickly intensifies into a powerful, howling force. It roars through the landscape, bending trees to their limits, sending debris swirling through the air and creating an almost deafening symphony of natural chaos. The rain arrives with a vengeance, starting with a few heavy drops that splatter against the ground and within moments, it becomes a torrential downpour as sheets of water cascaded from the heavens. The rain lashes against windows, beats on rooftops, and forms rivulets that quickly grow into streams, rushing along streets and carving paths through the earth. Visibility dropped to near zero, as the relentless downpour created a misty curtain that distorts the lines between sky and the earth.

Lightning splits the sky with blinding flashes, illuminating the storm's fury in stark detail. Thunder follows, booming and reverberating through the air, shaking buildings and rattling the nerves. The atmosphere is charged with electricity, each lightning strike punctuating the storm's violence. The air is thick with the odour of rain and an earthy aroma that permeates the nostrils. The temperature drops noticeably, adding a chill to the wind's bite. The people of the village watch in awe-inspiring wonder as the storm rages on, seemingly a living, breathing entity, its power palpable and its presence exhilarating.

As the storm rages, it creates a symphony of sounds, the howling wind, the relentless pounding of rain, the flash of lightning, and the rumble of thunder. Each element contributes to the overwhelming sensation of being at the mercy of nature's untamed power and the people knew it and to keep well away from the fury of nature.

Inside the house of John Cable at least it was dry; Isiah Blackwood was sat at a table.

John Cable sat down and looked at Blackwood. "Welcome Mr Blackwood!"

"Yes Mr Cable, I got your message, you have a problem here?"

"Yes indeed, we have had a series of problems here in the village, animals dying, sickness, all manner of things. The people of the village are angry and want something done."

"Have you any clues as to who is behind this?"

"The rumour in the village is that a family are practicing dark arts here and are responsible for all of the disorder, as I say this is the rumour, if it true, I no not!"

"Well Mr Cable, that is why I am here, if it is there I will find it and destroy it"

"I hope so Sir, the people become more agitated by the day!"

"Who are this family?"

"They live on the edge of the village, mother, Sarah Miles and two daughters Jane and Bess. The husband died some years back of an unknown illness, there have been questions."

"Alright Mr Cable we will get to work presently, do not fret I have this to hand."

By early afternoon the rain had mercifully stopped thought the sky was still an ominous shade of dark blue and purple. The Brownie Burn had been turned from a placid stream into a gushing tumble of water bouncing off rocks and spilling onto the land. The main river was fairing no better from the effects of the heavy downpour.

A raging river in flood is a breath taking, yet terrifying sight. The usually passive waterway was transformed into a powerful, unstoppable force of nature. Torrents of muddy, churning water surged headlong, sweeping away everything in the path trees and mounds of debris. The river's roar was deafening, a cacophony of crashing waves, snapping branches and the relentless pounding against anything that dares obstruct its pathway.

Banks that once contained the river were submerged, destroyed by the sheer volume and velocity of the water. The floodwaters spilled over, spreading across the land, turning fields and roads into a vast, inland sea. The normally distinct edges of the river were by now distorted and missing, replaced by a confused expanse of fizzing, turbulent currents. The air is thick with the smell of wet earth and vegetation, mixed with the faint, metallic scent of disturbed soil. Visibility is reduced as the spray from the river creates a misty haze, further adding to the sense of disorientation and danger.

Amidst the chaos, objects that were once familiar are rendered unrecognizable, battered and twisted by the force of the water. The current is relentless, its strength capable of moving boulders and carving new paths through the landscape. The river in flood is a stark reminder of nature's raw power.

The village of Greenslade was a mass of dirty puddles and mud that gripped the feet and slipped the soles of the unwary feet. Isiah Blackwood tramped though the mud and entered the barn; he stood in the doorway gazing at his two assistants asleep in the hay.

"Hey you two, wake up come with me and bring the dog!"

They jumped up rather quickly, untied the dog and followed their boss. They went immediately to the house of Sarah Miles and her two daughters. They banged on the door and it was answered by Jane Miles who questioned who these men were, but did not get answers.

"Grab her!" Blackwood cried aloud, one of his men did just that and tied her hands. Bess came out to investigate the disturbance and was also grabbed and tied.

"Mrs Miles, I am Isiah Blackwood, we have your daughters here, come outside now!"

Mrs Miles did come outside armed with a pitchfork and thrust it toward Blackwood and his men an aggressive manner shouting insults in the process.

"Who are you, what do you want with us, release my daughters now!"

Blackwood motioned to one of his men, "bring the dog forward."

The man came forward, the large massive straining to be loose but held tight.

"Give up Mrs Miles or I might have to set the dog loose!"

Mrs Miles brandished the fork again, "do as you please!"

Blackwood nodded in the man's direction, he let go of the rope and the dog sprung forward like a bolt from a crossbow. Mrs Miles was not intimidated, she stood her ground and as the dog approached she stabbed the fork with as much force as she could muster into the face of the mastiff. It was with a squeal and a howl of pain that the dog ran off shaking its head in panic and agony; it ran under a cart and laid there whimpering in distress. In the ensuing confusion the two assistants grabbed Mrs Miles and wrestled her to the floor. She kicked and screamed for a while before they managed to tie her securely.

Blackwood and his men marched the three women through the village and loaded them onto a cart. By now most of the people of the village were out watching the drama and there were a few shouts and thanks to the men as they were driven away. Sarah, Bess and Jane were taken south towards Durham City to an uncertain fate, doom adorned their eyes!

The journey was uncomfortable on the bumpy, mud soaked road especially for the three women trussed up in the back. They arrived at Durham and the women were transferred to the old goal at Elvet. As the three women got used to their new home, Blackwood went to see the sheriff and inform him of the day's work.

The sheriff and the mayor were in the town hall and were pleased to see him back.

"Now Blackwood, what news do you bring?" The mayor inquired.

"I have arrested three women suspected of witchcraft, they are in jail."

"Good work Blackwood, have they confessed to such crimes?"

"Not yet sheriff but they will in time!"

"Oh I see!" The mayor replied not surprised at this explanation.

The sheriff continued, "We have a Court of Session sitting in two days will you be ready?"

"Yes Sir we will, have no fear of that, we will get to work on confessions right away!"

To say the least life was not too pleasant for Sarah Miles and her daughters, Durham goal was a grim and fearsome place, designed explicitly for the interrogation and punishment of prisoners. The jail being underground, it was dark, damp, and poorly ventilated to add to the psychological torment, the walls were made of thick stone to muffle the screams of the victims. The chamber was dimly lit by torches, casting eerie shadows that heightened the sense of dread.

Sarah and her daughters were locked in separate cells away from each other, Bess was first to realise that she was in dire trouble as the guards came and unlocked the door. She was marched, manhandled into another room; the air was thick with the smell of blood, sweat, and fear, the stone floor was often stained. She was sat in a chair with her arms clamped to it, a man stood in front with a leather apron around his waist and malice in his eyes. She then in the corner on a stool the unmistakable shape of Isiah Blackwood, he came near.

"Now Miss Miles, you know why you are here, let us make this whole thing easy."

Bess said nothing, but shook her head in distrust.

"Miss Miles you are accused of practicing the dark arts, namely witchcraft, how say you?"

"Dark arts, I know nothing of such things!"

"Come now miss, make this easy on yourself, you are guilty and you know it."

"I am guilty of nothing Sir!"

Isiah Blackwood turned to his assistant, "fetch the screws."

His assistant brought two instruments and attached them to her thumbs.

"Turn the screws." Blackwood said.

The first turn was painful but the second and third produced agony in Bess Miles.

"Do you require another turn miss, confess!"

"No, no please I confess!"

She was untied and made to sign a confession before being take back to her cell. It was then the turn of her sister and the same procedure produced the same result. Then Sarah was sitting in her cell when the bolts of the door slid back with a scrape. Two guards entered and took her along the dark, damp passage to the interrogation room. She too was placed in the same chair and hands bound. Unlike her two daughters Sarah was somewhat more stoical as she refused to plead to anything and even as the screws were tightened, she would not speak.

After some time, they released the screws with something else in mind; she was moved from the chair and placed on her back on wooden structure, hands and feet bound. This was the dreaded Rack, a large wooden frame with rollers at both ends. Sarah's ankles were tied to one end and the wrists to the other and as the rollers, were turned, the body was stretched. Sarah screamed aloud, the sound echoing around the damp, dark wall as if it was trapped, eventually she passed out but did not confess to and crime let alone witchcraft.

Two days later the three women were standing in front of Judge Harris at Court of Session.

The judge looked at them from behind his desk, and asked them how they pleaded.

"Bess Miles, how do you plead?"

"Guilty but I was tortured!"

"Jane Miles, how do you plead?"

"Guilty, I was tortured also!"

"Sarah Miles, how do you plead?"

"I am not guilty of any crime, nor my daughters!"

Mr Blackwood, what evidence do you have as to their guilt?"

"I have signed confessions from Bess and Jane Miles Sir."

"What of Sarah Miles, she is of a different mind, what proof?"

"We discovered during out examination that she had several marks of the Devil, also when her skin was pricked with a steel pin, she did not bleed, she is guilty Sir"

"Very well I have heard enough, take them away!"

The next few days passed quickly for the three women as these were their last few days. Then one morning the time came as the guards came and marched them outside and onto a cart. They were then paraded slowly through the city as the local people threw any object they could get their hands on, along with shouts and screams of revulsion. They were transported up the hill to the north side of the city to a place called Dryburn.

A scaffold was already erected as this was the normal place of execution for any common criminal. They were blindfolded and guide up the steps, ropes were placed around their necks and as the priest said a final prayer they were dropped. A gasp came up from the watching crowd as the three women swung in the breeze still and silent. They were left there to hang for an hour or so until the crown had dispersed before they were cut down.

They were buried in the grounds of Dryburn next to the little chapel dedicated to St Leonard. There was no service, no ceremony of flowers not even a prayer to see them off. They were just another three victims of witch frenzy that had gripped the land with a fist full of suspicion and distrust that was almost a religion in itself!

Isiah Black wood left town considerably richer than when he arrived and moved onto the next town that required his assistance, wherever it may be.

CHAPTER 25

The city of Durham was enjoying the benefits of spring, if indeed there were any benefits to mention. At least the winter had passed for another year and the rain of the past weeks had ceased. The people of the city were about their normal business, there was no threat of attack by the Scottish raiders or anyone else, the plague had thankfully passed and life went on.

The sheriff of the county was in his office going through papers concerning the security of the city and the county, a knock came at the door and it opened with a creak.

The sheriff looked up to see Daniel Mathews enter with some papers of his own. Daniel had waved goodbye to his fortieth year some time ago and was well aware that the fate of all men, age, was coming up on him at a rapid pace. The lustre of fiery red hair, of which he used to be so proud, had slipped away to a better place, leaving a narrow strip around three sides of his head, with the centre being like a dessert where nothing would grow.

"Ah good morning Daniel how goes your investigations, what are you working on?"

"Good day sheriff, you remember a while past you sent me to the village of Elersly?"

"Well yes they were having a deal of trouble I recall, what of it?"

"I could not find the cause of the problems while I was there but the case has troubled me ever since. I have been searching in the university library and found some old documents."

"I see, please carry on, why manner of documents?" The sheriff inquired.

Daniel Mathews laid out his papers on the desk and pointed to them in turn.

"These are notes I have taken from the documents, there is it says in here that there is secret society of witches known as the Coven of the Silver Moon. They are a very ancient society and most scholars believe they were destroyed many years ago, I believe they have not."

"What Daniel you believe there is some sort of clandestine group causing all of this evil?"

"Yes Sir I do, I have found several clues and I would like to follow them up!"

"Well it could be an opening to this mystery, you have my permission."

"I will need to go back to Blackdale Abbey, the clues suggest that there could be books in there private library that mention this coven, if I can get in of course."

Daniel secured a horse from the sheriff's stable and with some provisions set off northward and then turned west toward Hampston Forest. The journey was to say the least uncomfortable as he did not like horses, let alone ride on top of one, they being too big and powerful with a tendency to panic at the slightest noise. However, this one did not seem so bad and he arrived at Blackdale Abbey without any broken bones or trauma.

He tied up his horse and was approached by a young monk. "Can I help you Sir?"

"I hope so young man; I would like to see the abbot, is that possible?"

"I am not sure, he is very busy."

"Tell him I am Daniel Mathews from the sheriff's office in Durham!"

The young monk walked away, "follow me if you please."

The monk led Daniel upstairs and along a long corridor then knocked on a door.

"The abbot will see you, this way."

Daniel waked into the room, "Brother Abbot, thank you for seeing me unannounced."

"Please come in, have a seat, we have met before I think?"

"Yes Sir I was here investigating a case of suspicious death, that of Brother Benjamin."

"Yes I remember it, how could I forget, a terrible business, he is still in our thoughts."

"Well Sir I have been following up on the case and I have found several clues in Durham University Library, they lead here."

"Here are you sure, why here?" The abbot questioned somewhat annoyed.

"The documents I uncovered at the university mention that there could be books or documents here in the abbey on this subject, I would like to see them if possible?"

The abbot shook his head, "We do not allow outsiders into our library, for any reason."

"Brother Abbot, there is a great evil about this land and I believe the answer could be here in your library. We surely do not want the misery of the past years to continue and what about Brother Benjamin, can he not lie in peace without justice!"

"Well, you do have a good argument; if as you say there is evil about the land, we must seek it out and destroy it, I will allow permission to study our collection."

"Thank you brother!"

The abbot called for the young monk waiting outside, he came in, "You called brother."

"Take this fellow down to the library; tell the librarian he has permission to enter."

"Yes brother, this way please."

They walked for a good while and Daniel was grateful for the guidance of the young monk. Through the cloister and past so many rooms and passageways he lost count, then down a long flight of stone steps, through the large wooden door and into the library.

The library was sanctuary of wisdom and history and stood as a testament to the enduring power of knowledge. Its towering, timeworn stone walls are adorned with intricate carvings that depict ancient symbols and forgotten languages, hinting at the wealth of information contained within. As he stepped inside, the air was thick with the scent of aged paper and leather, mingling with a faint trace of incense and old wood.

Rows upon rows of towering bookshelves, crafted from rich oak, stretched up to a high, vaulted ceiling. Each shelf was laden with countless volumes, their spines cracked and titles faded, but each book a treasure trove of ancient lore and wisdom. The books themselves were a diverse collection, some bound in weathered leather with intricate gold leaf designs, others in simple, rough-hewn covers, their pages yellowed and fragile with age. Soft, golden light filtered through stained glass windows, casting a medley of colours on the worn stone floor and creating an almost unearthly atmosphere. The windows themselves were masterpieces of design and artistic skill, depicting scenes from ancient myths and historical events, their vibrant hues illuminating the library's quiet corners.

In the centre of the library, a grand reading table, polished to a deep sheen, invites scholars and seekers of knowledge to sit and delve into the mysteries of the past. The table is surrounded by plush, high-backed chairs, their fabric worn but comfortable, offering a place for contemplation and study. Scattered throughout the library are various artefacts and curiosities: ancient maps, mysterious scrolls, and strange devices whose purposes have long been forgotten. A massive, ornately decorated globe sits in one corner, its surface marked with unfamiliar continents and seas, a reminder of how much of the ancient world remains undiscovered.

The silence in the library is profound, broken only by the occasional rustle of pages and the soft footsteps of the librarian, a guardian of this vast repository of knowledge. The librarian moves with a quiet grace, ever watchful and ready to assist those who seek the wisdom of the ancients.

"Brother this man has been given permission to examine your books."

"Oh and by whose hand was this given?"

"Brother Abbot!"

"I see, what manner of books interest you Sir?2

"Anything on witchcraft, superstition and especially secret societies, do you have any?"

"Over here we have somethings that might help you; this is a copy King James' book 'Demonologie' and a copy of 'Malleus Maleficarum', usually translated as the Hammer of Witches, is the best known treatise purporting to be about witchcraft."

"Yes they are impressive volumes but I believe you have another, book "Lupus In Fabula!"

The librarian stood back in a sort of shock, how do you know of such a book?"

"Because I am an investigator, it is my job to know these things, now where is it?"

With some reluctance the librarian opened a cabinet and produced the book and placed it carefully on the table, he opened it cautiously and began to read. The text was archaic and not easy to read, there were numerous symbols, cyphers and codes. Some of the text was in Latin and the librarian was able to help translate. He was there for quite some time studying the book, he would have liked to have taken it home to study in detail but he knew well enough that that was never going to happen. Instead he took copious notes on the things he thought were most important. Later that day he set off back to Durham before the sun set.

The next morning Daniel reported to the sheriff bright and early as usual, he entered the room and found the sheriff at his desk, he looked up. "Ah Daniel what news do you bring?"

"Yesterday I visited Blackdale Abbey and after some discussion with the abbot I was allowed into the library and what a library it is the collection of books and pamphlets is unmatched, they even have a work by one of our saints here in Durham Saint Bede!"

"So did you gain any knowledge from this library?"

"Yes Sir I have made notes and I will go and research several things today, with your permission of course."

"You have my permission Daniel but what research will it be?"

"During my research I have found that there is a secret society called The Coven of the Silver Moon. They had existed for centuries, its origins tracing back to a time when magic was woven into the very fabric of everyday life. This coven was unique, for it was not only dedicated to the practice of magic but also to the preservation of balance in the world. They were the silent guardians, intervening only when the scales tipped too far toward chaos or corruption."

"I have never heard of such a society, have you?"

"No Sir not until I researched these things, according to the book in the abbey, 'Lupus In Fabula,' a powerful warlock named Malachar, who had been banished centuries ago for his dark practices. From what I have learned, I think he has found a way to return and he is gathering followers, promising them power and immortality in exchange for their loyalty. His ultimate goal was to open a portal to the Shadow Realm, a dimension of pure darkness and malevolence, and unleash its horrors upon the world."

The sheriff shuffled nervously in his chair. "If this is true it could explain why there has been so much misery and torment unleashed upon this county, anything more?"

"According to the books the group have rituals at certain times of the year, I will try and find out what rituals or ceremonies they are and when and importantly where!"

"Please carry on you work Daniel, if this is real we must stop it for the sake of everyone!"

"Yes Sir I will get on with it right away, good day!"

Daniel Mathews took his notes and made his way up the cobbled road to Durham University and entered the library. His work was in no way finished and he knew there was a lot more to learn about this subject and his knowledge, although more was still thin. The head librarian of the university was kind enough to assign two students to help with the research and they were greatly welcome as his task was great.

He worked with his assistants long into the night and even after the students had retired and it was only when the library closed for the night he left, tired and hungry.

CHAPTER 26

Eliza was quite comfortable in her new home and as the days and weeks passed she became even more contented. There was plentiful food and drink and time passed in a pleasant manner. April was on its last legs and May was waiting in the wings, the weather was also improving by the day. Eliza was out and about on the moor taking in the fresh smells and sounds of the season, larks tweeted above and unmistakable sound of grouse filled the air. She walked for a fair while taking in the scene and revelling in the free and open space of which she was such a minute part.

After a while she found herself on the banks of Blackwater Lake, she stopped and gazed at the water glistening in the spring sunshine, it was serine calm and she wondered why this place had such a bad reputation. Was it once again the suspicious minds of the local people or was there more to it, truth has a way of merging with imagined events. She crouched down and put a hand into the water, it was cold, frigid and she could understand how someone falling into the lake would suffer an icy shockwave of panic.

After some time she made her way back to the cave and into her room, she stretched out on the bed. Sometime later Gaia entered. "Good rest now; we have an important night ahead."

"Important, why is that Gaia?"

"You still now nothing of our ways, tonight is the festival of Beltane, we all must attend."

Eliza pondered for a while, Beltane or something, what was Gaia on about? The day passed and Eliza was no wiser as to what was coming that night or where it was. She did know by the expression of Gaia that it was important but why was a mystery to her. As the afternoon slipped into evening Gaia came into the room with an outfit which she placed on the bed with some care.

"Put this clothing on Eliza, be ready, we will leave soon."

Eliza picked up the clothing, which consisted of a long black mantle, a black hood and a black cape with some sort of red symbols on the front, she put it on, it was a perfect fit. It was dark when she received the call to gather outside, she left her room and the cave. There outside were several people all dressed in the same apparel, each having a flaming torch they stood silent and still, without a sound or a gesture to each other, as if they were statues.

One of the people came toward her, "follow us Eliza, join the procession."

Eliza did not know who this person was but recognised the voice of Gaia. The procession set off out of the ravine and up the steep slope onto the moor, Eliza followed behind. It was an incredible sight, black shapes on the dark moor illuminated by flickering flame all in a straight line as if joined by some invisible cord, no words, no sound. They walked a long way over the moor; Eliza was keen to find out their destination but dare not ask. She knew the moor very well, she had after all been born and bred here but in the darkness she did not know even the direction they were traveling, she kept walking.

It was some time later that she realised the her steps were now in a downward slope as if they were descending off the high moor, she was correct as the procession made their way steadily downward. She could see in the distance through some trees flames dancing in the night air and realised they coming close to the location. She realised that all of a sudden the open moor was no more, the shapes of things were different, she could in the dappled light make out she forms of trees, old and twisted, she was in the heart of an ancient forest.

Then they left the trees and entered a clearing, a secluded glade opened up like a hidden sanctuary, bathed in the soft, flecked light of torches filtering through the canopy. The air was thick with the scent of pine and moss, and the gentle rustle of leaves the only sound. The gathering entered the glade and a circle of torches, was formed, their flames dancing in the darkness, illuminating the glade, casting long shadows and creating an aura of mystery. The participants move with reverence, their footsteps muffled by the thick carpet of fallen leaves and soft earth.

In the centre of the glade, an altar made of smooth, weathered stones, which is adorned with garlands of wildflowers, glowing lanterns, and sacred objects, each meticulously placed. One person stepped out of the circle and paced into the centre next to the alter, she held her arms outstretched as if praying to some god, with a voice both gentle and commanding, she spoke. The words, steeped in tradition and whispered secrets, echo through the glade, carried on the night breeze.

"I call upon the spirits of the forest, invoking blessings from the ancient trees and the creatures that dwell within. We carry out this vigil and its rituals in worship and dedication and as time shifts to become May Day morn we ask the spirits of the forest for your blessing. On this celebration of Beltane we ask you Freya for your guidance, we ask you almighty Mother of the Earth to open up to the fertility god, so their union will bring about healthy livestock, strong crops, and new life."

The woman collected a large jug from the altar and filled several cups; they were then passed around the gathering, each person taking a drink. It was then the turn of Eliza who sipped the liquid to find it was nothing more than natural water with an earthy, metallic taste.

"We take this gift oh Mother Earth; we thank you for this life giving liquid."

There then followed a series of chants and words of which Eliza could not recognise, the ceremony seemed to last for hours but was probably not that long. In the climax of the ceremony, a silent moment is held to honour the ancestors and the natural world, allowing everyone to feel the profound connection to the earth and each other. The silence is deep and all-encompassing, broken only by the soft sounds of the forest and as the ceremony concludes, a sense of peace and renewal permeates the glade.

The participants slowly disperse, leaving behind the altar and the glowing torches, which will burn through the night as a testament to their sacred gathering. The glade, now infused with the energy of the ceremony, returns to its serene state, a timeless witness to the ancient traditions and the enduring bond between humanity and nature

Eliza followed the procession back over the moor and into the cave, where she flopped onto her bed and sleep. When she awoke she found a woman standing in the doorway, still and silent. Eliza did not recognise this woman; she stood there tall with her flowing silver hair and piercing blue eyes.

This was Morgana, the leader of the coven, she was a sorceress of unparalleled power and wisdom, she commanded respect and reverence from all who knew her.

"Eliza Swann, we have not yet met thus far, I am Morgana."

"Well pleased to meet you I'm sure." Eliza replied a little confused.

"You did well at the ceremony earlier; you are now one of us, your new family. You now have permission to leave your room and explore these caverns and meet your sisters. I see that you have already dabbled in magic and with success, you will learn much more from our esteemed teachers. You have power and foresight and people will fear that, walk always in the shadows, what cannot be seen will not be trapped."

"Thank you Morgana, I will endeavour to be the best I can!"

With those words still in the air Morgana was gone and Eliza was once more alone, alone with only her thoughts to company her, she began to consider her life and future. Why was she here? Where was her mother? What would the future hold for her and the thought of the magic spell she conjured on Ann Simms? The woman was now dead, frozen into solid by her actions, if not directly by her hand, was this right, did she deserve it? She pondered for a while and decided that she did indeed deserve it, she was a ghastly woman and the world was better for her demise.

Daniel Mathews entered the office of the sheriff. "Good morning Sir."

"Come in Daniel, you look tired, what news?"

"I am a little fatigued this morning I was up late studying documents. I have discovered that the secret society known as the Coven of the Silver Moon worship a deity called Malachar. He is a powerful wizard who is intent on bringing darkness to the whole world."

"If this is true Daniel we must stop it, did you find anything else?"

"According to the documents they meet at certain times of the year in secluded glades and this map of the county shows glades around the county, one of them is up past the village of Elersly on the far side of Cross fell. I should go there and investigate right now!"

"I agree Daniel but take two men; you never know what you will find!"

"Yes Sir."

Daniel Mathews and two assistants left the city and made their way north and then west over the moor. The glade took a while to find, hidden in a deep hollow surrounded by trees.

"Look Daniel, down there is that it?" One of his men said, pointing an arm forward.

"Yes I do believe it could be, come on we must examine this place. They made their way down the steep slope, through the trees and out in to a large clearing, dismounting they tied their horses and began to explore. Immediately Daniel bent down and examined the ground, moving chunks of grass and pebbles.

"What have you found Daniel?" One of his men inquired bending over next to him.

"Look here, footprints, lots of them; in a straight line I think this could be the place!"

He stood up and followed the prints into the centre of the glade; several torches were stock into the ground now by now cold dim, he looked around at the scene taking in the evidence.

"There was certainly activity here and recently, what is that over there?"

They walked over and found what looked like an altar with flowers around and on top of it. Behind the altar there half hidden in the grass a serious of ancient stones. Daniel examined them carefully rubbing away the time gathered grime and dirt.

"The stones are made from what looks to be granite, chosen no doubt for their ability to withstand the elements over centuries. The stones exhibit signs of weathering, including surface erosion, cracks, and a discoloration that gives them a rough, aged appearance. This weathering is a testament to their antiquity and the natural forces they've endured."

The stones have a weathered, greyish or brownish hue, with a rough texture that adds to their ancient appearance. Moss, lichen, and other natural growths partially cover them, enhancing their mystique. The carvings include a variety of symbols, such as geometric patterns, religious or spiritual icons, runes, hieroglyphs, or pictographs. These symbols often reflect the cultural, religious, or social practices of the civilization that created them. Over time, the depth and clarity of the carvings may have diminished due to erosion. Some symbols might be faint and require careful examination to discern.

"These ancient weathered stones with carved symbols are not just relics of the past but are keys to unlocking stories, cultures, and knowledge from eras long gone."

"But who did these carvings Daniel and for what purpose?" His assistant questioned.

"That my friend is above my degree of knowledge I will take notes and go back to the university, they might know what they mean, as I do not!"

Daniel spent the next few days in the university library and discovered that the carved stones could have any number of meanings but scholars argued over what was true fact and what was theory. This mattered little to Daniel who left them to their discourse and returned to the more mundane tasks of keeping good order in the city and county.

CHAPTER 27

Time had moved on as it always does and the people of the region had moved with it, except for somethings for somethings will never change, superstition, the fear of God and the fear of anything that could not be explained by science or nature. To the west and far from the cities of Durham and Newcastle in the high Pennine hills there existed a different world. Life everywhere in this northerly region was difficult but here on the highest hills and deepest dales was the harshest, most rugged country in the whole county.

The hills towered above deep ravines through which silvered streams rushed and splashed over time worn rocks, purple heather stretched in every direction like some regal cloak. The landscape, although seemingly untouched by the hands of human kind were in fact a scene of industry, far away from any other form of business.

The land in these parts was rich with a mineral that was in demand not only in the region but all over the country and further afield, lead! It might not seem obvious at first sight but the dales were scattered with mines, some big but most on a smaller scale. Some of these mines were owned by individual companies but the majority were owned by the Bishop of Durham. The people who worked the mines lived in the small community of Westgarth, a few stone and slate cottages and not much else, a blacksmith, mining workshops, overseen by Thomas Page, appointed by the Bishop of Durham to make sure the mines kept working.

There was also a small church that had reportedly been there since Saxon times, this was not inhabited most of the week. On a Sunday a preacher would arrive to give a service, he would travel between the scattered hamlets of this area to spread the word of God. And they would need it as life here was hard at the best of times and in winter these hamlets would be cut off for weeks on end. The people of these places were self-sufficient; they had to be, catching fish from the rivers and game on the moors, deer, grouse and rabbits.

High on a hill overlooking the village was a small cottage, Margret Hodge lived here alone, an elderly, somewhat disagreeable and hostile woman, she lived away from the others by choice. Her husband, a hill farmer had died years ago and she was now alone and she liked it that way. She would on occasion enter the village to attend church or buy supplies. Her unpleasant manner and short temper she had something of a reputation among the people that did not endear her to the locals, who for the most part ignore her.

As in most communities in these times life was very much the same as anywhere else. The women kept house and cared for children. The men would almost entirely be employed in the mines; the only exception was Jack Lord who was a hunter and trapper who supplied food for the village. The men would start work early in the morning and work until late afternoon digging deep into the hillside in a series of drift mines. This involved digging a series of Bell Pits along a vein, Bell Pits were shallow, unsupported shafts dug on vein outcrops that widened in a bell-like shape as they were sunk. the lead ore was hewed and loaded onto carts that were pulled to the surface by pit ponies, before being taken away to be smelted.

It was now the height of summer and the work in the heat of the days was exhausting. Never the less it would be done or there would be no pay that day. The miners finished their shifts for the day and returned to their cottages in the village, tired, sweaty and dirty they washed as best they could before a simple meal of whatever could be bought or foraged that day. At least they could rest and with the thought that tomorrow being Sunday they could have a day to recover from their endeavours.

Next morning was fine, the sky an optimistic tone of sapphire blue with only the distant shape of white clouds in floating in the light breeze. All was well in the village when a man on a horse arrived, it was Reverend Stubbs. He dismounted and entered the tiny chapel and began to ring the bell. Before too long several people had arrived and were sitting at pews awaiting the service. Peter Bowe and his wife Susan were in early and had seats at the front along with their ten year old twin daughters Emma and Helen.

The reverend kept his sermon short as he had to be in the next village, this was somewhat of a relief to the congregation as they for the most part would rather be doing something else, somewhere else. They spilled outside into the fresh air; there standing stiffly was Margret Hodge, glaring at people as they left. She was old and not the prettiest of sights, weathered and bent, being propped up by a length of carved wood, long unkempt silver hair waving in the breeze. Last out were Peter Bowe and his family, who were immediately accosted.

"Why were you people sitting in the front pews, could you not have given it to an old woman, who has lived a much longer life than you?"

"Well we did not see you Mrs Hodge!" Peter replied considerately.

"Well I advise you to be more observant in future!"

"I advise you to get back to your hut on the hill!"

"Helen be quiet girl!"

"Yes, sorry mother but she deserved it!"

Margret Hodge shuffled off muttering something quietly before turning back. "Life was much better here in the hills until you lot turned up digging holes everywhere, miners huh!"

Jack Lord was sitting on a stone.

"Have you any game today?" Margret questioned with a look of distain.

Jack Lord looked up at her with equal measure distrust, the feelings were mutual.

"A Mrs Hodge, a fine morning is it not, good to be in the air?"

"Never mind the weather Jack Lord, have you any game?"

"Well it has not been a good few days; all I have is these two crows. He held them aloft tied together by their feet, "Freshly killed Mrs Hodge, plenty meat on these birds!"

"Tosh, why would I eat crows, filthy carrion eating creatures, I would rather eat heather!"

"Well you might have to Mrs Hodge, good day now!" Jack Lord allowed himself a smile.

Peter Bowe and his family walked past, "Can I interest you in two freshly killed crows?"

"No, not today Jack, would Mrs Hodge not have them either?"

"No Peter, she is a peculiar woman! How is the life of a miner these days?"

"Oh much the same, hot in the summer, cold in winter, damp, wet and dirty!"

"I have no deSire to be a miner; I will stick to hunting and trapping." Jack replied.

"My younger brother William is starting in the mine tomorrow, he is not too keen!"

"Nor would I be Peter, nor would I!"

Sunday came and went all too quickly, as Sundays always do and after a simple supper of pottage and rye bread the family went to their beds for the night. Overnight was not peaceful as a fierce storm lashed the hills and the small village. Huge rain like missiles pelted the slate roofs and the wind howled around the hills and dales like some angry beast. Peter was up early readying himself for work; he stepped outside and looked up at the sky. The rain had thankfully stopped but the sky was still a dismal shade of dark grey. Clouds hung low in the valleys and water ran from the hills percolated through the heather with a silvered flow.

"Peter!" Came a call, he turned around to find his younger brother William coming up the hill. William was six years younger than Peter and was somewhat timid and nervous of nature but he was young and strong and would make a fine miner.

"Good day William, are you ready to become a mine worked like your brother?"

"Not really Peter, I would rather be something else, anything else in fact but we need food."

"Yes I know what you mean, if I could leave the mine I would also but I cannot. Come on I will show you around and the foreman will set you a job, not too much for your first day."

They walked down the dirt path till they came to a high hillside an entrance had been cut in the hill and it was waiting, a yawning gape hungry and prepared. They made their way down the slope of the level lit by candles and the odd wall hung lamp for quite some way passing rumbling tubs pushed and dragged by boys which seemed like no age to be toiling in such a place. Eventually the turned off to the right and into a small, constricted tunnel where they stopped next to a newly excavated vein.

William turned to his brother, "I don't like it down here Peter, so dark, cold and wet and the feeling of constriction is almost overwhelming, do we have to do this?"

"Don't worry, this is a drift mine, it's much safer than other mines, just relax!"

Peter pointed to the face, "This is a fairly new vein, we have dug away the earth to expose the lead line and we have just recently begun to excavate the metal, we don't know how far it goes back, but it seems it is good amount, we should see the foreman."

"Peter look there is water running down the walls, is that normal?"

"Yes William it is, water runs downward and we are downward!"

Peter then suddenly stopped speaking in mid-sentence as a look of dreadful acceptance flashed across his candle lit features. The noise came upon them with a rumbling storm of thunder which engulfed them in rock and dust. It lasted but a few seconds, a few seconds of terrible violence in the lives of ordinary men, then nothing but the creaking and moaning of subsiding earth.

Peter lay still for a while trying to regain his senses, his legs were trapped and something warm ran down his head, it could have been sweat, it could have been blood. Blackness, he was engulfed in blackness, he held a hand to his face, but could not see it, he couldn't feel his legs, no pain, just a sort of numbness, he could be in some sort of shock however, it did not take long for this shock to turn to sheer panic as the reality of his situation closed around him.

"William, are you there?"

No answer.

He called again through the dust clogged air, nothing. Just a human sound would lift his spirit as the thought of being alone was pure terror. "Will, please answer." He lay back on the jagged rocks and contemplated a miner's death. Peter did not know how long he had been there or even if he was conscious, but he thought that he heard a voice. He sat up, "William, oh God I thought you were dead, were you knocked out?"

"It's alright Peter, I'm here, and I've been here all the time."

Peter gazed into the gloom, "You sound different Will is it the dust?"

"Ah the dust, it gets in your throat and lungs, it's not much of a life down here."

The voice vibrated through Peter, was his brother confused or had he lost his mind in the darkness? "Who are you?"

The reply was both harsh, yet gentle, "What you don't know me? I know you Peter Bowe, I know you well enough."

"You're not William are you, if not then who are you, what's your name?"

The stranger laughed softly, "Ah names Peter, names, I have many, I am every name and none, you decide."

Peter felt the icy finger of fear pass over him as he realised this was not his rescuers, was he dreaming or was his life force slipping away among the rubble?

"Help me; for God's sake get me out." He cried as he rested back in the darkness of his despair.

The voice continued, "Ah Peter you are trapped in the black belly of the earth, where is your God when you need him? You call out to him for salvation, but do you really think he will save you? No, the promise of paradise that you were brought up on is false, you must face the truth you are abandoned."

The rumbling earth had attracted the attention of the village several of who ran towards the mine. At the entrance they came across a miner who had been near the entrance who managed to escape the initial collapse and raised the alarm, he was unhurt apart from a few small cuts and bruises but in a state of some shock and bewilderment. He fell to the floor exhausted and could not give an accurate description of what had happened. Villagers and fellow miners rushed to the scene, armed with shovels and picks, to begin a desperate rescue attempt. They worked tirelessly, but progress was slow and dangerous due to the instability of the remaining tunnels.

The sudden collapse trapped some miners under tons of rock and debris. Those who survived the initial cave-in were left in darkness, with limited air supply and no means of escape. The collapse also blocked the main entry shaft, making rescue efforts incredibly difficult. However, some miners who were working in different seams began to emerge from the gloom; covered in dust and sludge and coughing wildly they stumbled out into the light. The women of the village helped the miners away and washed and treated their injuries, the men were busy digging frantically hauling rocks and rubble away as fast as they could.

Some of the workers would not be as blessed as some were either crushed by falling rock or suffocated by the lack of air. Others were injured, suffering from broken bones, cuts, and exhaustion. The injured were carried to the village and treated with the limited medical knowledge and resources available. The church was opened as a makeshift hospital where the victims were treated. Reverend Stubbs was overseeing the situation and providing as much help and resources as he could with limited means.

The men at the mine entrance were desperately moving debris away, these men were their friends and fellow villagers and the wanted them out! Thomas page the overseer of the mine arrived at the scene and began directing the men, who were already doing exactly what he said and was in no way any assistance, he questioned one of the miners sitting on a rock.

"You man, were you inside of the mine, what happened?"

"I don't rightly know Sir, at the start of the shift we noticed a lot of water running down the walls but we have had a lot of rain lately, we thought nought of it. Then after some time working there was an almighty rumble as if the earth had shifted and all hell followed."

"How the hell did you escape?"

"My and some others were working in a different seam to the collapse and we managed to find our way out through the rubble and dust, we were lucky!"

Thomas Page rubbed his face in a worried manner; he knew the collapse was likely caused by a combination of poor tunnel support, water seepage, and the weakening of rock due to continuous extraction. Wooden supports were used, but they were insufficient and prone to decay. He knew fine well as the mine's overseer he would face scrutiny and there was already talk of divine retribution or ill omens among the villagers.

Thomas Page shouted to another worker, "Have you made a count of missing persons?"

"Yes Sir, we think there are three people unaccounted for at the moment."

"Who are they?"

"Peter Bowe, his brother William and a twelve year old boy named Arthur Morris!"

"Thank you get the men to keep working, we must find them!"

"Yes Mr Page!"

Thomas Page went back to his house and wrote a note which he sealed with wax and a special seal recognising him as a representative of the Bishop of Durham. He called one of his men and into the house, James Burnell responded in a hurried manner.

"James get a horse and take this note to Durham it is for the Bishop or one of his staff, explain that it is very important, if you are stopped show this seal, they will let you through!"

"Yes Sir I will leave right away!"

"Good man James make haste!"

James Burnell left the village at a fair gallop and made his way south east through the high ills and deep dales, he was on an important mission and he was determined to succeed. Reverend Stubbs was at the entrance to the mine when a woman approached in distress.

Reverend Stubbs, have you seen my husband, is he still in there?"

"Yes Mrs Bowe I am afraid he is one of the missing, along with his brother William!"

"Oh no, please no, what will become of me and my daughters, with no husband?"

"Take heart Mrs Bowe, they are working to free any one trapped, go now your daughters need you right now, I will tell you if we have any news."

Mrs Bowe walked off sobbing gently into her hands; it was some time later before she found out the truth, the awful truth that neither her husband nor his brother would be coming home. The collapse was too extensive and there was no way that they could reach the far end of it without causing another collapse. The order was take to close the mine and seal the entrance, two men and a young boy would never see the light again and would spent eternity in the black bowels of the unforgiving earth.

Of course this being such a small community superstitions and fear spread among the villagers, with many believing that the mine was cursed. Later that day Reverend Stubbs visited the house of peter Bowe and spoke to his wife who was somewhat dejected.

"Mrs Bowe I am sorry for your loss, please except my condolences and the people of the village have asked me to pass on their thoughts, how are the girls?"

"Thank you Reverend Stubbs, it is a comfort of sorts, the girls seem to be coping well enough but soon the whole tragic reality will hit them with a huge shock!"

"Yes Mrs Bowe I understand, I have been saying prayers for them and your husband and we must not forget his brother and the young boy taken at such an age, he knew nothing."

"Thank you Reverend you are correct, his mother must be suffering, at least I have my girls, please send my wishes to her would you?"

"Yes Mrs Bowe I will do that and one more thing, the Bishop of Durham who owns the mine will be sending his condolences and compensation for your loss."

Reverend left with Mrs Bowe wondering what compensation would bring Peter Back.

Over the next few days rumour began to spread about the mine and stories of God being displeased in some way were begging to take shape. Another account suggested that the mine was somehow cursed and had been proven by such a tragedy. People looked at each other with a new found suspicion, glances were passed, names mentioned and whispers carried on the air like blossom in the breeze.

Reverend Stubbs did his best to calm the people ensuring them at his sermons that it was just a tragic accident and no one was to blame except the owners of the mine for not maintaining it sufficiently well enough. It did not work!

CHAPTER 28

The summer was by now passing and the chill fingers of another autumn were clawing at the land. The warm days were drifting away in to the distance as Mother Nature turned cold. Eliza Swann was sitting in her room in the cave pondering just what she was there for and how she even came to this place. Dreams, reality, what was real and what was not, she lay back in her confusion. What was her role in life, what was her destiny, did she even have one? The secret ceremony in the dark forest, why what was it for and how did it concern her? Nothing was clear and also nothing was explained by her so called new family, all will become clear when the time is right, what will become clear and when?

Eliza being of restless spirit and at home in the clean and fresh air left the cave and wandered up onto the moor. This was a place she knew very well having visited it since she was but a small girl, she was at home here, comfortable. She had come prepared with a woollen shawl knowing fine well that the high moor was temperamental and had the tendency to change in rapid fashion. She walked some way and after resting on her favourite stone for a while walked further.

Before long she found herself on the banks of Blackwater Lake, she gazed around it. It was a strange body of water, open to the elements, no trees, no bushes of bankside reeds, just cold, wind blasted barren openness. She had often wondered why this place had such a bad reputation, she bent down and lifted a hand full of water, if was even at this time icy, she shook her hand quickly. This is place where the two young boys disappeared and were never seen again, where they lying rotting at the bottom of this lake, two lost souls?

The lake was well named, Blackwater, it was dark and some say had no bottom as it opened up into another world of mystery and unknown things. She went on past the lake and had a mind to try and find the hidden glade where the ceremony took place, she did not know why but there was a compulsion there she had to resolve. She did not know exactly where the glade was as it was dark that night and she was in a little confused. She did however, come across the glade more through luck than endeavour.

It looked so different than the night of the ceremony, more spacious and open, she entered the clearing. Walking around she could see the remains of torches long cold and undisturbed and in the centre the stone alter. She paced around it looking at the symbols carved into it, there were by now no adornments, no flowers or gildings, just cold hard stone. She walked around the stones half hidden in the grass and heather; the runes carved onto it were in a different language from way back in history, what did they mean what was so special about this place and why was she brought here that night?

The day was moving on and a chill wind was beginning to whip around the trees moaning like some ethereal spirit casting a spell on the earth. Eliza decided to turn back as she did not want to be on the moor after dark, she left the glade and made her way back onto the moor. A cold wind from the north was beginning to blow and swirl around bringing a thick fog with it and she was becoming more uncomfortable by the minute. Before too long she was at Blackwater Lake, she stopped and rested for a few minutes; she put her hands in the water and lifted them up to have a drink. The water was icy on her hands and throat tasting peaty with a metallic flavour, she was about to leave when she heard a sound. It was quiet at first hardly audible, she looked around at the gathering mist for the source but could not see far.

Then it came again louder this time but still a whisper as though someone was speaking at a distance, a chill engulfed her and she did not know if it was the cold fog or fear! The sound grew louder and she could hear what sounded like groans roiling around the place as if they were trapped. The sound was by now everywhere, she could not decide where they were coming from but they were there, moaning and wailing like lost souls. She left the lake by quick motion and returned to the cave where she flopped on her bed and wondered.

As she dozed off she began to dream of people lost on the moor and drowning in the lake, so vivid, so real, then she was woken with a start, Gaia was standing next to her bed.

"Oh Gaia I did not hear you come in!"

"No Eliza I am a quiet soul, you have been out today have you not?"

"Err, yes I went for a walk earlier."

"You managed to find the glade and the lake."

"Yes but how did you know that, I was alone up there?"

"I know many things Eliza but be warned the glade is a sacred place and the spirits of the forest do not take trespass without permission lightly, you must take care."

"I heard strange noises at the lake, why does it have such a bad reputation?"

"The lake is also sacred but for different reasons, it is dark and holds many secrets."

"What sort of secrets?"

"You will learn all in time but you are not yet ready for such knowledge."

Eliza lay back and pondered what Gaia had said, what on earth could be so secret? Why did Blackwater Lake have such a reputation that stretched all about these northern lands? Eliza knew that Gaia was not easy to understand as she often spoke in riddles, teasing you with some knowledge, then closing it off again. She was a strange woman, the whole group were the same, none of them seemed to have a name, she knew none of them and it seemed mingling with other people as in normal society was forbidden or at least discouraged.

The whole thing was that of confusion, what was this place, why was she here? Sometimes she thought that all of this secrecy and clandestine behaviour was part of a bigger story, one not yet told but with a significance that was, at this time beyond her.

CHAPTER 29

The small village of Westgarth high up in the rugged north west of the county was still coming to terms with the tragedy of the collapsed mine. Mrs Bowe was visited by a representative from the Bishop of Durham who presented her with money as compensation. Not that it helped change her mood or that of her daughters Emma and Helen, who at the tender age of ten were now expected to grow up without their father. Mrs Bowe had noticed that her daughters had changed somewhat in their mentality; they seemed emotionally disturbed in some way, doing and saying things they had never done before.

The parents of the young boy lost under the rubble, Arthur Morris, were also visited and the same outcome was delivered to them and was received with no particular pleasure.

Mr Morris took the bag of coins with reluctance, "Thank you I will help I suppose."

Mrs Morris interrupted with a snap! "Help, will it bring my son back, it will not help Arthur too much I doubt, why did not the bishop maintain the mine in a safe condition?"

"Well Mrs Morris, his reverence the bishop has not time for such matters; he is a very busy man. That is why he leaves the running of the mine to his agent here in the village; Thomas Page is responsible for the day to day management of the mine."

"You go back to Durham and tell your bishop that he spends more time making money than looking after his flock, we have no time for him here!"

"Mrs Morris I know you are upset but you cannot speak of his reverence in that manner!"

"Why Sir, why can I not speak how I chose?"

"The bishop is God's representative on earth, do you deny him?"

"God, bishops, my boy lies lifeless and crushed, where was God then I ask you that?"

The next few days were tense in the village rumour and counter rumour skulked around every corner and in every house, some saying the mine was cursed, some that the whole village was. This was of little comfort to the parents neither of young Arthur Morris, nor in fact the Bowe family that had also suffered much these past days.

Thomas Page was in his office when a man entered covered in dust and seemingly tired.

"Yes Sir have you business with me?"

"I am a dispatch rider; I come with a message from the Bishop of Durham."

 He placed the dispatch on the table; will there be any reply Mr Page?"

Thomas Page opened it and read the short note, "No there is no reply good Sir, your mission is complete, but please take some refreshment before you head back."

"Yes Sir I will thank you!"

Thomas Page left the office and went to the foreman who was supervising the clearing of rocks and rubble from the mine, Page hailed him as he drew near waving his note.

"Have you news Mr Page?"

"Yes, leave this digging we will never find the bodies anyway, I have an order from the bishop. He wants a new shaft dug into a hill to the North West of here that will reach the same seam but from a different side of the hill. He wants work to begin immediately, no production means no profit and we cannot have that can we?"

"I see what you mean Sir I will gather the men and plot out a way forward."

The next day there was a measure of activity in the village as miners began moving equipment to the other side of the hill. The grasses and heather were cleared and a new entrance excavated hoping to find the same seam as before but from the other side.

Jack Lord was up on the moor having retrieved two rabbits from his traps and was on his way down when he noticed activity in a valley below, he watched for a while. When he arrived in the village he took his catch home and went to get some water from the natural spring nearby, he was approached by a woman from the village.

"Jack, what is all this activity concerning do you know?"

"I have just been up on the moor and I can see them working in the dale, it looks as if they are digging a new mine, I knew work would not stop for long, there is money involved!"

"You are correct Jack Lord, nothing will stop them making money!"

Later that night, the village was quiet, the darkness had enveloped it like a black cloak and the people were at rest as it would soon be morning again. The autumn sun was trying to break above the eastern hills and Mrs Bowe was up and doing chores about the house when her daughter Emma came in, she was in something of an agitated state.

"Emma dear whatever is the matter, you look worried?"

"It's Helen mother I can't find her, I have looked outside but there is no sign."

"Well I have been up for a while I did not see her go out!"

Mrs Bowe went outside and found Jack Lord preparing some traps.

"Jack have you seen my daughter Helen?"

"Why no Mrs Bowe I have not seen her today is there a problem?"

"She is not in the house she seems to have gone missing!"

Jack Lord was inspecting something on the ground kneeling down touching it with a finger.

"What is it Jack?"

"There are footprints made by bare feet, quite fresh they are heading toward the moor, I will follow them as far as I can, hopefully I will find her, do not fret Mrs Bowe!"

Jack Lord did as he promised and followed the tracks up the hill onto the high moors. They were relatively easy to see on the dirt road but then veered off into the heather. He followed as best he could but he had to hazard a guess as to which direction to head.

He persevered and reached the top of a high hill to the north where he thought he could see something white in the distance, it could be a stray sheep, he kept going. As he neared the place he realised that it was not a sheep as he saw a young girl standing still and silent dressed in nothing but a white smock, she was motionless as if frozen to the ground. He approached with some caution not knowing what to expect.

"Helen, Helen Bowe, you must be freezing what are you doing up here?"

Helen looked round at him with an expression of remoteness as if she were half asleep.

"Helen, who is Helen? Who are you?"

"I am Jack Lord, you know me Helen since you were a baby!"

She looked at him with a sense of distant distraction.

"Come on Helen let me get you home, your mother is worried."

He took her by the arm and led her off the moor with his coat around her shoulders.

Her mother was waiting at the door, "Helen where have you been Girl?"

Emma took her sister inside and tried to warm her up by the fire as Mrs Bowe stood.

Jack! Jack thank you so much for bringing her home you have saved us this day!"

"I was just glad I could help!"

"Well thank you anyway, I am afraid that I have nothing but gratitude in my purse!"

"It is alright Mrs Bowe, I will bring you a rabbit and you can make us all a stew!"

Helen was put to bed and she slept like a baby most of the day and when she awoke later she could remember nothing of what happened. She was questioned several times but could recall nothing. This was all a mystery to Mrs Bowe and her other daughter Emma who could not explain the strange behaviour. The next few days Helen seemed to be back to her normal self as if nothing had happened and she resumed the life of a ten year old.

Two days later Emma Bowe went to the spring on the edge of the village to fetch water. On her way back through the centre of the village she suddenly stopped dead in her tracks. The water jug slipped from her hands and shattered on the ground. Several people looked around at the noise as Emma stood rigid her eyes turned upward into her head leaving only the whites as she fell to the ground. People came running and tried to revive her, she began shaking and convulsing in a strange and uncommon manner, arms and legs flailing, head thrashing side to side, she made no sound.

The villagers picked her up and carried her home and placed her on the bed. Mrs Bowe was once again sent into a deep fear; she tried to give Emma a drink but could not manage. Her sister Helen stood over the bed, an understanding smile etched on her young face.

In a small, insular community such as Westgarth where fear and superstition loom large, tensions were already high, the society was tightly knit and bound by rigid religious and cultural beliefs. Rumours were already circulating in the village and even accusations against neighbours completely unfounded were washing around the village. Reverend Stubbs tried to calm the situation at his sermons and explained that accidents happen and there was no need of supernatural powers to cause a mind collapse, it happens all the time throughout the land.

The people of this village and indeed the whole parish were in no mood for compromise and the truth seemed to be irrelevant, this was not a natural event, some person caused this tragedy and some person must pay. Mrs Morris was busying herself around the village and at the entrance to the mine she placed a bunch of wild flowers on the ground and said a prayer. Another woman walked past and stopped, the two women looked at each other.

"How are you coping Mrs Morris?"

"Thank you for asking, I am doing as best I can under the circumstances but it is not easy!"

"No, I understand, it has been a trying couple of days for all of us, Thomas page has questions to answer, he is in charge of the mine and its workers!"

"You are quite right but I suspect something more afoot here, there is a curse on that mine!"

"A curse you say, Mrs Morris, you may be right but who would do such a thing?"

"There is evil on the loose in this village and more things will happen, mark my words!"

"That may well be but what can we poor folk do about it?"

"Well I do not know your mind but I am going to see Thomas page, will you back me?"

"Yes and so will the rest of the village but what can he do?"

"He can send a message to the sheriff in Durham and send someone to investigate."

Thomas page was approached about the matter but he refused to send word to Durham neither to the sheriff, the bishop or anyone else for that matter. He explained that the community should take care of its own business and bringing in outsiders would serve no purpose, or he did not want people to find out that the mine was not maintained properly! However, Mrs Morris was in determined mood and she arranged with a young man from the village to take a note to Durham.

Two days later a stranger entered the village, he was accompanied by a younger man who tied up the horses, he was directed to the office of Thomas Page.

"Mr Page are you the overseer of the mine?"

"Why yes sir and who might you be?"

"I am Daniel, Matthews, the sheriff sent me, I believe you have had some problems?"

"Who sent for you, we do not need help we can take care of ourselves, who sent you?"

"Calm down Mr Page, the sheriff of the county sent me, I am on official business!"

"I did no request any sort of assistance!"

"Well someone in this village did and I have an official warrant to search and or interview any person that I think necessary. He showed the warrant to Thomas Page.

"Very well, I suppose you have free will to do as you please, how can I help you?"

"I would like to start be examining and records or documents relating to the maintenance of the mine and any orders you were given about the safety of the workforce."

It had to be said that it was with some reluctance the Thomas Page provided the documents. Daniel Mathews and his assistant sifted through them for some time before speaking to Page.

"Mr Page you records on the maintenance and safety of the mine seem to be missing?"

"Oh I do not know where they are, they were there last I saw!"

Daniel and his assistant left the office knowing fine well that the records were not there as they had never been there. They went to the church and spoke to Reverend Stubbs who was much more agreeable and invited them into the small Chapple.

I am Daniel, Matthews, the sheriff sent me, you must be Reverend Stubbs?"

"Yes indeed I am, this whole area is my parish, it covers a lot of ground without many people, the villages are few and far between in these parts, are you here about the mine?"

"Yes reverend we are, how are the people taking it?"

"To be honest not very well, I think it happened because the mine was not safe."

"Yes we could not find any safety records in the overseer's office."

"I am not surprised, the less you spend on safety the more profit."

"What do the villagers think about it all apart from shock and sadness?

"Well Mr Mathews they are simple folk and once they get something in their heads it can be difficult to shift. Some understand that it was as simple accident but there is a large majority that think it must be something else."

"Oh, what else could it be reverend?"

"Evil Mr Mathews, witchcraft, dark magic, it's all the same, these people believe it!"

"Hmm, I have come across this sort of thing before, I think I will inspect the mine."

"Be careful down there Mr Mathews, it was not safe before and it is definitely not now!"

Daniel and his assistant made their way to the mine and began to inspect.

Daniel bent down, "Look here foot prints a lot of them there has been much activity here. Let us look at the entrance, here these channels were caused by water a lot of water, I wonder if there was a storm here before the collapse? It seems they tried to seal the entrance but stopped for some reason, look at the support beams, they are rotten, no wonder it collapsed."

"It seems as if this was a disaster that could have been avoided Daniel."

"Yes, this was natural, not supernatural there is no mystery here, let's go."

The men left to give themselves time to get back to Durham and report before darkness fell. Darkness was all encompassing in the village of Westgarth and the village fell quiet. A cold wind swept across the moors, winter was approaching rapidly and Thomas page was feeling the chill as it seeped under the door and rattled the small window. He was tired and went to his bed hoping to sleep through it all as the wind howled its cruel voice at the village.

He tried to sleep but it was not forth coming, his mind was racing with thoughts of the mine collapse, could he have done more, was it all his fault, would this be reported to the bishop? He did not quite know if he eventually fell asleep but there was a change in the room, dark shadows seemed to float around the place darker than the normal darkness. Noises came from corners, scratches, moans and sighs, harsh breaths clawed at his spirit, maybe there was a curse on this place.

His night was one of strange occurrences and as daylight seeped through the window he wondered if this was real of just a dream. He walked over to the corner where he had heard the noises and on the floor a pool of black liquid. It being like nothing he had seen before and it had the most revolting smell that stung his senses.

Later that day Mrs Morris came to his door and relayed the thoughts of the local people and demanded something be done. After the night he had witnessed he was now in agreement and accepted that there was something amiss here and that the presence of evil could get him off the hook. He sent a letter to the Bishop of Durham explaining the situation as he knew before too long the people would turn on each other.

CHAPTER 30

Eliza Swann was sitting on her bed when Gaia came in, she stood in the doorway.

"Eliza, you have an Aunt in Durham, you may want to visit her."

"Well yes Aunt Agnes, I have not visited for some time, why do you ask?"

"She could be in danger, you should go there now."

"What Aunt Agnes why would she be in danger, she never hurt anyone?"

"That is not for me to say Eliza but you should go!"

"Very well I will."

"I will arrange for you to be transported, one of our people will take you."

Eliza put some things in a bag and went outside to find a horse and cart waiting; she clambered aboard next to a man dressed in a black hooded cloak. The journey was not the most pleasant as the chill wind of autumn struck her skin with its biting tongue. The driver said nothing even when questioned the drive being even longer for the lack of dialogue. The cart entered the City of Durham and stopped, the man turned and motioned Eliza to step down, he turned the cart around and trotted off the way they had come.

Eliza made her way through the city and to the quiet little street; she knocked on her door, no answer. She knocked again, nothing, she tried the door and it opened with a scrape, she entered. She had just begun to look around when the door opened and one of the city guards walked in, he being in not too pleasant a mood confronted her.

"Hey, you are not allowed in here, who are you?"

"I am Eliza Swann and this house belongs to my Aunt Agnes, where is she?"

"I cannot tell you anything, you must leave now!"

"Oh I am sure we can come to some arrangement."

"Arrangement, what are you talking about?"

Eliza put a finger to her lips. "Let us see now, this is the house of my Aunt and I am worried about her. You let me look around for a minute or two and I will not report you to the captain of the guard, I am sure he would like to know how I was able to slip past you."

"Very well but be quick!"

Eliza began to look around, the place was a mess, the table turned over, stool on its side, a broken jug on the floor and further along blood spots. She went back to the guard who was by the door watching the street nervously.

"What happened here, where is my Aunt?"

"I cannot say Miss my orders are to remain quiet."

"Well at least tell me where she is?"

He leaned over with a hand to his face, "They took her to Saint Giles Church!"

"Thank you Sir and good day to you."

"Hey Miss do not forget our deal!"

"Fear not I will say nothing!"

Eliza made her way through the hustle and bustle of city life over the bridge at Old Elvet and along the long straight street to the east where at the end stood the old church of Saint Giles. She entered and unlike most churches that are havens of peace and tranquillity this was a hum of activity. People were moving around in every direction carrying jugs, linen and other items; it was a whir of activity. A man approached her dressed in religious clothing and it seemed that he had picked her out from the milling crown, he came near.

"Good day, I am Reverend Jones, you seem somewhat lost can I help you?"

"Well yes Reverend Jones, I am informed that my Aunt is here with you."

"We have an infirmary attached to the church, hence the activity, what is her name?"

"Agnes Swann."

"Yes I know of her, please come this way."

Eliza followed the reverend along a corridor away from the main infirmary and showed her into a side room, there lying on a bed was her Aunt Agnes, she was asleep or unconscious. Eliza looked at her; she had bruises on her arms as if she had been defending blows, her face was cut and scraped as if been beaten and dried blood mingled with her grey hair.

"She looks like she was attacked, what happened to her?"

"I do not know my dear, there is a man outside that could answer your questions."

The reverend led her back to the main vestibule where a small, stout man was sitting on a stool drinking from a cup, the reverend spoke to him and he came over.

"Good day Miss the reverend says that you are family to Agnes Swann, is that right?"

"Yes Sir I am her niece, what happened to her?"

"I am Daniel Mathews, I work for the sheriff, I have been given this case. I do not know exactly as you have seen your Aunt has not been able to speak to us. One of her neighbours found her early this morning, the house was ransacked and she has been badly beaten. We searched the house and found a purse of money and jewellery, if it had been a simple case of robbery why did the criminals not take these things?"

"I do not know!" Eliza replied, somewhat confused, why would they attack an old woman?

"That we do not know Miss but I can assure you we will not let this crime pass!"

Reverend Jones called her over and took her to one side. "You may stay here with your Aunt as long as you want, we do not have much food and drink but what we have is yours."

"Thank you so much reverend I would like to stay with her!"

Eliza did stay for a few days, her Aunt did not regain consciousness and her condition was becoming more worrying by the day. One morning Eliza was sitting in a chair half asleep when a sound jolted her awake.

"Eliza!"

"What, what, was that?"

"Eliza!"

She stood up and walked over to the bed, it was Aunt Agnes, eyes wide open but with a grey, unnatural mistiness to them, she moved closer and sat on the edge of the bed.

"Aunt, thank goodness you are awake, we were so worried, you are in the infirmary, can you remember what happened?"

"Yes dear I can remember every second, there was a bang on the door, I answered and was bundled inside by some brutes. They beat me and flung me around the room like a doll, they screamed at me in a wild eyed manner, it was terrifying, I thought they would kill me!"

"But why Aunt, what were they looking for?"

"They were looking for you Eliza!"

"Me Aunt, why would they want me?"

"I heard them mention someone called the witch finder, they are looking for you Eliza!"

"I do not understand Aunt Agnes, why me?"

"I do not know but I do know that you should leave now before they find you!"

"But what about you Aunt, I would stay with you here."

"No, I will be fine here and safe, you are not, go and go now without delay!"

Eliza left the room and walked back to the main foyer, Daniel Mathews was there. He assured her they would continue the investigation and was about to leave when she turned back. "Mr Mathews have you heard of the witch finder, my Aunt is awake and mentioned him."

"Yes he is a self-employed investigator he moves around the county searching for witches and making a handsome profit with his so called witch finding business."

Eliza left the church and walked back into town pondering the last few day's events when she heard a voice calling to her. "Miss Swann, Eliza Swann is that you?"

The turned to see Alfred Chase who held a small farmstead on the outskirts of Elersly, he would deliver goods to the city on most days.

"Mr Chase, is that you?"

"Yes my dear, what brings you to the city?"

"I have been visiting my Aunt; she has not been too well of late, now I must go home."

"Well you are in luck miss, I have delivered my goods and I am about to leave, jump up."

Eliza clambered onto the cart not quite believing her good fortune. It was getting dark by the time she reached Elersly, thanking Mr Chase she jumped down and skirted the village and up onto the moor and down into the ravine where she entered the cave. It had been a long and tiring day and she slumped onto the bed tired and confused at the day's events. There was a rustle in the doorway as Gaia entered and stood calmly at the side of the bed.

"What news of you Aunt Eliza, she fairs well I hope?"

"Yes she is much better; she was attacked by some men in her own home!"

"Yes I know of this!"

"But how do you know these things Gaia?"

"I cannot say Eliza, I just do!"

"My Aunt said the men were looking for me, why would they?"

"Because Eliza you are different and they fear what they do not know!"

"I was told that some witch finder was seeking me, who is this man, do you know?"

"Yes I gave knowledge of him his name is Isiah Blackwood and fear not he will know of us soon enough!"

CHAPTER 31

A week had passed and the village of Westgarth was not dealing well with the aftermath of the mine collapse. The community was nervous and uneasy, the normal life of the village disturbed and the people along with it. The villages were struggling to distinguish truth from lies, reality from fantasy, who could they trust and who not?

Thomas Page was in particular having a tough time as the people blamed him in some ways for the accident and he was keeping out of sight as much as possible. The morning was cold and crisp; an overnight frost was still clinging to the heather and gorse. The new mine shaft on the other side of the hill was progressing well but not yet open for work.

Reverend Stubbs was particularly busy trying to keep calm in these circumstances; he had visited the house of the young man killed in the collapse and was now at the door of Mrs Bowe. She let him in; the reverend observed she was not doing well by her tone.

"Mrs Bowe, how are you coping?"

"Coping Reverend Stubbs I am not coping at all, my family are shattered into pieces!"

"How are the girls fairing?"

"Not well Reverend Helen has been vomiting all night, she is now asleep. Emma has not been right for some time, she has episodes of panic and dreads and she worries me!"

Mrs Bowe hardly had time to finish her words when a scream came from the bedroom, piercing and shocking to the hearer, Mrs Bowe moved immediately to the room followed by Reverend Stubbs in quick fashion. Helen was sitting on the bed staring at Emma who was convulsing violently as if in some sort of seizure. Eyes white her stiff body was bouncing off the bed with such violence her mother screamed and tried to hold her down. The convulsions lasted a minute or so of utter terror before Emma seemed to calm herself lay flat and still.

"God be praised it is over!" Reverend Stubbs exclaimed hands clasped as if in prayer.

"My dear Lord, how can this be, is she is possessed by some demon!"

Reverend Stubbs leaned over the bed, "Listen she speaks, can you hear?"

Helen was still sitting on the bed in some sort of trance like state, Mrs Bowe listened.

"What is she saying, I cannot make it out, it sounds like a different language!"

Reverend Stubbs sat on the edge of the bed and put his ear close and listened carefully. Then like the sudden bang of a fire cracker Emma snapped forward sinking her teeth into Reverend Stubbs's right ear, the reverend screamed as much through shock as pain, that would come later. Emma held on tight sinking her nails into his neck, Mrs Bowe tried to loosen her grip but she struggled violently making growling noises as if a wolf had a sheep.

It was a minute or so before Emma collapsed back onto the bed still and silent, blood on her lips. Reverend Stubbs jumped up from the bed clutching his face; Mrs Bowe took him out of the room and cleaned the wound on his ear, he sat there in something of a daze.

"Is the wound serious?"

"No not too bad, you have a cut on your ear and it has bled some but it will heal well."

"What happened in there Mrs Bowe, is she insane?"

"I cannot tell you, she has not been right for some time but she has never attacked anyone!"

"Except for me, a man of the cloth, a religious man, does that tell you something?"

"Tell me, tell me what?"

"Who would attack a clergyman, someone who hates God, who is scared of his power and judgement? I believe she is possessed of evil, the Devil has a grip on here, we must pray!"

After a while they could hear words coming from the bed room, the entered. Emma was lying there talking aloud clearly and with purpose repeating the some words over and over.

Her mother listened shaking, her head, "I do not understand, is it a different language?"

Reverend Stubbs bent over the bed being careful not to get too close and listened.

"Mrs Bowe I know this language."

"You do, what is it?"

"It is Latin!"

"Latin, how could Emma know Latin?"

"I do not know Mrs Bowe but that is one of the signs of demonic possession!"

"No this cannot be true!"

"I am afraid it is true, when I was training to be a cleric I studied Latin, that was some time past and it is not fresh in my mind but I think I know some of it."

"So what is she saying Reverend Stubbs, what does it mean?"

"It is a bit fractured but she keeps mentioning the old woman on the hill."

Reverend Stubbs left the house and went back to his church holding his face. The rest of the day passed with relative calmness and as night grew older he took to his bed. He did not sleep well however, as his mind was troubled by the strange events of the day and the dull throbbing soreness of his ear did not aid restfulness. The next morning came with a chill wind sweeping over hill and dale, nature had decided to show how unpleasant she could be.

It was into this scene that a tall man on horseback arrived in the village followed by two other men on a cart with an iron cage fitted to the back, he dismounted. The tall man, being somewhat better dressed than the locals was causing some interest with his knee length boots, long leather coat and expensive looking hat, he stopped a young man.

"You there young man I seek Thomas Page?"

The young man pointed and arm towards a house but said nothing, the man approached and rapped on the door, it was opened with some caution by Page in an uneasy manner.

"Thomas Page I assume?"

"Well yes I am Thomas Page, who are you Sir?"

"My name is Isiah Blackwood I have been employed by the Bishop of Durham."

"Oh, for what purpose?"

"I have been informed that you have a problem here, a case of dark magic, is that right?"

"Well, there have been some strange events here lately, go and see Reverend Stubbs."

Blackwood left and walked around to the church, the door was open and he entered.

Reverend Stubbs, good day Sir, I am Isiah Blackwood."

"Oh did the bishop send you?"

"Yes I have been employed to rid this place of evil, tell me what happened?"

"It all started when we had an accident in the mine, three people were killed in the collapse, the village and its people have not been the same since."

"In what way Reverend Stubbs?"

"Thomas page told me he had some strange events in his house but the main problems have been with a family in the village. Mrs Bowe lost her husband and his brother; they have not been recovered as yet and probably won't be. Her two daughters have taken the loss of their father rather badly, it could be the effects of grief but they have been acting oddly."

"In what was reverend, can you explain?"

"I visited them one day and say the daughter Emma in some state of seizure; she bounced around on the bed for a good while before she settled down. She then began to speak in tongues, her mother could not understand these words, I listened closely and realised the words were in fact Latin, she had no education in Latin as I have."

"I see, Reverend Stubbs, you know what this means don't you?"

"Yes I am afraid to say I do, it seems like some form of Demonic possession!"

"You are correct, we must tackle this at once, where is their house?"

Isiah Blackwood made his way to the Bowe house and spoke to the mother.

"Good day Mrs Bowe, I am Isiah Blackwood, I have just spoken to Reverend Stubbs, he tells me you have had trouble with your daughters, please explain?"

"Well I do not know you Mr Blackwood you could be anyone!"

Isiah Blackwood pulled a note from his pocket and showed it to Mrs Bowe.

"Oh I see, it's from the bishop no less!"

"Mrs Bowe please tell me what you know, you and your daughters could be in great danger, we must stop this before it gets worse or who knows the outcome!"

"Did the reverend tell you about my husband?"

"Yes he did, a terrible event!"

"It started after that my girls began to act in a weird manner unlike their normal selves. Helen was found wandering on the moor barely dressed and freezing by a man from the village. Emma has been suffering with convulsions the like I have never seen and speaking a foreign language, it is not normal, the reverend thinks it could be an evil force!"

"Unfortunately so do I, did the reverend know what Emma said?"

"He said it was Latin and mentioned an old woman on a hill!"

"Thank you Mrs Bowe, I must continue my investigation!"

Isiah Blackwood left the house and began to mingle with the local residents of the village. He asked many question as to who could be the old woman on the hill and was surprised to hear the same answer from all of them, Margret Hodge! They were also quick to point out where her house was up on a hill overlooking the village. Isiah Blackwood gathered his assistants and went up the hill and found the cottage easily enough as it was the only one there.

They did not bother knocking on the door; they just barged in to find Margret Hodge asleep on the bed. She woke with a jolt and began to shout at the men in an uncouth manner.

"Who the hell are you lot bursting into an old woman's home? Get out you ruffians!"

"Margret Hodge?"

"What who are you how do you know my name?"

"My name is Isiah Blackwood, I have been sent by the Bishop of Durham to root out evil from this village, and evil I think you know well enough Margret Hodge!"

Margret Hodge jumped from the bed with surprising agility for someone of her advanced years and ran screaming at Blackwood, she did not get to him as his two assistants grabbed her in full flight and restrained her roughly.

Isiah Blackwood looked down on the woman who was being bound by the hands.

"Well Margret Hodge, you have much strength for an old woman where does that come from, some hidden power I expect, evil power, take her away gentlemen!"

Margret Hodge was manhandled down the hill and into the village where she was shoved into the iron cage on the back of the cart. She was no happier than before and screamed holy hell, cursing and swearing with it seemed taking a breath. The commotion attracted the people of the village who as Margret Hodge found out were not too unhappy at the sight of the old hag on the hill being locked up and returned some of her bitterness."

"Where are you taking her Sir?" A woman inquired of Blackwood.

"She will be charged with witchcraft, we are transporting her to Durham for trial."

A gasp wen around the village as the news filtered through and a cheer filled the air as the cart trundled off towards the city, Black wood following on his horse. It took a while to reach Durham and when they did Margret Hodge was pulled from the cage and thrown into a damp, filthy cell at the old goal near Elvet. As the iron door was slammed she looked around and began the understand the dire situation she was in. it was late afternoon and what little natural light there was began to fade into another night. The shouts of other prisoners and the screams of the tortured echoed off the cold stone, lost souls in the darkness!

The next morning she was dragged, still shouting her innocence in front of district judge Milford Lord at the Court of Session. He assessed her with some interest as she stood in front of him, struggling with the guard on either arm.

"Margret Hodge of the village of Westgarth you are here charged with witchcraft and of other and numerous dark magic, how do you plead?"

"I need not answer to you, I am an old woman tired and bent and I have an old woman's ways that some people do not like, I have lived a long time and I will be damned if I will bow down to you or any other person, here or anywhere else!"

The judge turned to Isiah Blackwood, "Have you any witnesses to present?"

"Yes I have, bring out the witnesses!"

His assistant showed two young girls into the room, they stood still and faced the judge.

"Who are these two girls Mr Blackwood?"

"They are Helen and Emma Bowe, we believe they were possessed by this woman!"

"You are referring to Margret Hodge?"

"Yes sir!"

The judge turned to the two girls, "Do you recognise this woman, say her name?"

"Margret Hodge!" They both said in unison.

"Do you think this is the woman who bewitched you?"

"Yes it was her!"

The judge turned to Blackwood, "Has she been examined?"

"Yes sir, we found several marks of the Devil about her person that cannot be explained."

"Very well Margret Hodge, I find you guilty of bewitchment of these two girls and of practicing the dark arts on the people of your village, you may take her away!"

Margret Hodge was taken back to her cell and as the door locked behind her she fell into a corner and waited. Two days past before the dreaded time when the door opened and she was taken out and loaded onto a cart. She was then paraded through the streets of Durham City to a place north of there called Dryburn. It was here that the common criminals of this county met their end, it had been this way for centuries. Here Margret Hodge took her last breath, at the end of a stiff rope, along with Alan Stott, a murderer.

They were buried in unmarked graves in the grounds of Dryburn as were so many others.

CHAPTER 32

Eliza Swann decided to return to Durham and see her Aunt Agnes; she knew fine well that this action was a risk as she knew the authorities were looking after her. She arrived in the city and pulled a hood over her head in an attempt to stay in secret, she made her way through the bustle to her aunt's house. She tried the door and it opened, she entered and found her aunt sitting next to the fire, she turned in surprise at the interruption. Aunt Agnes was both delighted and afraid at the coming of her niece and welcomed her warmly.

"Eliza my dear what are you doing here, you know it's not safe?"

"I wanted to see if you were alright Aunt, have you had anymore visits?"

"No, not as yet, that does not mean they will not come!"

"I won't stay long; I just wanted to see how you were."

"I am fine now, the physicians at the church infirmary patched me up well."

"Good, I must admit you are in a much better condition than the last time I saw you. Aunt Agnes can I ask you something, where is my mother?"

"Dear, dear Eliza I wish I knew where she was but I do not, what I do know is there is something going on here that I do not understand and you are in danger, be careful!"

Eliza stayed the night and they both decided that that was enough; she need not chance her hand further and set off back north, there being no carts heading that way, she decided to walk the ten miles to Elersly, she had done this many times before, even though she was somewhat older now she was confident of making it in a few hours. The day was cold but quite pleasant to walk as she paced up the main road to Newcastle. She was approaching her home village of Elersly and seceded with some wisdom to bypass it and go the long way around to her new home in that cave in that ravine.

She walked up onto the moor and to Blackwater Lake, she stopped and gazed into the water, it was calm and mirror like. She looked at her reflection and reflected on her life, her past life and her future. What lay ahead for her in her new life, she pondered at what she had become? She dropped down into the tree line on her way to the cave, she was but a few minutes' walk away when she heard a noise in the trees; she stopped and looked around but could see nothing through the trees.

She carried on a little further along the road and could hear the sound of the village through the trees and smell the fires and smoke rising. It was then that it happened, the trees parted and several men rushed out of the undergrowth. Eliza was shocked into stillness and silence, not expecting this and was unable to react by running away. The speed of the ambush was stunning and Eliza was grabbed by several strong arms, pushed to the ground and her hands tied tightly.

"What is this, who are you people, what do you want with me?"

She was marched to a cart with an iron cage on the back and pushed inside and the door locked. A tall man walked around the back and stood gazing at her intently'

"Who are you, what do you want of me?"

"Ah, Eliza Swann I do believe, we have missed each other so many times but alas in your case it ends badly, your evil ways come to an end right now, you belong to me now, enjoy your ride it is a nice day for a journey, hopefully it will be your last, Haaa!"

The ride south was not the most pleasant for Eliza as the road was full of bumps and holes; she clung to the bars tightly, it did not help that the cart was traveling far too fast for the conditions. Round a tight corner just outside of Elersly a famer was herding some sheep, the cart being so rapid did not have time to react as it scattered sheep in all directions. The farmer was livid as he tried to regroup his animals; the cart driver glanced behind but said nothing. Isiah Blackwood following behind on his horse did utter a response.

"Get off the road you old fool!"

The party entered the City of Durham much to the disbelief of Eliza who had only left this place a few hours earlier in the day. The cart pulled up outside of the Old Goal at Elvet and she was pulled from the cage and marched inside, where she was pushed forcibly into a cell.

The two men left immediately and she was alone for some time to think on her situation. What had just happened, why was she here, who were these people? These thoughts tumbled through her mind like pebbles in a stream, catching a glimpse here and there but never the answer. Sometime later there was activity outside in the corridor, a small flap near the bottom of the iron cell door opened and a hand could be seen. A clunk as a beaker was placed on the floor along with a lump of stale bread, the flat clanged shut.

Eliza jumped up and ran to the door. "Wait why am I hear, speak to me please?"

"Now now miss eat your food, we do not want you to go hungry, do we!"

Laughter could be heard from the corridor as the guards chuckled to themselves.

"Let me out, I do not belong here, let me out now!"

"Be quiet miss and make yourself at home and do not complain, we do not like that here!"

A couple of days past and Eliza was left in her filthy, dejected misery, left to rot but for what purpose, was it to kill her spirit or make her so distressed she would admit anything? The sharp scrape of an iron bolt jerked her from her desperation as her life was about to become worse. She was grabbed by either arm and marched down the dimly lit corridor into another room.

Some men stood in the shadows as she was placed on a chair, hands tied tightly behind. One man came forward and grabbed her face with a meaty hand and gripped tightly. Another man came forward and pulled his hand away with a look of annoyance.

"Do not touch her face you fool, we do not want her bruised when she meets the judge!"

Eliza tried to struggle but the ropes were too tight and she soon realised she could do nothing but sit there and hope the next few minutes were not as bad as she expected. A pair of hands from behind grasped her bodice and ripped it open, pulling it back to reveal her naked skin. Another man came forward, the same tall man she had seen earlier, he came close with a lamp in one hand and illuminated her face. He them moved the lamp over her body inspecting closely, what she did not know, he turned to another man.

"Look here; what do you make of that?"

The other man looked closely, "I would say that is not a natural mole, it is unusual to say the least, I would say it was a Devil's mark, no doubt!"

The tall man picked up something from a table, a small metal device and came close, he placed the instrument on her skin, she could feel the cold metal and flinched.

He then stood back and nodded to the others in the room. "It is as I thought, I pricked the withes mark and it did not bleed, she is the one we have been seeking, there is no doubt!"

Eliza, to her great relief was untied and taken back to the cell, redressing herself as the door slammed shut. She spent the night in her cold, damp cell, thinking of what might have been as she lay on her piece of straw in the darkness. Next morning came as the thin shaft of sunlight pierced the cell she awoke once more into a world of uncertainty and anxiety, feelings she was by now acquainted with. The door opened and once again she was manhandled out of the cell and marched along the corridor, in the other direction this time, up some steps and into another room.

There sitting at the front was a large rotund man, long grey hair dangling about his shoulders, he had obviously seen many summers, she was stood in front of him.

"Your name?"

"I will not tell my name as I have done no wrong!"

"Her name is Eliza Swann, from the village of Elersly Sir."

"Thank you Mr Blackwood, now madam, you know why you are here before me?"

"No Sir, I do not of what am I accused?"

"Witchcraft, Miss Swann, the practicing of the Devil's work, how do you plead?"

"I admit to nothing, I have done no wrong!"

"That is no defence Miss Swann, what evidence do you have Mr Blackwood?"

"She has been examined and we found several unnatural marks about her body, they did not bleed when pricked with a metallic spike. Furthermore there has been much bad news in and around the county, particularly in the village of Elersly, the place where she was born and bred. I have evidence that there is a secret society at work here, conjuring evil about the land and she is a part of that evil horde."

"It seems to me Miss Swann that you and your cohorts have been allowed to spread your foul stain for far too long, the people of this county have suffered enough, I find you guilty!"

"Very well it seems my fate is sealed, I declare that I Eliza Swann of the village of Elersly in this county am indeed a witch and have invoked dark magic upon the land."

She then pointed at the judge and Blackwood, I have from this time laid curses on al present here, this I decree you and all you hold dear be cursed for ever more!"

There was an audable gasp from the people in the room as they looked at each other. Eliza had no time to protest further as she was whisked away as Judge Milton Lord bowed his head quietly. He like all those involved knew the outcome of the trial before it even started! Eliza was taken back to her cell to wait and wonder what would become of her. She sat down on the straw and looked up to see the tall man in the doorway, smiling.

"You Isiah Blackwood are a liar and a fraud, how much will you earn from this one?"

"Oh enough to keep me going I expect, I have chased you from one corner of this county to another, almost catching you but now I have you in my grasp, the witch of Elersly!"

"What will happen to me now, will I be hanged like a common criminal?"

"Oh no, Miss Swann, we have a much more painful end planed for you!"

"What is that, I will be dead at the end of it, whichever way?"

"No, hanging is far too good for such as you, you will be burned and you will suffer!"

Eliza, not knowing her fate paced around her cell contemplating her end, she did that most of the night until exhausted she fell into a corner and fell asleep. Two guards were posted one on the main entrance and one outside of the cell, there not being a need for anymore as the prisoners had no way of escape from this hell hole!

It was by now two o'clock on a cold autumn morning, the guard outside was pacing back and forth in an attempt to keep warm. Nestled in a dark corner a man stood still and silent watching and as the guard turned his back he pounced on him. A steel blade stabbed into his neck in a second of severe violence, as the guard fell into his arms and was dragged into the shadows, blood pouring from a fatal wound. The man dressed in all black stood up and gestured to his companion to follow. The two men made their way through the main door and down the steps, crouching low in the shadowy underground world they crept along the corridor toward the cell.

The guard was sitting on a stool outside of the cell, nodding half asleep the two men hid behind a wall, one of them came forward into the light and whistled a shrill note. The guard jumped in shock and stood up looking around, then he saw someone standing in the corridor.

"Hey, you're not supposed to be in here, who are you?"

The guard paced forward with a pike in hand. "Stand right there do not move!"

The man held up his hands as the guard drew closer, it was then the second man stepped out of the shadows and grabbed the guard from behind around the nose and mouth as the first man stabbed him twice in the chest. He fell to the floor with a crump and was dead within seconds. The guard was turned over and his keys collected, they immediately opened the cell door, the noise awoke Eliza in something of a panic.

"Shush, quiet now Eliza, we are here to help follow us!"

They crept along the corridor and up the steps and just around the corner two horses waited patiently, the men mounted the horses and pulled Eliza up behind one.

"Where are we going?" She asked somewhat shaken.

"You are going home Miss, hold on!"

She did just that as the horses raced through the dark, quiet city streets and out through the north gate, past the killing fields of Dryburn and the sleeping village of Elersly to the ravine. Eliza dismounted and went straight to her room where she collapsed with exhaustion and relief in equal measure. She did not have time to rest however, as someone entered, it was Gaia watching her from the doorway.

Gaia what is going on one minute I am expecting to be burned and now I am back here?"

"Well we could not let them do that Eliza, not to one of our own."

"But how did you know I had been kidnapped and where I was?"

"We have our ways; it was obvious who snatched you and where you would be held. We have contacts who are trained in the ways of stealth and disguise, they are the hidden people, they are always ready if need be."

"It is cold in here!"

"Ha, you would have soon been warmed in a few days, they have erected a platform on Palace Green and built a pyre upon it ready for the big day which will now not come!"

"I see, they will be disappointed then!"

"Yes indeed Eliza, maybe they can burn some old woman instead!"

CHAPTER 33

Later that day at about seven in the morning two more guards were sent to relive those on duty overnight. They approached the main entrance and paused wondering why it was unmanned, they searched around pondering where he could be when one of them cried out.

"Here over here!"

The other man ran over and found the guard lying in a corner, a pool of blood collecting around him. They decided to go and investigate inside with some caution they entered the main door and down the steps. Along the corridor they tiptoed and as they approached the cell they saw the other guard lying in a heap on the cold stone floor, dead!

One of the men ran to inform his captain and his captain ran to see the sheriff. The place was then swamped with guards who were running around in an alarm, while the other prisoners shouted through the bars of their cells adding to the confusion. Daniel Mathews was at the jail and heard the commotion; he walked into the dungeon and inquired what the uproar was about. He was shocked when he was told and inquired just how it could have happened.

He decided to go to the interrogation room while people were busy with other matters, he had wanted to see what this room contained but was never allowed in. He entered and began to look around; several instruments were obvious to see. A chair with leather arm straps, on the far wall, chains and manacles and in one corner a rack with ropes and handles. He looked further and discovered something that he had heard about but never seen. The Scavenger's Daughter was designed to compress the victim's body into a compact position by using a metal hoop or frame with a central hinge. When the hinge was tightened, spikes or points attached to the inside of the hoop would dig into the victim's flesh, causing intense pain and discomfort.

He looked further and on a table he found thumb screws and a small metal device, he picked it up and examined it closely. It was fairly small with a sharp point at one end and had some sort of button on the top, he pressed it and the pointed end shot back inside of the casing. He then under stood what it was, the same instrument that was used by Isiah Blackwood and his men to convict witches by not drawing blood when they were pricked. He placed it into his pouch and left before he was discovered.

The jail was still in something of a commotion as he left, he had visited the prison many times before except for the interrogation room, so the guards did not question him. Daniel Mathews had long since questioned the authenticity of Isiah Blackwood, the so called witch hunter and now he had proof, he went without delay to the office of the sheriff.

On the way up the street he heard a whistle; he stopped and saw a man waving at him from an alleyway. Daniel was hesitant to enter the alley as he could not be sure that he would not be attacked and robbed but curiosity outweighed his doubt and he entered. A man was there looking around in a nervous fashion, "Come this way Shush quiet now!"

Daniel followed him along the alley to a backyard where he stood seemingly uneasy.

"Who are you, what d0 you want with me?" Daniel inquired a little concerned.

"You are Daniel Mathews are you not Sir?"

"Well yes I am he, what is this?"

"Sorry for the secrecy but I know you work for the sheriff, I work in the Court of Session as a caretaker. Something has been troubling me for some time and I must tell of it, that man Isiah Blackwood is a fake, he catches so called witches for profit and he makes a fine living from it. My conscience is calling to me Mr Mathews!"

"I see, well I must say I have had my suspicions for some time, I thank you for this!"

"That is not all of it, the judge, Milford Lord, I believe he is also involved, he is being paid by Blackwood to convict these people so he can claim the reward and no one is innocent!"

"I appreciate your honesty; I am on my way to see the sheriff right now."

"Please Mr Mathews do not say where you got this information or I too will next!"

"Do not worry yourself I will say nothing of our meeting, good day!"

Daniel Mathews left the alley and walked up the street to the sheriff's office, he entered the building and went straight to his office, he walked in, the sheriff was sitting at his desk.

"Ah Daniel come in, have a seat, how are you progressing with your investigations?"

"Well sheriff I have been side tracked by some other business."

"Oh how so?"

"I have mentioned before that man Isiah Blackwood and how I thought that he was involved in dubious practices, I have been informed by someone close that my suspicions were well founded. The man is a fraud and a charlatan; he is making money on the lives of innocent people, people who are guiltless of any crime save for being old or offensive."

The sheriff interrupted, "How do you know all of the Daniel, what evidence have you?"

"I have been informed that he, Blackwood is paying Judge Milton Lord a cut of his profit in return for guilty verdicts; I also found this in the interrogation room."

"Daniel, you know that place is off limits to all but a few, you should not be in there."

"I know forgive me sheriff but it was worth it as I have proof."

"Proof, what manner of proof do you have?"

Daniel placed the metal device on the desk; the sheriff picked it up and examined it.

"That is what Isiah Blackwood uses to prick his victims to see if they bleed, notice how the spike retracts when the button is pressed, no wonder they do not bleed!"

"Yes I see, thank you for bringing this to my attention Daniel, I will make further inquiries but say nothing of this for now, we do not want undue attention making our task difficult!"

"Yes sheriff, I understand."

Isiah Blackwood pleased with his latest work had given his assistants the night off and they were busy taking in the sights and sounds of the city, mainly the numerous taverns. Blackwood made his way through the streets and into Dun Cow Lane. This street being one of the oldest in Durham and being directly to the east of Durham Cathedral, it took its name from a depiction of the city's founding, etched in the masonry on the south side of the cathedral which depicts the original milk maid and her Dun Cow.

It wasn't long before he arrived at the place he was staying, The Dun Cow Inn Old Elvet. A traditional half-timbered building, black wood and white washed plaster giving a different appearance to the rest of the street. He entered through a narrow passage to the side and entered the Inn. There were but a few patrons drinking and joking as he entered and a pleasing fire lit up the grate. The conversation ceased as he entered as the local people recognised him instantly and knew the tall man well enough.

Isiah Blackwood took a seat in one of the corners and was brought a flagon of ale. He pondered at what a suitable place it was to stay as the executioner of the city would visit here for a fortifying drink before he did his duty. The executioner was well paid for his services but often increased his payment by selling souvenirs, such as pieces of the rope used for the execution which were widely regarded as lucky charms. This was a practise that had been carried forward for centauries when body parts from a hanged man or woman fetched a high price as ingredients in black magic spells.

It would be fair to say that Isiah Blackwood had a fine time in the Dun Cow and after several rounds of ale he was feeling somewhat well-oiled. A short time later the effects of such merriment came back to bite him as the past days of persecuting people caught up, he fell back against the wall and fell asleep.

The bartender looked at him with some distain at this man in the corner comatose.

"I hope he wakes up, I don't fancy carrying him upstairs look at the size of him!"

Another man spoke, "Aw just leave him, the man cannot handle his drink!"

Sometime later the other people in the Inn were thinking of heading home when the door burst open and three men entered, masks covering their faces, they drew their swords and told the customers to stand against the back wall and say nothing, they, surprised did just that! Two of the men walked over to the side wall and grabbing Isiah Blackwood by both arms dragged him outside and into a waiting coach.

One of the men turned to the patrons, "Sorry to disturb you gentlemen, please carry on!"

With those words he was gone, gone into the night leaving only questions. Isiah Blackwood was bundled into the waiting carriage still half asleep and they set off at affair pace. The crunch of dead leaves in their frosted forms and the crack of icing puddles accompanied the carriage on that desperate journey, iron rimmed the wheels, and iron willed the driver. He persuaded the two black horses with a whip cracked wrist, nostrils flared as they sliced the autumn air, black as the night, malevolent as their journey. Darkly dressed, the driver, cap pulled low over his brow, and scarf pulled high leaving only his eyes to reveal his evil intent.

The narrow country lanes to the north west of Durham echoed to the sound and the rush of spinning wheels, alarming owl and deer and roosting crow as it swished through the thick and tangled blackness. of Hampston Forest down into the deep, steep Leam Valley. Sturdy wooden gates open and waiting for the cargo of the night as the coach flashed under the high stone archway and along the road through the avenue of tall trees to a collection of out buildings where it stopped.

The man stepped down from the carriage and rapped twice with his cane on the small but stout door and it opened with a groan and scrape. He snapped his fingers a few times, a signal, a sign of admission of authorization into this place of soulful seclusion. His subordinates obeyed, bundling out their prize, their precious prize and with a secure grasp, marched him down a long and constricted passage deep underground. The passage emerged into a sort of underground court yard, dimly lit by unreliable wall lamps, other passages disappeared in different directions into the darkness and here and there heavy iron doors still and solid. The man stood expressionless as the party emerged from the tunnel, he observed them with unfeeling gaze as he tapped his cane on the dirt.

Isiah Blackwood was thrown into a cell and left to sober up, when he did come to his senses he looked around at his surroundings not even sure if he was fully awake. He was greeted by sight of pure despair, what happened why was he here in this place? Four walls of coarse stone enclosed the cold stone floor, no windows, no light except for a small oil lamp on the left side wall; it was dark, damp and held a distinctive earthy scent.

After a while he became aware of the array of sounds, his only companions in his lonely state, drips, creaks and taps, things moved in the corners of her eyes, in the shadowy places. Defiance quickly changed to fear and dread as reality came calling, he was cold and lost in desperation, no help for him, and no rescue here in his dungeon of despair, he was lost!

CHAPTER 34

The sheriff of Durham was in a state of blinding anger when the news was broken that Isiah Blackwood had disappeared, apparently kidnapped, he demanded to know why Blackwood had not been watched and his movements recorded. He was expecting things to improve as the evil element had been removed from the county, from whatever source it came. Reports had been coming in from various parts of the county, Elersly was quiet, Greenslade was no longer troubled by outside forces and even the mining village of Westgarth way up in the hills had returned to some sort of normality. Mrs Bowe and her two daughters were back to being a mother and her two young girls who had gone from convulsing to settled and normal.

Eliza was sitting in her room in the dark cold cave that was now her home, she wondered just why she ended up here and was basically bored of sitting around. She decided as was often the case to set out and walk up onto the moor. It was cold out but it was also cold in the cave, she set off, the sky had not brightened so far this day with heavy dark clouds obscuring the hills in the distance. She did not care as she walked for a while before sitting on her favourite rock for some time until her legs began to freeze.

Leaving the moor she was drawn to another direction, she had an uncontrolled feeling to visit her home village, not knowing why she felt this way, was it nostalgia or madness? She slipped down the slope and into Elersly, pulling a hood over her head she went to her old house and found it boarded up in a crude fashion with planks of rough sawn wood. On the door was a sign she recognised, a guard, a protection against witches and other evil forces. She continued into the village past Saint Andrew's Church, she stopped and watched, as the realisation dawned at why she felt so uncomfortable being in there.

Why did the people have such faith in such Gods and saviours, what had God done for them apart from abject poverty and misery of their very basic form of humanity, what indeed? She carried on for some time not being recognised by the local people who were oblivious to her presence and hopefully they would not realise who was walking among them. She waited a while before returning to the cave and into her room, she was not there very long when Gaia entered.

"You have been missing for some time Eliza?

"Yes I went for a walk."

"You must rest now, we have an important ceremony tonight, we must prepare ourselves."

"What ceremony Gaia, what is this one for?"

"Tonight is the last day of October, it is the festival of Samhain, the end of Summer and is the third and final Harvest, the dark, winter half of the year commences on this Sabbat."

"Samhain, what is that what does it mean?"

It has other Names, you may have heard, November Eve, Feast of the Dead, Feast of Apples, Hollow's Eve, All Hollow's Eve, they are all the same, you will learn all of this."

"I do not understand Gaia, what does it all mean?"

"It is the biggest festival of the year, Samhain is a time to remember those who have passed on, celebrate the summers end and prepare for the winter months ahead. The Sun God and earth fall into slumber, as the nights lengthen and winter begins, you must rest now."

Eliza did just that and lying back on her bed she pondered at what was to come. Sometime later, how much later she did not know but it was now dark outside, she roused herself. Gaia entered the room dressed in a black robe with red symbols stitched into it, she passed another to Eliza and told her to put it on and meet in the main hall. Eliza dressed herself and made her way to what was called the great of wisdom where she saw a fire burning bright in the centre of the room and around the outside several figures, dressed the same, Gaia was there.

"Eliza come forward."

Eliza walked into the centre of the circle as Gaia spread her arms wide, "Welcome Eliza!"

Another figure stepped forward; she seemed older and was probably an elder, she stood still and silent. Eliza recognised this woman; she stood there tall with her flowing silver hair and piercing blue eyes. This was Morgana, the leader of the coven, she was a sorceress of unparalleled power and wisdom, she commanded respect and reverence from all who knew her.

"Eliza Swann, we have met but once, I am Morgana, tonight we celebrate Samhain!"

The assembled people chanted something in unison before Morgana continued.

"It is a time to study the Dark Mysteries and honour the Dark Mother and the Dark Father, symbolized by the Crone and her aged Consort. Tradition also teaches that the aid of spirits and guides from the other world are easily enlisted at this time, so in the increasing moonlight of longer nights, we use this time to hone our psychic and divinatory skills"

Again a chant echoed around the cave, morgana beckoned to Eliza to come closer.

"It is time Eliza Swann to know the truth of life and the turning of the ages."

A figure stepped from the shadows, "I am Jane Frizzel and I am a witch!"

She stepped back into the shadows and another stepped into her place.

"I am Isabella Mosswood and I am a witch!"

Several others came forward and proclaimed the same and then another stood before her.

"I am Mary Swann and I am a witch!"

Eliza screamed at the sight of this woman, "Mother!"

"Yes Eliza dear daughter it is me you see before you, I did not want to leave you but my life was in danger, I had no choice. On a stormy night way back in the mists of time I gave birth to twin girls, one was left to grow with me and the other was taken away."

Gaia stepped forward, "Yes Eliza it is true, I am your twin sister, welcome to your family!"

Eliza was stunned at this news and after all of this time things were beginning to fall into place even though it was still something of a shock at these revelations. Morgana stepped forward and held Eliza by the hands holding them for a while.

"Eliza Swann, we will all fall victim to the fates of time and age and there will come a time when it will fall to you to keep this culture alive, it's various forms, its rituals and enchantments, you are the last of our kind, the last true witch of Durham!"

Although Eliza had always known that she was not like other people, she always knew she was different but did not know why, now she did. She did not have much time to ponder her situation as the group left the cave and set off across the moonlit moor a procession of dark figures, torches flickering in the chill breeze. They walked for some time; the moor was a sprawling expanse of rugged terrain, dotted with patches of heather, bracken, and gorse. The landscape was both stark and beautiful, rolling hills that stretched endlessly under the wide, open sky. In the distance, the outline of distant hills framed the horizon, their peaks shrouded in mist and low-hanging clouds.

Eventually they reached a place called Cross Fell and an ancient stone circle known as Hermit Henge. The stone circle, situated on a slight rise, commanded a panoramic view of the surrounding moorland, giving it an almost sacred prominence. A persistent wind swept across the moor, rustling the vegetation and carrying with it the faint, haunting echoes of the past and the air was crisp and filled with the scent of damp earth.

The ancient stone circle stood proudly on the wild, untamed moor, a testament to the mysteries of a bygone era. Composed of large, weathered stones, each one uniquely shaped and timeworn, the circle exuded an aura of ancient power and forgotten rituals. The stones, varying in height and girth, formed a rough yet mesmerizingly symmetrical ring. Lichens and mosses clung to their surfaces, adding a splash of green and grey to the earthy tones of the stones. Eliza had not been here before but had heard of it through tales and legends. Despite the harshness of the moor, the stone circle seemed to be a place of profound tranquillity and timelessness, inviting contemplation and reverence from those who ventured to this remote and mystical site.

In the centre of the henge a fire was burning, flames licking the sky with orange and yellow streaks. The atmosphere around the circle was charged with an eerie stillness, as if time itself had paused to honour the ancient monument. Standing within the circle, she could almost hear the whispers of long-gone voices, sense the rhythmic pounding of ceremonial drums, and feel the presence of the ancients who once gathered here for rituals some now thought lost to history and the Pagan past of long ago, this was not true, they were not lost!

They formed a circle around the edge of the henge and in the centre was Morgana who was chanting something in a language unknown to Eliza. Morgana walked away and was replaced by another, this was plainly a male figure dressed in a red cloak and a black mask obscuring his features, he stepped forward and in a deep, resounding voice he spoke.

"Bring him forth."

The men appeared with another man who was bound and blindfolded, the marched him to a large upright stone and tied his hands behind. The man in red approached and removed the blindfold revealing his face in the firelight, tied tightly, unable to struggle he stood there.

Eliza was standing next to her mother, "Mother, look it's Isiah Blackwood, the witch hunter!"

"Shus Eliza!" Her mother said in a whisper. "Who is the man in red mother?"

"He is Malachar, the supreme leader of the Coven of the Silver Moon."

The man in red in red stared at him intently for some time before he turned to the crowd.

"You Isiah Blackwood have disturbed our peace for long enough, now we will disturb yours, look yonder and witness the corruptions of your life, look there!"

From behind the stones there formed a line of dark shadows, human inform but without any human features more like a vaporous haze they walked through the circle and passed Isiah Blackwood in a procession of deathly silence, he struggled and protested, "What is this?"

The man in red spoke, "Look well Isiah Blackwood, these are the people you have killed, a parade of dead souls, innocent souls that you will meet again, in another world!"

Malachar took a large ceremonial dagger from his cloak and stabbed Blackwood with one firm and fast blow to the throat. The blood immediately spurted out in a flow of deep red as Blackwood slumped his head forward groaning in his final moments as his life slipped away. malachar held the bloody dagger aloft for a time showing it to all.

"Oh mighty Lord of the Dark, we walk in the shadows to worship you, please accept this man as a token of our devotion and thus we prevail as we always prevail!"

The body of Isiah Blackwood was taken down and thrown onto the bonfire where it crackled and melted like a hog on a spit. Next morning in the ancient Henge was bright and clear except for the slender plume of grey smoke rising into the autumn air. The fire was still smouldering with the ashes of burned wood and burned flesh still lingering, here and there a bone was protruding from the pyre all that was left of Isiah Blackwood and his crimes!

CHAPTER 35

Summer

1680

Many years later in the village of Elersly things had moved as always into a new and different scene. The physical nature of the village had not changed much nor had it improved. The people of the past were now the past, as life began and ended, Reverend Marshal had passed onto a higher plain, Ealdorman Hudson also and most of the local people were also dead.

Into this scene walked an old woman, crooked and bent, long white hair tied back she rested on a wooden stick for steadiness. She staggered into the village square and sat down on a wooden bench; there she sat still and quiet seemingly oblivious to passers-by. After some time a woman passed by and stopped, gazing at her the old woman, closed her eyes and slumped to one side.

The woman called for help but it was too late the old woman on the bench was dead! A crowd gathered around, she was a stranger, nobody seemed to know her, until a man stepped forward and looked at her sitting peacefully on the bench, his name was Edward Jacobs.

"I think I know this woman, she helped me when I was a child and I was sick, her name is Eliza Swann, late of this village, the last witch!"

Eliza Swann was buried outside of Saint Andrews Church Yard, in un consecrated ground, a stone tablet featuring the Eye of God was placed on top. The fearful parishioners surrounded it with wild garlic, which according to folklore provides protection against witches, so that her spirit could never be conjured from the final resting place or her body to return to torment the people of Elersly with her evil deeds once more. The stone now hangs on the west wall of St Andrew's' beneath the round Eye of God window as a permanent reminder to the villagers of the frightful history of this place.

The End.

Printed in Great Britain
by Amazon

45883098R00106